THE SON-IN-LAW

BOOKS BY ELLIE MONAGO

The Secret Mistress

The Marriage Test

THE DIVORCE SERIES

The Custody Battle

The Divorce Lawyer

THE SON-IN-LAW

ELLIE MONAGO

Bookouture

Published by Bookouture in 2025

An imprint of Storyfire Ltd.
Carmelite House
50 Victoria Embankment
London EC4Y 0DZ

www.bookouture.com

The authorised representative in the EEA is Hachette Ireland
8 Castlecourt Centre
Dublin 15 D15 XTP3
Ireland
(email: info@hbgi.ie)

ISBN: 978-1-83618-703-5
eBook ISBN: 978-1-83618-702-8

NOW

ONE

DIANA

I'm alone, and primed to make excuses for my husband. Story of my life.

No, not my life. Just my marriage. Stories have plot twists and marriages end and life goes on. I'm thirty-nine, which isn't that old, depending who you ask.

"I reserved a table for four," I say to the hostess ruefully, "but there will be only three of us. I'm sorry."

"No problem at all!" She beams at me and tosses back her voluminous blonde tresses, so similar to my own. We're separated by about twenty years, but this is Houston, a town built on oil, gas, and big blonde hair. "Just let me know when the rest of your party arrives."

My nerves intensify. Will it actually be a party?

I sure hope so. I'd really like this to go well. The last time I saw Lizzie was at her college graduation two months ago, when she announced that she wouldn't be moving home for the summer. That she'd never live with me again, in fact. She was staying in Austin. "I don't need your money anymore," she said. I asked why, did she have a plan? Because she didn't have a job. "I'm figuring it out" was her curt reply.

Has she figured it out? I don't know, she's barely texted me back since then, and when she does, she skirts even the most direct questions. How's she paying her bills? Is she still in the same studio apartment?

Tonight, it should all become clear. I'm about to meet her fiancé.

I was shocked by the invitation and hurt, too, because I hadn't known about a boyfriend, let alone a fiancé. I thought she'd been preoccupied with finding a career that would put her degree to good use.

Her dad hates that she majored in communications. He told her that was just a hop, skip, and a jump from business, the far superior major. In business, you have to communicate, too, does she know that?

But Ron isn't here to patronize, belittle, and harangue her. He bailed at the last minute and couldn't even be bothered to send Lizzie a text to say sorry; instead, he told me to do it.

Soon, I won't have to take his orders anymore. I'm so close to getting out with the help of the $50K I have squirreled away.

I don't like to think how I got my hands on that money, but it's essential. I'm sure Ron's got plenty of hidden funds, and he'll hire the most cutthroat lawyers this town has ever seen to make sure I walk away with the absolute minimum.

Tonight, he's made it clear that I'm on my own, which is both a relief and an annoyance. My primary feeling right now, though, is anxiety.

Will Lizzie seem prickly or warm, or alternate unpredictably between the two poles? What's her fiancé like, and will he like me? And does she really have to get married so young? I hope she's planning on a very long engagement.

Lise, she goes by Lise now. I have to keep reminding myself of that because when I accidentally call her Lizzie, her face either darkens or closes off entirely. Elizabeth has at least a dozen potential nicknames, and when she was born, I was drawn to the idea that someday my daughter would exercise an agency that I've never experienced. She could be whoever—and whatever—she chose. She could christen herself.

But in my heart? She'll always be Lizzie.

And there she is, walking into the steakhouse that she suggested (to my surprise; I thought she'd stopped eating meat), her long blonde hair in a French braid, wearing a shapeless asymmetrical dress with one shoulder exposed. It's incredibly short, emphasizing her endless legs, and fashionable in a way that I can't quite understand, which signals tremendous confidence. Tears prick my eyes.

This is all I've ever wanted: for my daughter to move through the world feeling like she owns it; no, like she owns herself. A full and complete person, something I've never managed to be despite my expensive, well-tailored clothes and trips to the salon and the cosmetic dermatologist for preventive Botox. I've always tried to fit in rather than stand out, to be good enough in everyone else's eyes, and my adult rebellion had been a disaster, a fever dream of manipulation that I mistook for love, but Lizzie—sorry, Lise—is charting her own course. She's writing her own ticket. She's—

Oh my God. It can't be.

She's taking the hand of the man who's entered the restaurant just behind her and now they're coming straight for me. I try to adopt the proper expression, but I can't seem to control the muscles in my face. The shock and horror are too potent.

I'm overwhelmed. By the present, and the past. By the apocalyptic, unforeseen collision between the two.

"Mom," Lise says, "you know Gavin."

Unfortunately... terrifyingly... "I do."

TWO

LISE

I'm thrown by the look on Mom's face. I knew she'd be surprised, but *revolted*? How can anyone be disgusted by Gavin? Mom, in particular, knows how much he did for me when I was in high school. Or maybe she doesn't. I've kept a lot from her, then and now. But she's always been pretty opaque herself.

We don't really know each other, Mom and me. And she definitely doesn't know Gavin.

To her, he's Mr. Axelrod, my high school English teacher. It's time for her to see him in a whole different light.

"This is my fiancé, Gavin," I say proudly.

She gives a wide smile, trying to cover up her initial reaction, which wasn't just disgust. There was fear in the mix, too. But then, she's always been afraid. She's never wanted her little girl to grow up.

This is a whole other level, though. She's moving slowly, almost like she doesn't want to shake his hand, like she has to force herself to touch him, as if he's a serpent or a shard of glass. Normally, you can count on Mom to have impeccable manners. So what the hell is going on here?

I glance at Gavin, hoping he's not offended, that he'll realize it's not about him. This is why Mom and I had so much tension and dissension when I was a teenager. She wants me to live a bubble-wrapped life, but I won't do it. Gavin and I have talked about this plenty over the years, first when he was my teacher and then later, after we'd become acquainted in an entirely different way.

So he's taking her behavior in stride. As she hesitates to shake his hand, he switches his body position to a hug. "Since we're going to be family," he says. She goes rigid in his embrace.

Does she have to make everything so awkward?

I stifle my annoyance. This is supposed to be a new beginning for Mom and me. Soon, I'm going to be a married woman and she'll have to finally respect me as an adult. Right?

Gavin gives her an authentically warm smile, the kind I wish she seemed able to return. "It's good to see you, Di," he says. I must have told him she's "Di" to her friends.

"Good to see you," she murmurs, so low that I have to strain to hear. She looks over at me. "I'm sorry, I just didn't expect this. You'll have to give me a minute to adjust."

"I told you I'd be bringing someone," I say.

"But I didn't know..." She tips her head forward, hair cloaking her face. "Just a minute, okay, Lizzie?"

"Lise." In the correction, I'm not even hiding my irritation.

I tried to make this easy for her, picking the kind of restaurant where she's most comfortable. Gavin had agreed instantly. He said that a woman of her age would like the darkness; it camouflages crow's feet. I told him she's not that old, she's not even forty yet, and she's actually still unlined and really pretty, though he hasn't seen her in five years, not since parent-teacher conferences when I was a junior in high school. But the point is, he was trying to be sensitive and so was I, which is how we wound up in a steakhouse that admits no outside light. It's all dark wood, brown leather, and brocade, with portraits of

Venice and the founding fathers on the walls. I miss Austin already.

I take a deep breath. Reset.

"You're going to love Gavin," I tell Mom. I look at him affectionately; he looks back just as affectionately.

My sixteen-year-old self would have died if she'd known how it was going to turn out, that only five years later she—I mean, I—would be sleeping next to him every night. I had a mad crush on him back then, but he could not have been more appropriate. The first time he ever laid a hand on me was ten months ago.

I used to put him on such a pedestal, and now we're standing on equal ground. Or maybe we're both on pedestals because he's always telling me how much he admires and adores me. I really never knew love could be like this. It definitely wasn't modeled at home.

Poor Mom. I doubt she's ever felt anything close. She's saddled with Dad, who treats her like dirt unless other people—outsiders—are around. He'll probably be on best behavior tonight.

"How late is Dad running?" I ask.

"Too late," she says. "He really wishes he could have made it but it's almost the end of the quarter and there was a last-minute emergency—"

"Healthcare never sleeps," Gavin says, taking my hand soothingly. He wants to make sure I'm not upset by what a nonevent this is for my father, what a nonpriority I am. After all, Gavin's only the man I'm going to spend the rest of my life with; why would Dad deign to show up?

It's okay, though. Now I can just focus on my mother since that's the relationship that's worth saving. Mom and I might not always see eye to eye but she's a decent person. At least I know she loves me. Too much, in fact. That's come with its own problems.

But not anymore. New beginnings, remember?

"I'm sorry, Liz—Lise," Mom says.

"It's not your fault. You're not the one standing me up to work on a quarterly report or whatever." I roll my eyes in a way that's meant to be good-natured. It's meant to show that I'm unaffected by his selfishness and callous disregard. I wonder if she's affected after all these years, or if she fully inhabits her subservient role. I've watched her embark on entire apology tours on his behalf without breaking a sweat. She's a real Texas lady, my mother.

"Thank you," she says, and I can tell she's grateful that I'm not blaming her. She glances at Gavin and I see it again—that flicker of fear.

She's probably worried that he's not going to like her. It's so important to her that a) everyone likes her and b) no one's uncomfortable. I refuse to see my relationships through such a superficial lens. Gavin's been instrumental in that. He wants a woman, not just a lady. He accepts all of me, an experience I know she's never gotten to have.

After all, Dad's the only man she's ever been with. She got knocked up at sixteen years old, when he was twenty and already in college, a big man on campus from a good (i.e., wealthy) family, and that was it for her. Her life course was decided.

But I'm not her. I'm a person with agency. I smile to let her know it's all going to be okay, that I know exactly what I'm doing.

"I'll get our table," I say, walking toward the hostess stand.

This is going to be great. How could it not be?

Everyone loves Gavin.

THREE

DIANA

The menu is large and leatherbound, so I hide my face behind it while trying to regain my composure. It doesn't matter what I order, I won't be able to eat. My stomach has just announced a hunger strike.

I'm terrified of Gavin. Terrified for Lizzie—no, Lise. She's a grown-up now, responsible for her own choices. She can protect herself.

I'm telling myself that, but I don't believe it. Not only because of Lise's youth or inexperience but because I know who Gavin really is and what he's capable of. I discovered it the hard way. I can't bear the idea of her going through anything close to what I did.

Maybe she won't have to. Maybe he's changed.

He certainly looks different. There's gel in his hair and he's wearing a navy blazer with a crisp blue button-down. He's dressed like an upright citizen in that savvy little meet-the-parents outfit, an ingratiating smile on his face. But it has to be an act.

Someone like Gavin could never change. He can only get

better at what he does. More dangerous. And when I knew him, he was already so good at being bad.

My poor daughter. She has no idea what she's up against. If I try to explain what kind of person he is, she'll ask how I could possibly know. Telling her the truth would mean outing myself. It would destroy what's left of our relationship. She'll never forgive me.

Lise is not Lizzie. She's poised, with no slouching or skittering eyes. Her skin is luminous, all traces of teenage acne long gone. Now that she doesn't have her hair in her face, trying to hide, she's unbearably lovely. Gavin used to comment on my appearance all the time, talking about how gorgeous I was, how I should wear my hair swept back, just like Lise's is now.

He's controlling her, like he used to control me.

I hate to admit it, but he's right, the hairstyle suits her. She looks like a younger, more confident me. A better, fresher model. He traded up, didn't he?

I really might be sick.

"Wow, Mom, it's like you've never seen a menu before!" Lise jokes. She's nervous, too, I realize. She wants this to go well. She's hoping I'll like Gavin, and if I say anything to the contrary, I'll only alienate her further.

I have to remember how my mother raised me. Indoctrinated me, I guess you could say. No matter what happens—whether it's your father talking over you or your mother licking her finger to wipe your face clean or some strange man looking down your shirt or touching you without permission, which they now call "consent," you smile like it's a beauty pageant. No one should see you sweat, and if anyone needs to be uncomfortable, let it be you.

"What are you having?" I ask Lise. I flick my eyes quickly to Gavin as if to include him in the question.

"Tomahawk," he answers quickly. "Forty-eight ounces."

Lise laughs—no, she giggles. Lizzie was never a giggler. "You just had Jack in the Box during the drive!"

"I'm a growing boy," he says, and the flirtatious look they exchange is truly nauseating. I can't tell if they're putting on a show for me or if they've momentarily forgotten I'm here. "How about a bottle of red for the table? Do you like wine, Di?"

My skin crawls at the familiarity of the nickname. He's staring right at me, his expression friendly and open, as if he's got nothing to hide. Nothing to atone for.

I try to mirror him, though I can feel that I'm failing miserably. My mother would be so mortified.

I force a nod. Consent given. No, consent taken.

"He's basically a wine expert," Lise tells me. "He's even thought about becoming a sommelier." She's glowing with pride and happiness.

I recognize myself in her. I remember the early stages with Gavin, how I felt like I was levitating. She must still be in the honeymoon period. When will he show his true colors? How can I get him to show them during this visit?

"You'd give up teaching, Gavin?" I ask. "That would be a real shame." I don't mean it to sound sarcastic but it must sound *something* because Lise's eyebrows knit ever so slightly. "He was such a great teacher," I add, directing it toward Lise.

"He still is." She's basically batting her eyelashes at him.

This is what he craves, what he cultivates: constant ego boosting by the woman who loves him. I don't believe he's capable of loving back, though he can present all the trappings of it.

Like now, he's gazing at Lise as if she's his queen. I'm not sure how I'm going to be able to watch this for the next ten minutes, let alone an entire dinner, let alone an entire week while they stay under my roof. Perhaps worst of all, I can see how much Lise wants my approval.

When she was in high school, I would have killed to feel like my opinions mattered. But now, it's agony.

Gavin reels off the name of an Italian red, using what sounds like a perfect accent. (Though how would I know? I've lived only in Texas.) Still, I cross-reference with my wine list and I'm pretty sure that he's picked a bottle that's nearly $400.

Is that because he's going to offer to pay for this dinner, prove what a big shot he is? Or because he knows that I'm picking up the check, on Ron's dime?

I would have liked to work, would have liked to go to college, but Ron's old-fashioned. He wanted a stay-home wife and mother. Gavin knows that I've always been embarrassed that Ron's wishes overpowered my will so completely. I've never even spoken up, just bowed down.

Gavin is jabbing at me, I'm sure of it. But Lise is completely oblivious, and for now, it has to stay that way.

"It's an excellent Sangiovese," Gavin says. "I'm sure you'll enjoy it."

I force another smile. "I'm sure I will." It's not enough for him to just have it all his way; you have to show that you like it. He's a puppet master, and all these years later, he's still pulling my strings.

Lise is looking back and forth between Gavin and me as if it's ping-pong, and I wonder for a second: *could* she have some idea of what transpired?

No, there's no way. She's no actress, and she's never been manipulative.

Unless Gavin has rubbed off on her. I, of all people, am well aware of how influential he can be.

He's smiling at me in a way that could seem kindly to the untrained eye. But I'm picking up the undercurrent of sadism. He knows he's got me cornered. If I expose him to Lise, I expose myself.

"I'm not very hungry," I say. "I think I'll have the bone

marrow appetizer, or maybe the seven-ounce filet. Unless you want to split a steak, Lizzie?"

"It's *Lise*." She looks instantly annoyed and it's a flashback to high school. I'm oddly relieved. Despite her protests, despite the sophisticated façade, the feisty girl she once was is still in there.

"I'm sorry," I say. "Sometimes..." Tears prick my eyes and I can't continue. This is humiliating. You don't cry at the dinner table.

"It's okay." Her tone softens. "I know you don't mean anything by it. Old habits die hard."

"Lise isn't the same person anymore." Gavin twists the knife. "It's time you realized that. You've always had a hard time letting her grow up, haven't you, Diana?"

I don't answer, so he goes in for the kill.

"Lise tells me everything. I know her whole past and all about your family." He gazes at her lovingly. "I'm her number one supporter."

"That's true." Lise turns back toward me. "I know it's a shock, seeing me with my former teacher, but I promise you, we're equals. Partners in crime. My relationship with Gavin is nothing like yours with Dad, and I hope that you're happy about that."

Wow. That was a low blow.

"I don't mean that to hurt you," she says. "But it's important to me to live in honesty and to speak the truth. I'd never pick a man who treats me like Dad treats you. You deserve better and so do I. And I have better. I have the best." She and Gavin trade gooey looks.

Ah, the self-delusion of the young, as if no one else has ever been in love. But then, I never got to feel that myself. I always knew exactly what I was getting with Ron. I just had no other choice. I was a pregnant teenager in Houston from a conservative family.

I could've done much worse than Ron, though. That's what I've told myself all these years.

Lise is doing much worse than Ron, and she hasn't got a clue. I need to tell her.

I broke free, but it sure as hell wasn't easy, and Gavin is definitely the type to hold a grudge. Is that what this is about?

There's nothing that could hurt me more than hurting Lise. If they really do get married, he'll make her suffer, I know it. I'd have to live knowing it was all my fault because by getting involved with him years ago, I'd put her in the line of fire.

I'm reduced to hoping that it is true love, that he really has changed, that he is, in fact, my daughter's biggest supporter. But deep down, I just can't believe it.

This must still be early days for them and he's showing what he wants her to see. The mask will have to slip at some point. But by then, will she be in too deep to get out? Gavin's quicksand.

We're blessedly interrupted by the server. I'm having an out-of-body experience as I watch Gavin order for all of us. It's like I'm floating above, my head filled with white noise. I can see that the server's eating out of his hand, falling for his nice-guy routine. Lise has, too. Fallen hard. But she hasn't hit the pavement yet, hasn't gone splat. It can't be too late.

But what do I do? My mind's a blank.

I've been feeling so hopeful lately. When I got the text from Lise asking me to meet her fiancé, I thought it was serendipity. A fresh start for us, just when I was planning one for myself.

I didn't stay with Ron all these years because I was afraid to destroy our seemingly perfect life. It's not because he looks good on paper, or because he circulates well at parties. It's not even because of how brutal our prenup is.

Ron's always been self-centered—my life has had to revolve around his—and he can be caustic but it's never risen to the level of physical abuse. He's more dismissive and thoughtless.

But he can be controlling, particularly financially, and while he allows me to make small domestic decisions, he expects to handle all the major ones. He can be vindictive and on the few occasions that I've crossed him, he's made me pay (quite literally, placing a hold on my credit cards for periods of time as punishment). But that's okay, I can take all that.

What scares me is that as Lizzie grew up, he seemed less emotionally invested in her all the time. So if I'd dared to cross him by leaving, if he was humiliated and faced any sort of public loss of face or status, he might very well have taken out his anger on Lizzie. His own mother told me that was a valid fear, and a mother knows the child she's raised. She understands the man he's become.

I've stayed with Ron all these years for Lizzie. I've been a buffer, ready to absorb anything. I made sure to put in these last four years so that he'd pay off her college tuition.

Now she's graduated debt-free, and that was going to mean freedom for both of us. I've never touched my rainy-day fund. I did, however, make the mistake of telling Gavin about it and I have a feeling that might come back to haunt me.

Lately, I've been so upbeat, fantasizing about this next chapter of my life. Who do I want to be? What am I capable of doing? Could I finally find true love or have a second family? Or could I find some other calling or purpose, maybe finally going to college myself and launching a career? Or could it be all of the above?

Until tonight, I was starting to feel like anything was possible, including rebuilding my relationship with my daughter.

Then I walked into this restaurant and saw Gavin.

Now he's telling anecdotes about teaching in Austin that are supposed to be both humorous and charming. There are all sorts of humble brags sprinkled in as he pretends to be self-effacing, but really, he wants me to know that he's still out there changing lives.

Don't I know it.

He can't just be a fiancé hoping that his mother-in-law will support the union. This is Gavin. So what does he really want with Lise? And with me?

Lise excuses herself to the restroom and I want to cry out, "No! Don't leave me alone with him!" I was never supposed to have to lay eyes on him again.

He regards me with a smile. The cat that ate the canary. But who's the canary, Lise or me?

I can feel that he wants me to break the silence, and I never want to do anything he wants ever again.

It's agonizing, though. The not knowing.

Is it possible he'd just tell me if I asked? If I said pretty please? He used to say that he was wrapped around my finger, that he could refuse me nothing. He claimed I was the one with power over him.

So I ask, nicely. "Why are you really here, Gavin?"

He picks up his wineglass and holds it up to the light. He starts talking about the hints of currant, smoke, leather, and rock. Rock?

He's stalling. Torturing me.

I glance over his shoulder and see that Lise is coming back. "What do you really want?" I interrupt, all my sweetness gone, replaced by desperation.

He sets down the wineglass and leans back, completely relaxed. In his cruel element. "I want what we all want. Love." Slight pause. "Though I could also use money. Who couldn't?"

Love and money.

Is he saying that if I pay him off, he'll leave Lise alone? But he'd also expect me to take her place?

No, I could never go back. Not even for Lise.

But the fact is, he has all the power. He's the one who knows my secret. The only one who knows I'm a killer.

FOUR

LISE

Dinner ended uneventfully, I guess. Now Gavin and I are in his car, heading for my parents' house.

I feel uneasy and dissatisfied. Is Mom ever going to change? So often with her, it's about what goes unsaid. Tonight, I was trying to show that I'm not like her, that I'm going to speak my mind, because I'm Lise now, not Lizzie, and soon I'll be Mrs. Gavin Axelrod. I'd hoped she'd be inspired to say something real. Ever since I hit puberty, we don't speak the same language and maybe I thought Gavin would serve as some kind of interpreter, that his presence would embolden her like it emboldens me.

But nope, she's still Mom. Except that... "Was it just me or was my mother acting a little strange?" I ask Gavin.

"I don't know her like you do," he says, his eyes on the road. "But she was pretty much what I expected."

"What do you mean?"

"I thought it would be all superficial pleasantries. You know, the usual bullshit." He shrugs. "I warned you: people don't really change."

"I know. I shouldn't have gotten my hopes up."

I feel my brow furrowing as I replay the night. Mom's social niceties and surface placidity were camouflaging something else. At times, her hands were shaking. She went from ignoring her wine to gulping it, almost as if she wasn't sure whether she needed to keep her wits about her or to anesthetize. At one point, she knocked her glass over and apologized so profusely that it was like she'd ruined someone's life instead of a restaurant's white tablecloth.

What if it's not really about me and my announcement? I haven't stayed in very good touch since I moved out four years ago, and when I have been around, I've hardly been attending to Mom's well-being. Living alone with Dad would take a toll on anyone's mental health. I feel a surge of guilt for having abandoned her like I did.

Or could she be physically sick and on medication? Could that be why her hands were shaking? Maybe she's not supposed to drink alcohol at all but she couldn't resist. She wanted to celebrate my engagement.

Not that her demeanor had exactly been celebratory. When she raised her glass to toast us, her voice nearly faltered and that's when her hands shook the most.

I glance at Gavin. I don't want to say this out loud and risk hurting his feelings, but she wasn't really happy for us. I'm pretty sure she was frightened.

Which makes no sense. Mom had such a high opinion of Gavin when he was my teacher. Could it be that she's a snob, that she doesn't like the idea of me marrying a teacher? Well, I'd rather stay with Gavin in our one-bedroom apartment forever than live in a McMansion with someone like Dad.

I'm not her. I certainly don't want her life. And I wouldn't have thought that's what she'd want for me, either.

Maybe it's not that. It could be the nine-year age difference. She should just look around at her own social set, though, where rich men are often on their second or third marriages to women who are decades younger than them.

Or it's the teacher thing. I just have to make it super clear to her that Gavin and I weren't romantically involved back then, that he was more than a perfect gentleman. He was a trusted adult, someone who was there for me when I needed him. But he never crossed any lines.

The problem is, my mom's always been hard to talk to. Her anxiety's just so palpable. That's why everything went haywire when I was in high school. Now it's rearing its head again.

I can't lose focus. I came here hoping for a relationship reboot, and one way or another, I'm going to get it. When I was little, Mom and I were so close. Planning the wedding together could bring us together again.

I feel bad for her, being stuck in a loveless marriage with no career of her own. Now that she's largely done with her mothering duties, she must feel so useless.

Mom and I actually want the same thing. We both want me to have a better life (and marriage) than she has. She just needs to see that I'm on my way. I'm a strong, independent woman who has the love of an incredible man.

"How did I get so lucky?" I say. "Sometimes I still can't believe it."

He smiles over. "Believe it. Because I'm not going anywhere. Ever."

"I'm making a big deal out of nothing." It was only the first dinner, and we're here for a week. "When Mom sees us together more, she'll realize that there's nothing to worry about."

"The problem is, your mother doesn't know you," he says. "You're more mature than women my age. More than women her age."

"I just want her to respect my decisions."

"We all want a lot of things. Sometimes you have to let go of the dream, if it's never going to match the reality."

Gavin might be right; he usually is. It could be time for me to give up certain childish dreams and accept what is.

But then, sometimes childish dreams actually do come true. Just look at Gavin. "I love you so much," I say.

"I love you," he responds, "and I don't care what your mother thinks. I've always thought she was kind of a bitch, though she hides it well."

"You've never said that before." It feels a little like a sucker punch.

"When I first met her, I was your teacher. That's a whole different context, but even then, I had my suspicions." He reaches out for my hand and his voice softens. "Hey, I didn't mean to upset you. I thought we could tell each other anything. Isn't that what you told your mom?"

"Yes." It comes out small.

"Our relationship is built on the truth, no matter how brutal. We can't shield each other, but we can help each other face it. I'll always be here to pick up the pieces and to see the absolute best in you. But that doesn't mean lying to myself—or letting you lie to yourself—about anything, including who your parents are."

"I know. You're right."

His opinion of Mom came out harsh but I don't think it's fixed. If I can get her to be more vulnerable with him and with me, he'll see her good heart.

"Mom can be slow to warm up," I say, "but even if she never does warm to you, it doesn't matter. She can't change how I feel about you."

"That's what I'm banking on," he says.

THEN

FIVE

DIANA

Mr. Axelrod was just what I'd expected.

It wasn't from what Lizzie told me since she didn't tell me anything anymore. But I'd overheard his name when she talked to friends, and why would a teenage girl be talking about her English teacher that much unless he was young and attractive?

I was thirty-four and I suspected he was hovering around thirty. He had sandy hair, mussed but not moussed, eschewing vanity. He wore an untucked button-down shirt and jeans. Tall and well-built, not bulky. Like a runner, not a football player.

He extended a hand. "Call me Gavin," he said.

"Diana." His hand was as warm as his smile and when I clasped it, I found myself blushing. What was wrong with me?

It must have been that I wanted to make a good impression on the teacher who'd made such a good impression on Lizzie. But I was being ridiculous. It wasn't as if Mr. Axelrod—Gavin—was going to tell Lizzie at school the next day, "Your mom's really cool!"

I'd been reduced to grasping at straws. Lizzie's attitude toward me increasingly ranged from dismissive to scornful. And

I knew that despite the stereotypes, not all sixteen-year-olds were like this; my friends' kids still talked to them. Still valued them.

I took the seat across from Gavin. The desk between us was covered with numerous folders filled with student work. The classroom was decorated with quotes from different authors, some of them inspirational, others much darker and more philosophical. I hadn't read any of the books. I wondered if Lizzie had and if so, what she thought of them. She's so bright and always had such interesting opinions. I wished she'd start sharing them with me again.

"Will Lizzie's father be joining us tonight?" Gavin asked. His hazel eyes were intense on mine.

I flushed again. Ron's a workaholic and there's no changing him. I gave up trying a long time ago. Actually, who was I kidding? I'd never tried. I'd always been much better at adapting to circumstances than altering them. "He had to work," I said.

"He's a corporate VP, right?"

I was a little surprised. "Lizzie told you that?"

"She tells me a lot of things. I really appreciate how open she is." He was rooting around on his desktop, looking for a particular folder. "Her writing is incredible. So insightful and vulnerable."

"I haven't read any lately." When she was younger, she liked to share her poems and stories. She used to enjoy my praise.

"It's okay, Diana. She'll come back to you."

I was startled. Even my husband didn't speak to me so softly, with such care and intimacy.

I had the strangest reaction. I found that I wanted to cry. It had been two years and I still felt so much guilt and self-loathing over what I'd done. Ron didn't know about it, but whenever he treated me badly, I thought maybe he actually did, and that he hated me for it. I deserved that.

When you hold on to a secret that big, when you do something so unforgivable, when you take another person's life, and when you're equipped with a conscience, you never really get away with it, or from it.

I moved through my community like a loving wife and mother, but I knew I was an impostor. I was a monster and nobody knew. But I could never forget.

That's why I was trying extra hard to make sure that Lizzie stayed on the right path.

From how Gavin was looking at me, I knew that he must be a very kind man. Lizzie had good taste.

"Lizzie's in the process of finding her voice," he continued. "For some young women, that means pulling away from their mothers. Temporarily."

"It feels like forever."

He laughed, though I wasn't joking. I had the sense that he liked me, and I wasn't sure why. Probably because he seemed to have such a high opinion of Lizzie that it carried over.

He slid the folder along the desk. "Would you like to read one of her poems?"

"Do you think she'd mind?" He'd insinuated that her writing was quite personal. "I mean, does she know you're showing them to me?"

"What she doesn't know won't hurt her." He smiled at me encouragingly. "Read the top one. It's my favorite."

I hesitated because I didn't want to violate her privacy. My mother violated mine constantly, was overbearing in every way. I'd tried to do it differently with Lizzie. But then, this wasn't Lizzie's diary. It's a poem for her English class, and this was a parent-teacher conference. I was supposed to learn more about her work. Besides, Gavin seemed so insistent and so caring. I envied his surety.

It felt like he knew my daughter better than I did, which was unsettling. But it was also reassuring because he clearly liked her. He was looking out for her. Maybe this poem would help bring Lizzie and me back together.

I opened the folder. The poem was called "Insecure."

It started with all the things that she didn't like about herself, from her appearance to her personality, and I was filled with sadness and a desire to tell her no, it's not true, but then it was like she found her own counterarguments. By the end, she recognized that the insecurity made her human, and that vulnerability could be a strength.

I looked at Gavin, my eyes slightly wet. "You're right," I said. "She's incredible."

He nodded but he was no longer smiling. I could tell that he was a little troubled, perhaps even debating whether he should go on. "I do believe that she's going to be okay in the long run, and that she'll find her way back to you. But in the short run..."

As he trailed off, my heart seized. It felt like all my worst and most unspeakable fears were about to be confirmed. "What is it?"

"The conclusion is trite, isn't it? Full of false bravado. All the conviction is in the early stanzas. The ending feels almost tacked on, doesn't it?"

"You'd know a lot better than I would." About poetry. About Lizzie. "I'm so afraid for her." It just slips out, surprising me.

"I can understand that."

"She seems so unhappy. With the world, and herself." Now the words were rushing out, like an oil spill. "She hates that she's so skinny, and her acne's improved some, but I know she's still really self-conscious."

Should I have been telling him all this? Was it breaking her trust? No, he already knew. It was right there in the poem.

Strangest was how quickly and deeply I trusted him, that I

was suddenly the one baring my heart and soul. Lizzie *was* my heart and soul, and I didn't know how to help her. But I had to hope that he did.

"She won't see a therapist," I said. "But she does keep a journal. Has she shared it with you?"

"No. I wouldn't ask her to."

"Of course not. I just thought…" I was flooded with embarrassment. How desperate I must have sounded. How pathetic I was. I had one real job—to raise a happy, healthy young woman—and I was failing.

"You thought that Lizzie and I are close, and you're right about that." His tone was exceedingly compassionate. "You thought that I care about Lizzie, and you're right about that, too. She likes talking to me about her work and her life. Plus, writing is a form of therapy."

I hadn't realized I was holding my breath until it came out of me in a whoosh. I couldn't recall the last time I'd felt this grateful toward anyone, and never toward a virtual stranger.

But he wasn't a stranger. He was Lizzie's English teacher, and he's on her side. On my side, too, it seemed.

"Thank you so much," I said. "I haven't really talked to anyone about how concerned I am." I couldn't tell my friends, not with how well their lives were going and their kids were doing. I couldn't talk to Ron because he said it was "just teen-girl angst bullshit."

It was so nice to interact with a man like Gavin, someone who really got it. That could have been part of Gavin's appeal to Lizzie, too. She may have been looking for a father figure since she and Ron had such a distant relationship. My own father had been detached, too, not counting that brief period toward the end of his life. I wished I could have done better for Lizzie, and in the early days with Ron, I really thought it might turn out differently. But then, we were so young, just kids ourselves.

I didn't want to think about Ron and the other disappoint-ments of my life. I had a lot of regrets about my actions and inaction. Not to mention the abiding shame over the worst action anyone could ever take. Even if I turned myself in—and I had considered that plenty—it would only cause more suffering to people I loved.

There was no penance big enough. The punishment was living with the knowledge every day that I wasn't who I appeared to be.

But right then, I was just a concerned mother and all I wanted was to keep talking to Gavin. I wanted to pour out all my unspoken fears: about my parenting, about my child.

Lizzie was so underconfident that she didn't even want to learn to drive. She barely went out on the weekends. And on the one hand, that meant that I didn't have to worry about her drink being spiked at some party, but on the other hand, I did have to worry that she was alone and miserable in her room on Saturday nights, scribbling in a notebook. I could never entice her to hang out with me.

But maybe the scribbles were a good thing. Like Gavin said, they could be her therapy. She wouldn't share them with me, but if she'd share them with another trusted adult, someone like Gavin...

"I'm so sorry," he said, glancing at the clock. "These confer-ences are way too short."

"Thank you." I stood up, hastily gathering my jacket and purse. I'd already taken up too much of his time.

"My door is always open," he said. "I'm sure we'll talk again."

"I'd like that," I said, smiling. It not only seemed appealing, but wise.

Because Lizzie must have trusted Gavin. She'd revealed herself to him and, I suspected, would allow him to influence her.

In other words, he had power. And I had to protect my daughter, make sure that all that power wasn't in the wrong hands.

Keep your enemies close and your kid's teacher closer.

SIX

LIZZIE

I was lying in wait but trying to seem casual. Still, it was suspicious, me being in the living room at all. These days, I tended to cloister in my own room.

I liked the word *cloister*. I'd bet Mr. Axelrod does, too. It was one of the things we had in common, one of the things that was sorely lacking in my friends, family, and everyone else I knew in Houston: an appreciation for language, and for nuance.

I liked the word *nuance*, too.

The thing about Houston—or at least the suburbs where I spent all my time—was that it took so little to be weird. And weird was seen as innately bad. Like, disqualifying. But for college, I intended to go less than three hours away, which was also a world away, to a magical place with the motto *Keep Austin weird.*

I set down my book when I heard Mom open the front door. That was another weird thing about me, that I liked actual physical books I could hold in my hand, spines I could crack open. Mr. Axelrod totally agreed. He said the smell of old books was incomparable.

I didn't like hanging out in the living room because it's

sterile and cold. We'd moved here two years ago because my dad wanted to upgrade from the house we'd been in my whole life, even though he and Mom were going to be empty nesters soon and should have been downsizing. But Dad wanted to show off how well he's doing professionally and he seemed sure he was in line to be the next CEO of his healthcare company. He must have anticipated lots of parties and entertaining in his future since that's what this house was built for, with the crazy-high ceilings and chandeliers and double ovens and grand sweeping everything. It was only ten blocks from our old house, but palatial, with a view of the pond.

I preferred the old house, but really, what did it matter? I'd basically aged out of this life. When I was little, I loved living in a planned community. Mom and I could walk to everything (a huge community wave pool, playgrounds, and ponds), and bands of kids roamed freely on foot or by bike. But once you get older, it's just so small and you feel so trapped. You can't walk to *anything*. Not that you want to anyway because it's so hot and humid most of the year, and I couldn't drive because I had one lesson and said never again, not when road rage is epidemic in these parts and it takes forever to get anywhere interesting.

The first thing people need to understand about Houston is the loop. The suburbs where I lived were outside the loop; all the cool stuff was inside. Of course, my parents decided to raise me on the outs; of course, Mom was terrified of the big bad city.

I'd heard rumors that Houston is diverse and multicultural and I wished I could verify that for myself, but none of my friends with licenses were allowed to go inside the loop. In these parts, they parent by groupthink. I wanted to have experiences that didn't feel stale and mass-produced. I wanted to really live. Was that so wrong?

Mom seemed to think so. She pretended that her negativity toward "the city" wasn't only about safety, that it was about aesthetics, too. On the rare occasions we ventured into the urban, she was always commenting on how ugly it was because of the lack of zoning laws. In Houston, your house could wind up sandwiched between a Walmart and a taqueria. Mom thought that was a bug; I thought it was a feature. She wanted everything planned and controlled, but I was hungering for randomness. Not everything needed to be pretty (though Mom herself was, to an irritating degree).

It sucked to look like me when your mother could easily pass for Miss Texas. Maya said that I was going to be as good-looking as Mom someday, that we shared a lot of the same features, and I was destined to grow out of my gawky period. Or maybe, Maya suggested helpfully, I could just spend some time on my hair, makeup, and clothes?

Screw that.

When your best friend is that totally off base, you know you really have to get out of town.

Since it was almost November, the humidity had finally died down and hurricane season was supposedly behind us. But hurricanes won't be confined by the calendar; they're unruly. They have minds of their own, just like I did. Natural disasters and me, we both stressed Mom out. Maybe a kid was kind of like a natural disaster, out of control and capable of leaving detritus in its wake.

If Mom was honest with herself, deep down she was probably as eager to let me go as I was for release. She just didn't want to admit it, even to herself, so she had to cling harder. This might sound mean but she's like a barnacle and I couldn't wait to shake her off when I set sail.

College was salvation, glimmering in the distance. The only bummer would be leaving Mr. Axelrod behind. But I could always see him when I came home on breaks, and besides, he was my teacher, not my friend. I did get that distinction. I wasn't stupid or naïve, contrary to what my mom seemed to think.

She was always fussing over me like I were still a little kid. It's *Don't forget this, don't forget that* and *Are you eating enough?* and *I haven't seen Maya lately, is everything okay?* and *Maybe it's time to make some new friends!* Mom was a big part of why I wouldn't go to Rice for college, even if I could have gotten in. Also, Dad went to Rice and it would make him way too happy if I followed in his footsteps. So... nope.

"Oh, hi," Mom said, with that exaggerated startle reflex of hers.

"Hi." I was trying to sound cool and disaffected. But really, I wanted to know what my teachers had said. What Mr. Axelrod said. He was the only one who mattered.

Lots of girls at school were wearing their short skirts and shaking their asses at him but that wasn't my way. I didn't even care what he looked like. I wasn't that basic or superficial. And he wasn't some pig. I'd never once caught him eyeballing a teen girl. If I had, then I would have lost all respect for him.

In class one time, he happened to mention that he's twenty-five, which wasn't really that much older than I was. But I understood that at this particular moment in time, it was older enough. Too old. Also, it's impossible because he was a teacher and I was ugly.

It shouldn't happen and it wouldn't happen, but still. I was curious what he'd told my mom, what he thought of me, and what's wrong with being curious? A writer should be curious. He'd said that a few times.

Mom walked into the living room tentatively, as if she wasn't sure she'd be welcome. Then she sat down in the chair opposite me, all ginger like she had a hemorrhoid.

"I'm so proud of you." It was her standard line. "Your teachers said loads of nice things. Especially your English teacher." I tried to suppress my smile. "He said your writing shows maturity as well as talent."

"Really?" He'd been giving me A's but somehow it seemed

more official now that he'd said it to my parents. Well, one parent. I kind of would have liked for Dad to hear it, though he might have just found a way to insult me or Mr. Axelrod or both of us. He had no respect for writers, or for teachers.

"Really," Mom said.

"Did you like him?" I surprised myself with that one. I didn't know I cared so much about her opinion.

"I did. Mr. Axelrod seems like a real gem." She was studying my face. But what was she looking for? "You're lucky to have him for a teacher."

She had that right. I'd felt my good fortune since I walked into his classroom in September, since I listened to his first lecture.

When it came to words, Mr. Axelrod and I both cared about precision. He'd been speaking to my mother in code about my *maturity*, and I'd heard him loud and clear.

My life needed to change, and he was the man to change it.

Now I just had to give him the green light.

NOW

SEVEN

DIANA

I arrive at the house first, aware that Gavin and Lise aren't far behind. I shut the front door behind me, trying not to hyperventilate. I can't believe I managed to survive that dinner. Everything Gavin said rankled and/or frightened me. I'm sure that was his intent despite the amiable and innocent expression he wore throughout.

Lise hasn't even begun to suspect; she thinks she's landed the perfect man. But when she'd been away from the table, he'd confirmed that he has an ulterior motive. Can he really be bought off, or is he just toying with me?

It seems extreme, handing him a suitcase full of cash, but my options are limited. If I tell Lise about the affair, she might be so disgusted that she's done with both Gavin and me. But given his substantial charms and penchant for manipulation, he could very well convince her that it had been all my fault, that I was a spider and he'd gotten stuck in my web.

What if his hold on her got even stronger? I'd be cut out, and it would be the two of them against the world. She could wind up entirely at his mercy.

If the affair was my only secret, I might take the risk. But what if he tells her that I'm not only a seductress, I'm a murderer?

I scan the interior, heart racing. I'm not even sure what I'm looking for. A weapon? It's not like he's going to walk in and attack me. Not physically. Not in front of Lise. But make no mistake, he's on the attack.

My home is spotless and I can just imagine what Gavin is going to think about that: "So Ron still has you at his beck and call, scrubbing every surface until it gleams?" I can also imagine what Gavin will think about the bland décor. Ron had scoffed at the notion of hiring an interior designer, so I had to do it myself.

I lack confidence in my taste and never want to stand out. I'm not the type to visit art galleries, and Ron would never be willing to shell out for original art anyway. So I found a section on an online decorating site called "Upscale Hotel." That's where I ordered everything for my walls and tabletops, in one fell swoop.

I'm neither proud nor ashamed of that; it was simply pragmatic. But I know that Gavin is a romantic, in his way. In his own special, diabolical, supervillain way.

I think of that dress Lise was wearing tonight. Had Gavin picked that out for her? Or had she picked it out herself, with Gavin's voice in her head?

It's taken me a long time to purge Gavin's voice from my head.

Now I'm forced to hear him again as Lise opens the front door without knocking. The two of them are laughing about something. I'm hiding out in the kitchen, not wanting to go back and greet them. I wish Ron were here. At least he could take up space, serve as a distraction.

Finally, I return to the foyer. "Welcome!" I say. "It's getting late. We should get you settled into your rooms."

"Rooms?" Lise raises an eyebrow.

"You'll be in yours, and Gavin will be in the guest room."

"I thought we'd both sleep in the guest room," Lise says.

I'd thought that, too, before I realized who Lise's new fiancé actually was. Now I don't see how I can stomach it. She told me at dinner that they're living together, so obviously they sleep together, but they don't have to do it under my roof. "You're engaged," I say. "You're not married."

Gavin is wearing a half smirk. Lise glances over and mirrors him.

"Come on, Mom," she says. "It's not like you and Dad didn't have sex before you were married."

"We're all adults here," Gavin adds. "Why pretend?"

My insides tighten. I'm doing nothing but pretending and he knows it. I say to Lise, "It's not me, it's your dad. You know how traditional he is."

As if on cue, like we're in some kind of demented sitcom, the front door opens. "Well, hello!" Ron booms. "I didn't think you'd all be right here, waiting on me." He looks at us in turn, landing on Gavin last. "So you're the fiancé."

"I am." Gavin thrusts his hand forward. "Gavin Axelrod."

Ron shakes Gavin's hand aggressively, as he's wont to do. It's a way to establish dominance, though Gavin is giving it right back to him. They're sizing each other up.

Ron is still a handsome man but he's not aging especially well. His hair has thinned and his face has lined considerably. Gavin, on the other hand, is every bit as handsome as he was five years ago. Maybe even more so, though I'm loath to admit it.

Ron seems to be struggling to place Gavin; he must think he's seen that face or heard that name before.

Ask, I think. *Ask where you know him from.*

I want Ron to make it clear how peculiar it is that Lise is engaged to her high school English teacher. I can't say it, but he can.

Only Ron rarely does anything I want him to do. We think

differently, and beyond the first few years of our relationship, he's never been very invested in pleasing me.

I guess he just doesn't care that much who Gavin Axelrod is. This is only his daughter's future husband that we're talking about.

"Good to meet you," Ron says. Then he glances at me. "You're about to give Gavin the tour?"

"I can give him the tour," Lise says. "Hi, Dad."

"Hi, Lizzie." She doesn't correct him on her name, and they don't hug. They never do. And he doesn't tend to give me a hug or a kiss or any affectionate greeting unless there are important people around to impress with his perfect marriage. Again, Lise's fiancé doesn't rate. Which means Lise doesn't rate. Which pisses me off, but it won't do any good to say it.

I should probably be glad that Ron is so self-absorbed and oblivious. If he'd realized that I was on the verge of divorcing him, if he knew that I'd once had an affair with Gavin...

I don't even want to think about what that could mean. In Texas, you have the option of a no-fault divorce when it's amicable or there are no skeletons in your closet. But if I was found to be "at fault" for adultery, Ron could reduce my settlement even further. As if I haven't already been screwed enough by the prenup.

But I have a more immediate problem that Ron could actually help solve. "We were just talking about sleeping arrangements," I tell him. I'm sure we're aligned about separate rooms. He doesn't know yet that Lise and Gavin have already been living together.

"Gavin and I are taking the guest bedroom." Lise looks straight at Ron as if daring him to object. I guess this is how we know she's Lise, and not Lizzie.

We're all waiting to see what Ron is going to do now that she's fired her shot across his bow.

"Well," he says, "you are practically married."

Since when did Ron get so progressive? So easygoing? It must be because he doesn't know the full truth, and I guess I'll have to be the one to tell him.

"Gavin is Mr. Axelrod," I say. "He used to be Lizzie's teacher in high school." I watch Ron's face closely. His expression remains unaltered.

Why isn't he surprised? Did he already know about Gavin and Lise before I did?

No, there's no way Lise would have shared more about her life with Ron. My relationship with Lise is distant but Ron's is practically nonexistent.

Or is it the other way around?

I'm silently urging Ron to say something. He's Lise's father! He should be her protector. And even if you don't know what Gavin is capable of, anyone can see that this is weird. Not the good weird, as Lizzie used to say. It's very bad weird.

"Are you still a teacher?" Ron says. Gavin nods. "Noble profession."

What is going on here? Ron doesn't respect anyone making less than six figures.

I'm standing, watching Ron and Gavin make nice while Lise looks on happily. It's a moment of humiliation for me—Ron's just shown me to be the old-fashioned one—but even more than that, it's a moment of profound disappointment.

Sure, Ron's always been disengaged, but I've wanted to think that when there was a real need, he would rise to the occasion. He'd show how much he truly loves his daughter. I'd hoped for the same with my own father, and I'd only had those few brief months at the end. For a little while, I'd thought people really can change for the better.

Unfortunately, Ron's largely changed for the worst. When we were young, he'd given me the most beautiful and heartfelt proposal, pledging to love and take care of me. It had been just the two of us there on the beach in Galveston, and I swear, I would have married him right then. It had felt like a vow. And I made my own silent vow in return: while I didn't love him then, I would someday, and then always.

Only nothing's gone the way I planned. The way he promised.

Gavin turns to me. "You seem really upset about this sleeping situation, Di," he says. "If it really bothers you that much, I can be solo in the guest room."

"I didn't say it bothered me." It comes out defensive, and both Lise and Ron look at me quizzically. "You and Lise can sleep where you want."

It feels like waving the white flag, admitting I'm at their mercy in my own home, but then it occurs to me that maybe Gavin really didn't want to be in the same room with Lise. That he was hoping I would steal away in the night and come see him. Because there's a hint of flirtation—of seduction—that I recognize from long ago. Gavin likes dancing close to the fire, upping the ante, creating the potential for getting caught. He thinks that turns me on, too.

What's his endgame?

I never could read his mind the way he used to be able to read mine. Right now, I have no idea what he's really playing at.

I do know that he's using a lot of his old moves with Lise. At dinner, I observed just the sort of charm that he used to practice on me, how subtly he guides her in the direction of his own desires, all those micro-expressions to indicate pleasure or displeasure.

I remember all too well how persuasive he can be, all the things that I once did that I still can't bear to think about. It's like I was a car that Gavin was driving closer and closer to the edge of a cliff. Even when I was the one doing things that would have been previously unimaginable, he'd been the one steering.

Not that I have any excuse. I own my own mistakes. My

own bad deeds. I've been paying for them for years now. And the worst deed of all was before he and I even met.

I don't want Lizzie—Lise—to go through anything that I did. I don't want her to have to pay.

While Lise and Ron are engaged in small talk, I allow myself a glare in Gavin's direction. He's not even trying to disguise how much he's enjoying this.

And it's only Night One.

He knows everything about me, even my worst secret (which I imagine would be the worst secret anyone could have), and I know so little about him. He was probably lying to me the whole time about his past.

The last time I saw him, I'd been focused on self-preservation. I didn't even try to bring him to justice for the way he'd stalked me because the personal costs would have been too high. But now I see the error of my ways. When he walked free, I hadn't even considered the damage he'd do to the others who came after me. Never even imagined that my own daughter would be among his next victims.

I have to keep Lise and me from becoming two more skeletons in Gavin's closet.

Two more skeletons, period.

EIGHT

LISE

"You know what's funny?" I say, lying beside Gavin in the guest bed. "I've never slept in here before." I look around at the white walls with the black-and-white photos of flowers. Mom's decorating is so nondescript and inoffensive that it's peculiarly maddening. I feel like Dorothy in monochrome Kansas, yearning to get back to the Technicolor of Oz.

Gavin puts his book down on the nightstand and rolls toward me. Reading physical books was one of the first things we bonded over, though right now, I'm on my phone instead.

He kisses my neck, and I find myself starting to squirm. "What?" he asks.

"I guess I'm just tired."

It's not that, not entirely. I mean, I knew that we weren't going to sleep in my old room, even though there's a queen bed in there, too. But I couldn't have been with Gavin at the site of Lizzie's fantasies about Mr. Axelrod. I needed a neutral setting.

I never had sex in my old bedroom, didn't even lose my virginity until sophomore year of college when I decided to just get it over with. But I didn't discover myself sexually until Gavin because he's a real man, and a real man is interested in giving a woman pleasure. That's what he always says. And man, is it ever true.

But I'm not comfortable receiving pleasure right now, not in my parents' house. It would feel perverted somehow.

I don't want to say that, not when Gavin's hands are roaming my body. I know that this is going to be a night when he doesn't want to take no for an answer, though of course he will. A real man respects a woman's bodily autonomy.

"Sorry," I say. "I just don't think I'll be able to relax. I can't switch gears." I hold up my phone to show him the WhatsApp group chat. "I'm coordinating for tomorrow night, making sure everyone comes out to meet you."

"I've already met most of them." His tone is unusually dismissive.

"Years ago. But that was completely different. You were a teacher then."

"I'm a teacher now."

"You know what I mean. You're not *their* teacher now. You're certainly not my teacher anymore." I say that last part coquettishly, though he's not biting. Which makes sense; I shouldn't be teasing him, not when I've already said no to sex.

"So who's going to be there?" He still sounds none too pleased. As I reel off a few names, he cuts me off. "Are you serious? *Denver?*"

"I thought Denver would be right up your alley. He's smart and he's original. An iconoclast." Gavin loves that word. "I'm honestly surprised he stayed in Houston, but then, he did get into Rice, which is a pretty great school."

"You shouldn't judge people by what school they attend. That's elitist."

"I wasn't." I stare at him in surprise. What brought this on? "I just meant—"

"Denver was a legend in his own mind."

I'd never gotten that impression from Denver. But then, Gavin did have a different vantage point.

This conversation is filling me with apprehension. I'd thought Denver was the person who Gavin would enjoy the most at the bar tomorrow. If not, we might be in for a long night.

"I remember when they were in my classes," Gavin says. "How they could barely conjugate a verb, let alone analyze poetry. You always had depth. They didn't."

"I just really want to show you off. Please?" He doesn't immediately answer. "Well, would you rather I go without you?"

"No." That was instant.

"Can you go with a positive attitude then?" Now I'm the one rolling toward him, cajoling. "It'll only be a few hours. Do it for me."

"I'd do anything for you." His face has turned serious. "But would you do anything for me?"

"Obviously."

I'm not sure he quite believes me. "I'm worried," he says, "about the effect this house has on you. That your parents have on you. Especially your mom."

"There's nothing to worry about." Especially not Mom, who's basically afraid of her own shadow.

"You don't even want to have sex with me. You know how I feel about you, how irresistible you are. I can't go a week without."

"You won't have to." I touch his face. "We'll be together soon. I promise."

"I love you so much, Lise, but I've been let down before. You know that it's not easy for me to trust."

He had an affair with a woman years back—the mother of a student—who seduced and abandoned him. Who made all sorts of promises and told all sorts of lies. I used to wonder if it was Mom's best friend Mari—well, former best friend, since they had a falling out years ago. Gavin said he didn't want to name names, and that made me even more sure it was Mari. Because why else would he keep a secret from me?

He's got one, and I've got one, which makes us even. We're a perfectly matched set. "You can trust me," I say. "Always."

He finally smiles. "Always and forever."

THEN

NINE

DIANA

Mari—short for Marianne and pronounced like "marry," reminding everyone of her appalling level of matrimonial bliss—reached across the table and poured brandy into my coffee mug, then added a generous glug to her own. It was classic Mari. She cosplayed the consummate host, seemingly anticipating your every whim and desire, when really, she was setting it up so that she could help herself to whatever she wanted most.

Deep down, though, Mari was a good person and she'd likely be a supportive friend if I ever gave her any indication that I could use support. But I'd been raised to keep my feelings and problems to myself.

My real problem with Mari? She just seemed so deeply, truly, gratingly satisfied. If I were actively choosing a friend, I would never have selected someone who constantly triggered my sense of inadequacy.

But I rarely chose; I allowed. That was how I approached life, and I was increasingly realizing that it was one of the reasons Lizzie seemed to have such disdain for me.

She recently told me that she intends to grow up to be "a person with agency." I had to ask what that even meant. She just rolled her eyes and found a reason to leave the room, so I started Googling. I discovered I was, most emphatically, not a person with agency. I was the opposite, a person who followed all society's rules (written and unwritten) and everyone else's preferences. It just felt safer that way.

Mari was a person of agency.

She wasn't just about minimizing risk but about maximizing pleasure. She'd launched her charm offensive after I first moved into the neighborhood twelve years ago, and when Mari helps herself to you, you're helpless.

Not that it's ever really mattered who my best friend is. I'm a locked vault. But so nice. Easy to be around, never making waves. My whole life, I'd been busy and popular and lonesome.

I'd never understood why Mari liked drinking so much, and so early in the day, given her advantageous circumstances. We were sitting in a sun-drenched atrium overlooking the pond. Everything around Mari seemed to glitter, from her blonde highlights to her large and immaculate home to her husband, Nelson, who was in his forties and every bit as hot as the hot new English teacher. Nelson was affable and sweet, could say "whatever you want, dear" with twinkling eyes, ironic and sincere at once. He plainly adored Mari, and if that was an act, it was a damn good one. I'd heard nothing to the contrary from Mari or the local gossip. And there was always plenty of local gossip, much of it dispensed from Mari herself.

I was a little envious of her marriage, but I was rabidly jealous of her relationship with her children. Two of them, a daughter and a son. Sixteen-year-old twins. Who by all accounts—again, hers and local gossip—also adored her. They were physically attractive, socially adjusted, and academically accomplished. He was Harvard-bound and she was Yale-bound, which sounded oddly kinky, didn't it? All that bondage. As if Mari's perfectly attractive, perfectly perfect twins were engaging in S&M practices.

As if.

There was nothing to sully Mari or her family, and it was hard not to resent that, just a little, especially since my own daughter was typically so withdrawn. Her waiting in the living room on parents' night, ready and willing to talk to me, had been a notable exception. I'm sure it had more to do with the hot English teacher than with me.

That wasn't Mari's fault. So whose fault was it?

Mine, it had to be. Because I was the adult, and Lizzie's the child. So many times I'd looked at her surly, sulking, disapproving face and thought, "How could I possibly have become a mother at that age? What did I really know?"

I became a mother but clearly not a very good one. Otherwise, why would Lizzie hate talking to me?

Other women had the kind of confessional relationships where they could share insecure thoughts with their best friends. But every time I tried, I'd get lockjaw. My mother always said that weakness begets contempt. Expose your jugular and people will be tempted to slice it. Oh, sure, they might appear sympathetic at the time, they might even offer reassurance, but underneath what they feel is smug superiority. "Mark my words," she said, "they'll lose all respect for you. Then what will you have?"

Those words have guided every relationship I've ever had.

"So what kind of things did you hear during the teacher conferences?" Mari asked, taking a large sip of spiked coffee.

"Lizzie's doing well. Not Ivy League well but..." I smiled as I prepared my pivot. My deflection. I couldn't mention Gavin because I feared my face would give away that our interaction had been more than just another conference. "How about you? How are the twins?"

"They're doing well, too." Mari was happy to elaborate, providing specifics about the twins' accolades. I tuned out until I heard the name *Axelrod*. Then I was all ears.

"Are the twins in his class?" I said, with feigned casualness.

She nodded. "They each have him but not at the same time. Remember, I went to the school at the end of last year and asked that they be separated this year. It's like a trial run for college. They have to start individuating now."

"Makes sense," I murmured, though I didn't know what individuating was. "What do they think of Mr. Axelrod?"

"Beefcake, right?" Mari pretended to fan herself. "But what's strange is that Genevieve hadn't even mentioned the way he looks. I don't mean she should have focused on that exclusively, but it was kind of an oversight, don't you think?"

"Even Lizzie mentioned it." That wasn't true; I'd just overheard her on the phone to friends and gathered as much.

Mari leaned forward. "I wouldn't trust that man as far as I could throw him."

"What do you mean?" I was stunned. And a little worried, since Lizzie seemed to have taken a shine to him. I had, too, a little. "What have you heard?"

"Things have come way too easily to that man. You can just tell." She was certainly one to talk. Maybe like repels like. It's just a principle of physics, not that I took physics.

"So you haven't heard anything specific?" I persisted. Mari shook her head and I felt some measure of relief. "Lizzie really likes him."

"Of course she does. All that talk about how writing is a revolutionary act, that it can change the world. He's catnip for teen girls. Teen-nip."

Before I could respond, I heard the sound of an incoming text. I peeked at my phone and saw it was Ron: *I'm craving Florentine lasagna.*

Ugh. Lasagna. That's three hours of work, on virtually no notice.

Mari looked at my phone, too. She'd never been shy about that, and I'd never really had anything to hide. "Tell him to fuck off. But politely. You know, say, 'Bless your heart but Mari and I have plans all afternoon. I'll get a bucket of fried chicken.'"

"Yeah, right."

I'd long held the impression she didn't like Ron or how he treated me but wasn't about to launch a full-scale intervention. It was no secret that she wanted me to speak up for myself more.

"Men are trainable, you know," she said. "You think Nelson came out of the box like that?"

"I've been married for seventeen years." The template was fully set. And Lizzie loves that lasagna, too, so why pick fights?

"It's never too late. Old dogs can actually learn new tricks."

Another text came in. It was a little humiliating, how Ron expected me to answer him instantly in the affirmative.

Only it wasn't Ron. It was from an unknown number.

Hi, Diana! It's Gavin. There are a few things I forgot to mention about Lizzie. Maybe we should schedule another meeting.

I hadn't covered my phone, and Mari fixed her gaze on me, eyes alight. "Who's Gavin?" she said.

"Mr. Axelrod." Hadn't he told all the parents to call him Gavin?

"Ah. Intriguing."

"It's really not. I think he's worried about Lizzie." Not that I wanted to go into any details; I never did.

I hoped Mari would say something reassuring and positive about Lizzie but she just nodded. "I can imagine that, Lizzie writing poetry like Sylvia Plath."

I didn't know who Sylvia Plath was but I didn't let on. Mari's older than me, more educated, just like all the other moms in this neighborhood. They went to college before getting married.

Mari revealed a slightly lascivious smile. "So Mr. Axelrod—excuse me, *Gavin*—wants to meet up. You have to say yes, if only to keep your daughter from putting her head in the oven."

I stared at her, my heartbeat accelerating. Lizzie seemed down sometimes and often irritable, but suicidal? What had Mari heard?

"Don't look so panicked. It's a Sylvia Plath reference. You know, the tormented poetess who killed herself by carbon monoxide poisoning?" Now she was staring at me. "I meant it as a joke, but once I explain it, it's hardly funny. And I know Lizzie can be, you know, a handful but she's probably not clinically depressed. She's just an introvert. She's a deep thinker."

"Do you really think so?" I didn't like my tone, how pleading I seemed. "I mean, of course Lizzie's fine. She's wonderful."

"Go meet *Gavin*. Then tell me all about it." There was a glimmer in her eye. But that didn't mean she wasn't watching closely. Mari never missed a trick.

I hoped she couldn't see through me, that she couldn't tell how much I liked the idea of seeing Gavin again. Far more than I should have.

TEN

LIZZIE

"Oof!" Denver said as his elbow went into my head (not by his own power or volition). He'd been pushed. Again.

"Ow!" I said back, more in solidarity than in pain. Denver had been having a rough time since moving to Houston, targeted by jock boys. I felt for him since his parents gave him such an on-the-nose name. He was from—you guessed it—Colorado. I wasn't a fan of Elizabeth in its totality, but as Mom said, it came with options, which I intended to exercise once I went away to college. I was thinking of becoming Elle. Or maybe even Zizi, if I could pull it off.

My school had these absurd mini-lockers and mine was below Denver's, a particularly unfortunate spot given all that jostling in the hallway from the toxic masculinity crew. Denver was as much of a beanpole as I was but he was new and I was old, having gone to school with all these kids since elementary. I was largely left alone. I wasn't a pariah; I could get invited to a party if it was big enough. I just never wanted to go.

"It's been two months." Denver slammed his locker door emphatically. "When's the hazing going to stop?"

"I don't know. I'll never understand the troglodyte mind."

He smiled down at me. "I love your vocabulary."

I looked away, blushing. I'd inherited that condition from my mom, except when she blushed, it accentuated her beauty, made her seem more approachable. When I did it, my whole face turned as red as my pimples.

Denver really was odd. No other guy in this school would pay such a direct compliment without a trace of self-consciousness or passive aggression.

Actually, Mr. Axelrod could, but then, he wasn't a guy; he's a man.

"You're weird," I said to Denver, my version of a compliment.

"Glad you noticed. I'm not trying to fit in with assholes or the bystanders who enable them."

I felt a trace of shame. I wasn't one to speak out much. Or really, to speak at all at school, except in Mr. Axelrod's class where I couldn't help myself. I was just too inspired to keep quiet. I needed Mr. Axelrod to know the real me.

I stood up, placing my bulging backpack over my shoulder. I was taking AP classes to make sure my grade point average stayed high enough to get me into UT Austin. No sense leaving anything to chance. Mr. Axelrod had livened up this place but that didn't mean I intended to stay.

I started walking up the hall and Denver fell into step beside me. Despite the social antagonism he was experiencing, he had this loose-limbed gait as if he didn't have a care in the world. That was probably part of what pissed other guys off, that they weren't getting under his skin the way they wanted. He was one of the only boys in school with long hair and he knew that if he cut it, at least some of his harassers would back off. They would feel like they'd beaten him into submission. He'd know that he wasn't so special after all, that a nail that sticks up will get hammered down. But he'd told me that he'd never give them the satisfaction.

I envied his confidence, and I wasn't the only one. Some of the other less conforming members of the student body were definitely drawn to him. He could probably be their king, if he was interested in that, but he didn't like "hierarchical power structures."

See? Weird. But in a good way.

As I got closer to Mr. Axelrod's classroom, my mood lifted with each step. Denver loped along beside me, trying to engage, but honestly? I could barely formulate a response. All I could think about was what I was going to say in class (and maybe after class) about the previous night's reading. I really wanted to impress Mr. Axelrod with my critical acumen. Hadn't he told Mom I was insightful? I needed to live up to that.

It was hard for me to be anything but impatient with everyone around me. I was antsy for my real life to begin, and Mr. Axelrod was the shape of things to come, a harbinger or an omen, assuming harbingers or omens could be associated with anything positive and not just doom.

In college, people were going to be deep. They'd care about substance. About words. About insight.

I looked right past the other girls in the hallway, the ones who were always putting on lip gloss and studying their asses in the changing room mirror like that's all the worth and value they had. I wouldn't have chosen to be like them, even if I could.

Not that I could.

I was too spindly for hot pants, and even though my stomach's flat, no one wanted to see a midriff with protruding ribs. Over the years, I'd been occasionally mocked by people saying they should donate $5 a day and adopt me through Save the Children. Who didn't want to join the fight against malnourishment, starting in our own backyard? Hardy har har.

I'd just been marking time here until Mr. Axelrod came along. He was my saving grace. He gave me hope that someday, I'd find my people. My person.

If I ever got married, which was doubtful, it was going to be to someone like Mr. Axelrod. We were right outside his classroom now and I had to suppress a grin.

Denver shot me a pointed glance. Or as pointed as a sweet goofball could muster. "You really like him, huh?"

"Who?" I decided to play dumb.

"Mr. Axelrod."

"Everyone likes him."

"I heard that you talk all the time in Mr. Axelrod's class. But you hardly say a word in any of the classes I have with you."

"Didn't know you were keeping tabs on me." I wasn't sure how I felt about it. Was it good weird—flattering weird—or just creepy?

"I'm keeping tabs on him." Denver jerked a thumb toward Mr. Axelrod's door.

"You don't need to," I said. "Just a tip since you're new: Mr. Axelrod's the best they've got."

"Best at what, though?"

I felt myself blushing. Because one way or another, I intended to find that out myself.

NOW

ELEVEN

DIANA

"I thought I'd find you here."

Though Lise's voice is playful, I look up in slight alarm. I can tell she's trying, that she wants this visit to go well, and of course I do, too. But what are the odds, when Gavin is on the loose in my house? When he's on the loose in her life?

"Good morning," I say, forcing a smile. Then I go back to the quiche I'm making. It's good to have a distraction, not to have to look deeply in her eyes.

I have so much to conceal. So does Gavin, but he's probably getting off on the duplicity, and on my discomfort. Two for the price of one.

What does he *really* want from me, and from her? As much as I dread the thought of being alone with him, I need to pin him down. If it's truly about money, then I'll have to figure out how I can persuade Ron to part with his. It won't be easy, but I'd do anything to save Lise.

I'd planned this large Sunday brunch to welcome Lise's fiancé to the family. That was before I knew he was a sociopath. Now I'm going through the motions, hoping he chokes on it. I can't recall how to perform the Heimlich, can you?

Lise settles herself on a stool at the kitchen island. She's still in her pajamas, her hair in a messy bun. It feels like we've gone back in time to her high school days, except for the friendly and open expression on her face. Oh, and how clear her skin is. She really is glowing. I hate to think that's the Gavin effect.

I feel myself tensing up. The last thing I need right now is some mother-daughter bonding time.

All I want is to blow the whistle on Gavin, to tell Lise everything I know about the man she loves. But what if he turned around and told Lise that I'm a murderer? From the hold he appears to have on her, she's more likely to believe him than me. And actually, he should be believed. He'd be telling the truth.

I continue chopping. "How did you sleep?" I ask.

"Pretty well. The mattress in the guest bedroom is way better than my old one."

"It's barely broken in." Ron and I both grew up in Houston and our families are local. The guest bedroom doesn't see much action except when he gets in late from work or from required shmoozing and sleeps in there. He says it's so he won't disturb me but it's far more likely that he has something to hide. Of course, I have little interest in his secret dalliances.

Silence descends on Lise and me, broken only by the staccato sound of chopping. "What do you think of him?" she finally blurts.

"I told you he was a good teacher—"

"Not your old opinion. Your new one." She looks so heartbreakingly hopeful. But since when is she suddenly so obsessed with my good opinion? It's a little bit bizarre. It makes me wonder if Gavin's putting some sort of pressure on her. I can just imagine the sadistic pleasure he would get from me being forced into giving my verbal blessing. Maybe he'll want me to officiate their wedding.

Their wedding.

The bile rises in my throat, making it momentarily difficult to speak. Lise is watching me closely.

I avert my eyes to the white marble countertops veined in gray. They take a ridiculous amount of maintenance, but Ron had insisted. Quartz wasn't good enough for his dream palace, no sirree.

I shouldn't be thinking of countertops when I need to come up with a proper response to Lise.

I had plenty of time since I barely slept last night. But my thoughts were frenzied and terrified, like I was in a waking fever dream. I was sweating, too. Maybe the stress of Gavin's reappearance has catalyzed early menopause. Ron slept through, undisturbed. I'm still disappointed in him for not seeming to care about the obvious inappropriateness of a teacher engaged to his former student. But it's not like Ron knows who Gavin really is or what he's done. Outrage is too much to expect.

I should probably be glad that Ron's not outraged, because if he were, it would be with me first and foremost. He wouldn't take betrayal lightly. No, Ron would make for a very vengeful cuck.

Gavin must know that. Is he planning to tell Ron—about the killing, or the affair, or both?

Lise is staring me down, refusing to let this subject drop.

"It seems like Gavin makes you very happy," I hedge. Which is, unfortunately, an honest answer.

"He really does." She gives me such a pure smile that I know the social graces my mother instilled have served me well once again. Maybe I should become a diplomat someday. Join the foreign service. If Gavin really does become my son-in-law, I'll want a continent between us.

What if he becomes the father of my grandchildren?

I pick up the knife and attack the pepper. The recipe said chopped but I'm entitled to liberties. I need to mince.

"I could tell you were a little freaked out last night," she says. "And I get it, I really do. I never thought I'd be engaged this young, either. You don't need to worry, though. I've got a good head on my shoulders. I would never have gotten engaged until I finished college. I told Gavin that was important to me. I know it's important to you, too."

"It is," I say, not looking up.

"You probably noticed I'm not wearing a ring. I've never been big on diamonds or anything like that. I didn't want him wasting his money. Well, our money. We're a team."

I make a noncommittal noise and continue chopping.

"I thought that might have been one of the reasons you didn't look so happy. In your eyes, if a man proposes, he's supposed to have a ring, right? But he was listening to my wishes. That's the most important quality in a husband, that he respects how I feel. Right?"

"Right." I'm gritting my teeth. My suspicion? That Gavin manipulated her into thinking those were her wishes. Given the chance, he'll probably backseat-plan their entire wedding, and all the while, she'll be telling her friends what a great listener he is. So supportive. All he wants is to make her dreams come true.

He used to pull that same shit with me. Then he pulled the rug out from under me.

My hand tightens on the knife's handle. I don't know how long I'm going to be able to tolerate this, hearing her extol his virtues as if he's some kind of feminist hero.

As she prattles on about how fantastically considerate he is, I picture myself hurling the knife with all my strength. I can see the blade lodging and then sticking out horizontally from the custom cabinetry while I shout, "Enough! He's not who you think!"

Instead, I wait politely for an opening and say, "So what about your career?"

"What do you mean?" She looks at me askance, like I shouldn't have dared to interrupt her reverie with something so mundane. Another sign that beneath the veneer, the shellac of Gavin's influence, she's still Lizzie.

I never thought I'd be so excited to have my daughter roll her eyes at me.

"You were talking about how you and Gavin are teammates," I say, "how you help each other realize your goals. I'm just wondering what those are for you, career-wise."

"I'm not sure exactly. Communications is a really versatile degree."

"That's what I always told your father. I've stood up for you." Not that it did anything because Ron never changes an opinion on my account. "But you did graduate a few months ago. I thought maybe you'd have narrowed the possibilities by now?"

"I'm keeping it broad." She's also keeping her cards close to her vest. Did she really think she'd show up here with no true job prospects and her former teacher as a fiancé and I'd clap my hands with glee?

"Where have you applied?"

"Lots of places. Look, I don't really want to talk about this." She stands up and walks to the refrigerator. Then she brings champagne and orange juice to the island. "Do you want a mimosa, too?"

"Yes, please." I wish I could swig directly from the bottle. And chase it with some morphine.

Lise pops the cork and starts pouring into the flutes. Without looking up, she says, "I just want you to be happy for me. Can't you do that?"

I hesitate. Despite everything, I really do hate telling lies. I got to be quite proficient during my time with Gavin but it's not a skill I relish.

Lise is only here for a week, though. I'm going to have to tell a lot of lies, and I'm going to need to work fast.

I have to get back on solid footing with Lise. Maybe I can

get her to agree to a long engagement, which will give Gavin the time to display his uglier aspects. If I manage to stay close over the next year, I can be the voice in her ear pointing out all his tricks. Lise may be young and inexperienced but she's smart, too. By the time this is over, she'll have picked up valuable lessons about red flags, honing her gut, and who can and can't be trusted.

Gavin is a great teacher, after all.

Can I play the long game like that, or will this have to be quick and dirty? I have no choice but to corner him. Then I'll know how bloody this is going to get.

I picture him waltzing into the kitchen with that smirk of his just as I pull the quivering knife blade from where it's embedded itself in a cupboard and then I plunge it into—

"Yes," I say, "I can be happy."

TWELVE
LISE

Mom has us eating outside next to the pool even though it's hot as balls. Sure, we're under the covered veranda and occasionally the misters come on to sheen us with water, but still. It would have been way better inside.

If I'd protested, Mom would have blamed Dad, saying he insisted on a backyard brunch. And while a great many things are, legitimately, his fault, sometimes I've wondered if his assholery is her camouflage. Like last night when she wanted Gavin and me in separate rooms and then Dad came home and… Busted! He obviously didn't care about our premarital sex. Which meant that she was the one who did. So why couldn't she have just said that? Why can't she ever just say what she means?

I'm a fine one to talk, I guess, seeing as I'm sitting here silently playing the easygoing houseguest. I'm letting myself feel uncomfortable so that no one else has to be.

Oh no, am I actually becoming my mother? *Already?* I thought that wouldn't happen until after I had kids of my own. Not that that's in my immediate future, much as Gavin says he'd love to have a little me running around.

"This is really excellent, Di," Gavin says, waving a forkful of quiche.

"Diana," she corrects.

That's no way to treat a houseguest, is it? I noticed this at the steakhouse, too, that she occasionally abandoned her social graces. For her, that's truly bizarre. I'm going to need to watch her closely to figure out what's going on. Because she sure as shit isn't going to just come right out and tell me.

"My mistake," Gavin says, taking it in stride. "I was being presumptuous. Or Lise, did you tell me to call her Di?"

"I said her friends call her that," I affirm, though actually, I can't recall saying it. But one member of the couple is supposed to swoop in for the other sometimes—socially speaking, that is. Not to the extent that my mom does for my dad, but every now and again, there's something romantic about catching the bullet that's intended for your partner. It means you're really paying attention, and that's something that I've felt from Gavin ever since he was Mr. Axelrod. Nothing's getting past him, in the best way.

"Call her Di," Dad says, which peeves me. He's never looking out for Mom. He doesn't mind making things harder for her. Maybe he even enjoys it.

"If Mom prefers Diana," I say, "then that's what Gavin will call her. Right, babe?"

"Absolutely." Gavin widens his lips in a smile that he then directs toward Mom. "I wouldn't want to act overly familiar."

Gavin could not be any nicer, and yet Mom appears to tense up. I seriously don't know what's with her.

"Ron," she says, "did you and Gavin ever actually meet before? When he was Lizzie's teacher?"

"I'm Lise!" It comes out petulant, which is annoying. I don't want to sound like a little kid when this whole visit is about demonstrating the opposite.

"You were Lizzie then," Mom says, her eyes still on Dad. It's like she really cares about this particular answer.

"I'm not sure." Dad turns to Gavin. "Have we met?"

"I don't think so, sir." Gavin's in suck-up mode, which I don't love, but it's probably normal when meeting the future in-laws. Who would have thought my mother would be the harder sell?

"You never attended many parent-teacher conferences." Mom's tone is neutral but it's hard to miss the underlying air of judgment. "Really, I could count them on one hand."

Dad's face tightens, and so does my stomach.

I've never seen him be violent. But psychological control can be way scarier. Mom is totally under Dad's thumb and always has been. Except for right now, when she's poking the bear.

What's gotten into her?

She's basically swigging mimosa. Gavin and I are both staring at her as he says, "We can talk about the elephant in the room." She freezes. "Lise and I didn't exactly have a romcom beginning. I mean, I would have preferred if she and I had met some other way. I understand how it looks."

She sets the champagne flute down, not answering.

"Gavin and I haven't done anything wrong," I say. "He's an amazing teacher but that's all he was to me then."

Mom's eyes are on the table. Dad looks from me to Mom to Gavin, his face inscrutable. My heart speeds up. He can be a real dick when he wants to.

There's a long fraught moment. Then Dad's face relaxes into a smile. "If you say so, Lizzie, then I believe it."

"Really?" Now I'm smiling. For once, I don't even mind that he called me Lizzie. I didn't think he'd be the one on my side. Does that mean Mom's against me?

"Really," Dad says. "Everyone has to grow up sometime. Get married and you'll age a decade."

Mom leaps up, knocking over the mimosa (her third, but who's counting). "Sorry," she says. She's on the verge of tears, which is just not like her, especially not in front of company. And she's made it more than clear that Gavin is company; he's not family.

But he will be soon, and she's going to have to accept that.

I get to my feet, too, helping to wipe up Mom's area of the table with my linen napkin. Dad stays seated, of course.

"Thanks, honey," she tells me, "but there's no need. I'll go inside and get a sponge."

"Grab me another beer while you're in there," Dad says. No "please" on this end and there won't be a "thank you" on the other. If she hadn't spilled her glass and needed to go inside, he would have told her to get his beer anyway. He probably thinks he's being considerate by preemptively instructing her when he still has a few swallows left.

I'd glower at him but he did just come through for me. Besides, any strong display of negative emotion toward Dad would ignite Gavin's equally strong protective instinct. I'd like to make it out of this week without Gavin and my dad getting into it.

I'm worried that might be impossible. Dad's a prick at heart, and Gavin has an irrepressible chivalric streak. He can't help it. He's a Texas boy. It's baked in. He's not going to let anyone hurt the woman he loves.

But Dad's not the problem this trip. It's Mom who's acting stiff and jumpy at once. She knocked over her wine last night at dinner, too.

Wait, am I the world's worst daughter? All full of indignation and irritation when something might be truly wrong with Mom? She hasn't just seemed shaky at this brunch; she's been off kilter in every way from the second I first saw her at the steakhouse.

"Are you sick?" It comes out borderline hysterical and I

guess it's true that you don't know how much you love someone until you think you might lose them.

"What?" my mom says, jolted.

"Is something wrong with you physically? Or, I don't know, mentally?" I say. Gavin lets out a bark of laughter and I'm surprised because usually he knows when I'm kidding and when I most definitely am not. "Mom, are you all right?"

"Oh, honey." She takes me in her arms and how natural it feels is the biggest surprise of all. "I didn't know you cared."

"*What?*" I wrench my head back to stare at her. "You didn't think I'd care if you had some neurological disease?"

Now Dad is laughing, a scornful, snide laugh that cuts through me like a gale-force wind.

Gavin watches Dad, eyes narrowing, but before he can open his mouth, I blurt out the first thing that comes to me: "I'm just so glad you're not dying!"

Mom smiles as if it's the sweetest thing she's heard from me in ages, and maybe it is, which is a horrid thought.

It's true, I'm glad that Mom is going to stick around, but if she's not sick, then what is she? Why does she seem so agitated and afraid? And why can't she look my fiancé in the face?

If I didn't know better, I'd think Mom had something to hide.

THEN

THIRTEEN

DIANA

"Hello!" My voice sounded falsely bright as it echoed in the empty classroom. I wasn't nervous to see Gavin, seeing as he'd put me so at ease during our first meeting, but I was concerned about what he had to tell me.

His texts had been cryptic and insistent. We needed to meet. There was something I had to know.

I told myself to be grateful for this window into Lizzie. Gavin was about to offer me insider information when I'd become such an outsider over the past few years.

Lizzie was in trouble, that much was obvious. But would she let me help? It seemed doubtful.

Gavin was smiling as he ushered me into the room. "So good to see you again," he said. "You look lovely."

The compliment caught me off guard. "Oh." I blushed. "Thank you."

I moved toward his teacher's desk, assuming we'd take the same spots we'd occupied during the parent-teacher confer-ences, but he was heading toward the student desks. They were the same as when I was in school, a curving wooden arm bolted to an iron chair.

Gavin picked two up and turned them so that they'd face each other. The rows were awfully close together—meaning he and I were awfully close together. My blush deepened.

"For you, madam," he said, gesturing toward one of the desks. I sat down and he followed suit.

I waited for him to plunge in, given the urgency of his texts. His eyes were warm on my face. "How are you?" he asked.

"Nervous, to be honest. For a while, I've suspected that Lizzie's really struggling. I wanted to be wrong about that but you calling me here confirmed it. I'm right, aren't I?"

"Yes and no." I could tell he was choosing his next words carefully. "During the conference, I told you that I believe Lizzie will ultimately be okay. But this is a pivotal moment. How you respond as a parent—how I respond as a teacher—can have a determinative effect."

"I'm sorry, I don't know what that means."

"This is a perilous time for Lizzie. You and I need to work together because what we do could have a significant impact on her future."

My heartbeat accelerated. "Perilous? What kind of danger is she in?"

"Relax. It's going to be okay."

"But you said—"

"Let's slow this down. Breathe with me, Di." He closed his eyes, did a deep and performative inhale, and a long exhale.

I just stared at him. I wanted him to get on with it. Tell me what was wrong with my baby.

He opened his eyes. "You didn't breathe, did you?"

"If I wasn't breathing, I'd be dead, right?" He laughed. "Don't keep me in suspense. I've been worried since I got your texts."

"Okay, okay." He laughed again. "Your breathing is your own business. My texts weren't a five-alarm fire. I really think we've got time on this one."

I didn't answer. He was trying to help me relax but it felt like he was stalling, as if he didn't want to deliver the bad news. So my anxiety just kept growing.

"I've noticed a bit of a change in Lizzie. In how she relates to boys. Her interactions have seemed more... sexualized."

"Sexualized?" I echoed.

He nodded. "I've seen her sort of draping herself over their lockers, or bending over and tying her shoes right in front of them, or—you know the tricks, right?"

I nodded. Unfortunately, I did.

This was tapping into my biggest fear. The last thing I wanted was for Lizzie to follow in my footsteps. If she got pregnant, Ron would insist on marrying her off just like my parents had married me off to him.

Lizzie was supposed to have all the opportunities I never had. I couldn't let her get pregnant and derail her entire future.

But could I really stop her?

"I see you spiraling," Gavin said. He reached out and put his hand over mine. "The important thing is that you're here. That we're talking. Nothing's going to happen instantly."

"It only takes one time. One time without protection and a girl's life will be..." I was about to say "over" but that's not what I meant. Becoming a mother was hardly a death sentence. No, it's more of a life sentence. "I don't want Lizzie to be me. I got pregnant at sixteen."

It came out in a whisper, and once it had, I was mortified. This wasn't how I talked to near strangers.

But he didn't feel like a stranger. He felt like a confidante, which was crazy. Because I didn't have those.

His hand was still on mine.

I stared down at it, and he pulled away, seeming self-conscious. "I don't know what it is, Di," he said. "There's something about you, and about Lizzie. I just want to keep you safe."

"I appreciate that." I really did. It wasn't something I had even been feeling from Ron lately. "But what do we do? How do we help Lizzie?"

"I think it's a watch-and-wait situation. You and I both keep our eyes open for further changes, and then we keep in touch. We compare notes."

"You don't think I should say anything?"

He shook his head. "I'll talk to her. Tell her what I'm observing. Give her the guy's perspective. I'll say that the way she's acting isn't going to earn anyone's respect, and she deserves to be respected."

"You'd do that for her?" *And for me?* If I said anything, she'd accuse me of spying on her. She'd dismiss anything I said, and the behavior would likely intensify in defiance. She'd show me that she can't be controlled.

I remembered that from my own childhood. I'd been rebelling against my overbearing mom, and look what happened.

I stared at Gavin in amazement. I couldn't believe my luck, that he was willing to invest his time and attention in Lizzie. And in me.

His smile was dazzling. "I've got you, Di."

FOURTEEN

LIZZIE

"Mr. Axelrod!" I called. He was just about to get into his car. It was a battered Mazda 3 and looked like it hadn't been washed in about a hundred years. I loved that it didn't suit this neighborhood at all.

"What are you doing here so late?" he asked. He turned around and leaned against his car door, seeming in no particular rush.

Now that I'd approached him, I wasn't sure exactly what I even wanted to say. It felt different somehow, being outside of not only the classroom but the entire school building. I hoped my skin didn't look too terrible in the late afternoon sunshine.

"I was painting scenery for the school show." I gestured toward the messy smock I was still wearing over my clothes.

"Will I get to see you onstage?"

I made a face. "Absolutely not. I don't like painting, either. But you know how it is. I need to bulk up my extracurriculars if I want to get into UT Austin."

"What about UT Dallas? That's where I went." I liked how casually he told me personal information. He probably didn't do that with all his students.

"I think Austin needs me more. I'd be good at keeping it weird."

He laughed. "You'll have to tell me about that sometime."

Was that an offer to, like, hang out? My face went up in flames, which was way annoying. It made it hard to think about what to say next.

"Maybe you could do an extracurricular that you actually care about. I've been thinking of starting a literary magazine. You think you'd be interested?"

My eyes lit up. I'd bet he wasn't proposing this to all the girls in hot pants. "Definitely! What would I do?"

"You could write. You could also help me pick from the submissions. Critique and edit other students' work. That's a great skill to have, supporting people in their growth."

"I can see that." It's what he did for me.

"Glad to know you'd be on board. I haven't decided for sure if I can fully commit to the lit magazine. I've just started on a personal project, and if all goes well, it might take up a significant amount of time." His face took on a faraway, almost dreamy look. "I shared your poetry with your mother at the conference. Did she tell you?"

"No. Which poem?" *Not "Insecure." Anything but that one.*

"The one about feeling insecure. I thought if she knew what was going on inside, you two could have some meaningful conversations."

I couldn't be mad when he was only trying to help, though he was barking up the wrong tree. "Mom doesn't do meaningful. Like I said, she never even told me she'd read it."

"It really moved her. She cares a lot about your pain, Lizzie."

"I'm not in pain." It wasn't like I was some abused child. I was privileged, and I knew it, even if I kind of hated everyone and everything other than Mr. Axelrod.

"You don't need to lie to me. Vulnerability is a beautiful thing."

I looked past him, making sure no one could overhear. The faculty parking lot was empty but for a few cars. "I guess life is hard sometimes."

"You're a very thoughtful person. A very internal person. But sometimes it can help to externalize."

"What do you mean?"

"I mean, most of your clothes look kind of like that smock." He gestured. "It feels like you're trying to hide in plain sight."

"I just don't care about things like clothes." That was part of my identity, how I separated myself from the other girls who cared way too much. But was he telling me I looked ugly? This was basically my worst nightmare.

"Even when you choose not to participate, you're still participating."

"I don't understand."

"You can't opt out of life, Lizzie. It's happening whether you like it or not. You can't disappear for the next two years and just reappear once you get to college, fully formed. You have to show up, now."

"What do you think I should do differently?"

"Put yourself out there. Be bold."

I felt disappointed in him. A little defiant, even. "I'm not going to show off my tits and ass like all those other girls."

"Of course not. You're better than them."

My spirits lifted instantly.

"Personally, I think what matters most is subtext versus text. It's about suggestion versus obviousness." He pulled out his phone and started scrolling. Then he held it out. "These are just a few examples. It's about finding your own style. Dress to feel good and be seen."

I stared at the screen, making mental notes.

"It's as if you've just given up on how you present," he continued, "like you think you're not even worth the effort."

He was right; I did sort of feel like that. I had been opting out. But how could he know? Had anyone ever put such time and effort toward figuring me out before? It made me feel almost... compelling.

Was it possible that the most charismatic and awesome man I'd ever met saw something in me?

"You're worth it," he told me.

I felt like I was glowing. Because he was worth *everything*.

NOW

FIFTEEN
DIANA

I'm supposed to be out running errands. That's what I told Lise I was doing. She gave me a funny look and said, "You couldn't have picked up Dad's dry cleaning before I got to town?" I told her I was sorry, but I'd been so excited about the visit that some things had just flown out of my brain.

The first part was true: I had been genuinely excited about the visit and rebuilding our relationship. The second part was the lie. I'd made sure to clear my to-do list so that I could be entirely available to Lise and her fiancé for the whole week.

Now I'm sitting in the mall parking lot, trying not to cry or scream or vomit. I couldn't have spent one more second in that house. I'd needed to get away from Lise and Gavin and their constant public displays of affection.

I've been trying to get Gavin alone for a conversation but it's like he's been thwarting me, making sure he's glued to her side.

This isn't only about money or love; it's also about vengeance. He wants me to suffer.

I wish I had somewhere to go, someone I could talk to, a friend I could fully trust. Every time I spy Mari, I run the other way. On the very few occasions I haven't been able to avoid her, she's looked openly venomous.

I don't know if she's told her other friends—my old friends—the whole truth of what happened between us, and the disgusting things I've done. I avoid them all. If only I could outrun my own bad deeds, but it doesn't work that way.

I killed someone—someone I loved—and there's no outrunning that. It's with me, always.

But I do my best to fill my time and occupy my mind. I have a new group of "friends" now. They live in other prosperous planned communities. They're the wives of the other VPs whose husbands are jockeying for power. The CEO is already seventy, so the successor will be anointed soon. As you'd imagine, given those politics, there's an automatic ceiling on how close the other wives and I can really be, which generally suits me fine.

But it does mean that this is all on me. I have to figure out this Gavin situation alone. Ron doesn't seem even slightly concerned, and this week he's going to be working his usual long hours. I'm on my own.

How can I expose Gavin without exposing myself? Without him turning around and exposing me?

I defeated him once, but he's like the villain in a horror movie, the one who gets slashed and keeps getting back up.

He knows my secrets. He knows my weaknesses. But what do I really know for sure about Gavin Axelrod? How do I stop him?

SIXTEEN

LISE

This night is not going well.

Why am I surprised, though? The day didn't go well, either.

After that bizarro brunch, Mom announced that she had errands to do. Yes, errands as pressing as picking up my father's dry cleaning. I tried not to feel rejected. I mean, Dad really would have laid into her about his missing shirts. But when she said that she'd been so excited about my visit that she'd forgotten her wifely duties, she hadn't sounded convincing. I've always said Mom was a terrible liar, and she proved it again.

For dinner, Dad insisted on going back to the same steakhouse where we'd just been because it was his favorite. Who does that? Well, Dad, obviously, but the bigger question is, who goes along with such bullshit? I'm embarrassed to say the answer isn't only Mom, but me, too.

I sat there fuming the whole time, which was part of why the conversation was so stilted. Poor Gavin. He carried the whole thing on his back, asking Mom and Dad lots of questions, trying to joke me into a better mood. It didn't work.

Now I'm here with my old friends at a sports bar just down the street from my parents' house because no one felt like driving into one of the cooler parts of Houston. I guess none of them thought my homecoming was worth the effort.

I shouldn't blame them. I haven't put any effort in over the years, either. I stayed in Austin for practically all my breaks while occasionally "liking" their social media posts.

Maya's changed a lot. Her hair is dyed jet black and intricately shaved. She's in baggy, ripped clothing and her face is dotted with piercings. I might have said she'd come into her own except that she's twinning with her girlfriend, Bree.

Kristina's here, too. She hasn't changed a bit. She's still easy to overlook and to forget, so sweet that you feel guilty for finding her boring, and she's flanked by her boyfriend, Bill, who seems to be exactly the same way. They're both dressed preppy, like they came from the country club.

Then there's Denver.

He's the only one without a significant other, and he looks good, I'm not going to lie. Once it was no longer a badge of honor or a point of rebellion, he finally cut his hair. He's got some muscle definition. While I can't picture Denver lifting weights, he must. He's in a black band t-shirt (as in, a t-shirt that just says BAND) and jeans.

All I wanted was to see everyone and hear what they're up to and brag just a little about having landed the hot English teacher. I mean, I knew that it might initially raise a few eyebrows, but ultimately, they'd see it as a sign of my maturity. Gavin chose me. The thing is, if he and I had met under different circumstances ten months ago, we would have fallen in love anyway. We're meant to be, and I wanted them to see that. After keeping our relationship under wraps this whole time, never posting even a single picture, I was looking forward to the big reveal party.

But it hasn't been anything like what I'd hoped.

Maya practically wrinkles her nose as she turns to Bree and

explains, "Gavin's Mr. Axelrod. Our English teacher. From high school."

Bree's expression is muted horror, and Denver stifles a laugh. Kristina and Bill smile politely. Beside me, Gavin's body tenses up. He hates being the butt of a joke. But then, who likes it? My cheeks have gone scarlet.

"So what's everyone else been up to?" Denver says, and he probably means well with the change of subject. Instead, it feels like Gavin and I are such freaks that they all just want to look away.

Maya and Bree start talking about the preparations they're doing for their student show. They're both fifth-year art students at the University of Houston. They finish each other's sentences, punctuated by the occasional open-mouth kiss.

"So what are you going to do next?" Gavin asks them.

"What do you mean?" Maya says. Bree stares at him challengingly. I wonder why she seems to instinctually hate him. It's not like she would have heard anything about him previously; no one knew that he and I would be showing up together.

"Once you graduate, what are you going to do for a living? You need money, right?" Gavin is staring back, hard.

I hate those kinds of questions, the kind my father asks, and doesn't Gavin realize that he's already the old man at this table? He's got almost a decade on us, which I normally don't mind. In fact, usually I like it. He's older and wiser and sexier than anyone my own age.

Usually.

"We're sculptors," Maya says.

"Yeah, didn't you hear us the first time?" Bree adds.

"He just meant, it's hard to make money as an artist," I say. "I mean, I used to hope I could become a novelist but—"

"You still could," Maya interrupts. "If you finished your novel. Have you finished it?"

"No." I look down at the table. Now my face is so hot I fear spontaneous combustion. "I'm not working on a novel right now."

"Didn't you used to encourage her writing?" Denver says to Gavin. His tone is mild but it feels like there might be something sharp within it, like a shard of glass baked into a cake.

"I still do," Gavin says, and I'm surprised because that's kind of a lie. We haven't talked about my writing in months.

Then again, that's my fault. I haven't written since Gavin and I got together.

"Why do you think it's too hard to be a novelist?" Now Denver's talking to me, gently.

"Everyone knows how brutal publishing is," I say. "How is anyone supposed to earn enough money to live on in a creative field?"

"That just means you have to work harder," Bree says. She's ignoring Gavin completely. "It means you can never give up, no matter what."

"People are always going to try to dissuade you," Maya says. "They want to cull the herd, you know?"

I can feel Maya's judgment. It's like I don't even know her anymore, even though we were best friends for six years.

Kristina and Bill are nodding. I've forgotten what their voices sound like. But I envy the way they're casually leaning into each other. Gavin and I are both so separate and rigid. I think it's because we're under attack.

Or are we? Gavin might be the one who fired the first shot, with his condescending questions.

I think of Gavin as being so socially adept, but then, we don't actually go out with anyone else. It's always just the two of us in our own little bubble.

"I saw Genevieve the other day," Kristina says. She and Maya exchange meaningful looks, laced with pity.

"How is she?" Denver says. So he's not in the loop either, which makes sense. He stayed in Houston, too, but he went to

Rice while the rest of them all go to the University of Houston.

"Let's just say, it's not pretty," Maya says, and I think that's probably for Bree's benefit. Back in high school, I always thought that Maya had a crush on Genevieve. Lots of people did, though. Mari's twins were destined for greatness.

Gavin shifts in his seat uneasily. No, he was just reaching for his beer. Maya and Bree both stare at him pointedly.

What is their fucking problem? It's getting old, fast.

"How did you and Gavin meet?" Denver asks me. Another subject change, this time toward us instead of away. "I mean, I know how you initially met but how did you remeet? Or had you stayed in touch since high school?"

I look at Gavin, hoping that he'll look back at me lovingly, and then I'll melt, and we can get this night back on track. We can show everyone what we're really like.

Instead, he's guzzling beer like a Neanderthal. Maybe he can burp out "Happy Birthday" while he's at it.

What's going on here? I'm almost never irritated by Gavin. This isn't me, this isn't Lise; this is Lizzie. High school had been profoundly aggravating, and now it's like I'm right back there.

"Do you want to tell it or should I?" I ask Gavin, trying to make my voice sweet.

"Not much to tell," Gavin says. "When I was her teacher, obviously nothing happened. Then maybe a year ago, I was in Austin. She was in Austin. We realized it on social media and we started to hang out. That's all."

That's all? That's how he wants to tell our grand origin story?

"So *nothing* happened during high school?" Maya is talking to me, like she doesn't quite believe Gavin.

"Of course nothing happened in high school!" I feel the heat rush to my cheeks.

"You have to admit, it could look a little bit creepy," Bree says. "To the untrained eye."

Gavin does this derisive snort. "And you have a trained eye, artist that you are?"

"I try to have an open mind." The way Bree says it, you can tell it's now closed. She thinks Gavin's an asshole. A creepy asshole.

"You guys have it all wrong." I look around the table. "We weren't together then. That would have been gross. He was my teacher, and I respected him."

"Don't you respect him now?" This comes from Bill, of all people. Bill, the mute.

"We respect each other." Gavin's practically baring his teeth.

But I can tell that they don't believe it. They're seeing this strangely aggressive version of the man I love—they've provoked this version—and now they're sitting back to watch the show.

"We should probably go," I say. I can't storm out. I've got too much of my mother in me. "It was good seeing everyone. I'm just kind of tired and—"

"Don't go," Denver says.

I meet his eyes, and they're as kind as I remember. But I can't stay, can I? Not with Gavin in his current state. Not when Maya and Bree are so determined to antagonize him.

I have to make a choice, and I'll always choose Gavin. Because he'll always choose me. That's what marriage is, right?

I can feel Mom coursing through my veins as I hug every last person goodbye.

Maya holds me close and whispers, "Are you really okay? Because I'm here if you need me." I can feel her sincerity, and it's both touching and mortifying.

Could this have gone any worse, truly? I thought I'd be an object of envy, that they'd all be impressed, thinking, "Wow, Lizzie ended up bagging the hot English teacher!" (I wasn't even expecting them to remember to call me Lise; my parents still have trouble with that.)

Instead, I'm an object of pity.

It's like Maya thinks I'm some abused woman and I don't see how I can convince her otherwise. She'd probably twist anything I said, just like she and Bree have been twisting all Gavin's words. Maybe when Maya went punk, she became a man hater. She could be the one under the control of her partner and she's just projecting that onto me. She's the one who needs an intervention.

They're the reason this night has been such a disaster. It's not Gavin's fault at all.

He's my person, and no one can tell me otherwise.

THEN

SEVENTEEN

DIANA

I was pounding the steaks with a mallet, and in between the blows, I heard the front door open. I was excited to see Lizzie, to find out what she'd bought, but sorry to have to take a break. Cooking dinner was a necessary evil but pounding meat into submission with a mallet was pure delight (whatever that said about me).

I walked out of the kitchen and waylaid Lizzie in the foyer. I could tell that she was eager to scurry upstairs. As I'd hoped, she was holding bags. I'd given her my credit card and told her to go wild.

"You don't have to act like a thief in the night!" I meant it to be playful but as had become usual with Lizzie, the joke didn't land. "I'd love to see what you picked out."

"It's just some clothes." She was practically muttering, avoiding my eyes. The bags were clutched tightly in her hand, close to her side.

Why was my daughter so secretive? It made no sense. I spent so much time and energy looking out with her. Yet the misperceptions, misunderstandings, and miscommunications just kept coming.

Maybe she was secretive because deep down, she knew that I wasn't the kind of person she wanted to let in. She couldn't know that I'd committed a crime—no one did—but she might have sensed that there was some dark and sinister strain running through me. There had to have been because how else could I have done what I did? It was a split-second decision but it came from somewhere.

"Don't clothes make the woman, though?" I said with a weak smile, trying to be playful and cover my awful roiling thoughts.

"Women are a lot more than what they wear, Mom," she said sharply.

I was always letting her down by being too much of something or never enough. I encouraged her all the time, but in her mind, I still wasn't a feminist.

I just wanted to see the clothes. I just wanted to have a moment with my daughter. Why was it all so exhausting?

My own mother would never have tolerated this kind of disrespect. I would have gotten a backhand to the face if I'd ever spoken to her the way Lizzie routinely mouthed off to me. But my mother believed she had moral high ground. I knew I didn't. Not after what I'd done.

"Lizzie, please." I was desperate to get back on track. Just one nice moment, was that too much to ask? "It would mean a lot to me to see what you picked."

She seemed to be thinking it over. Then she started pulling clothes from the bags quickly, stacking them on top of the console in a big heap. I lifted various items, my stomach plummeting.

"What?" Lizzie demanded. "What's that expression?"

It was fear. Because hadn't Gavin told me we needed to watch and wait for any changes? It hadn't taken long. His instincts had been dead right.

"I would have thought you'd be happy." She sounded accusing. "You hate the way I dress. You've always told me that I should 'show off my shape more.' Isn't that what you said?"

"But you never listened." So why now? Because she was determined to get attention from boys however she could? "And I never said I hated the way you dress."

"Oh, come on. It's obvious. You're not much of an actress, Mom."

Under normal circumstances, I might have been pleased with Lizzie's wardrobe selections. They were body conscious but they didn't seem low-cut or especially revealing (not like the tacky stuff I hid in my high school locker and changed into in the restroom). But the timing of it, the motivation behind Lizzie's makeover—that's what raised my anxiety. Because Gavin knew teenage behavior way better than I did, and he'd recently sounded the alarm.

At least I wasn't alone in this. He was here for Lizzie, and for me.

"The clothes are beautiful," I told her. "You've got great taste."

"See?" She shook her head in disgust. "You're a terrible liar."

"You've got me all wrong." She really did. I'd proven two years ago that I could be a great liar when I needed to be. After his death, I'd fielded all their questions. There'd never even been a police investigation. "I really like your new clothes."

"Save it." Lizzie was throwing everything haphazardly back into the bags. "I know what you really think about me."

"What are you talking about?" I was mystified. "You're beautiful and smart and—"

"Save it," she repeated. Then she stalked up the stairs to her room, the bags slamming against the banister.

I watched her go, confused and crestfallen. Then I grabbed my phone out of my back pocket and started texting before I could think better of it.

Sorry to bother you but you were right. She's changing. She bought all new clothes. This is not the Lizzie I know.

He didn't respond immediately because why would he? He's not an ER doc on call; he's a teacher.

But I couldn't control myself: *I need you.* Then I added quickly: *I mean, I need your help.*

I sounded like a lunatic. What I should have said was that I'd really appreciate his help. I couldn't text that now because four unreturned messages? I'd look like some kind of stalker.

This was entirely inappropriate, and mortifying.

I was about to send an apology and a promise to observe reasonable boundaries in the future when my phone pinged.

We've got this, Di.

EIGHTEEN

LIZZIE

I hate being a cliché kind of teenager, snapping at Mom and flouncing out of the room. I'm not proud of having outbursts. I don't like being a bitch to my mom or even to my dad. That's not how people should treat each other, even if they are family.

But she just made me so mad, the way she lies to me. Or maybe she's lying to herself. I don't know and I don't care. I just want her to stop breathing down my neck.

So at least I'm writing and trying to get it out on paper like Mr. Axelrod told me to instead of bottling up every feeling like she does. I'm never going to show this to anyone. I'm never even going to reread it because it's so cringey. A lot of time that's how I feel about strong emotions, like they're embarrassing. Strong emotions are a sign you're weak, that you can't control yourself.

Or is that just what Mom thinks? Or it's what Grandma thinks and she basically spoon-fed it to Mom. Mom's parents really fucked her up, you can tell. Otherwise, she would have left Dad a long time ago.

I think she married her dad. How cliché is that?

Well, it will never happen to me. I know that much for sure.

Mom is definitely weak, how she lets Dad treat her like she's nothing, how she acts like she has no needs of her own. It's all service with a smile.

Say what you want about Grandma but she's strong. She doesn't take anyone's shit. I don't like her but I respect her, you know?

It's hard to respect Mom but I do try sometimes. I feel sorry for her because she probably doesn't even get that my dad is abusive. He's like the emperor of our little kingdom. He doesn't hit us or anything, but he rules over us, making pronounce-ments. I don't think he's ever once been truly proud of me.

Mom must be taking her cues from Dad. Lately, nothing I do can make her happy or satisfied.

I really did think she'd like the clothes, though. I mean, I didn't go to Hot Topic or any of the stores in the mall that Maya kept suggesting. At one point, I came out of the dressing room and Maya said, "That looks like something your mom would wear!"

That hadn't even crossed my mind. I'd just been trying to replicate one of the looks from Mr. Axelrod's phone.

I can't wait for him to get a load of the New Me tomorrow. I feel kind of warm, picturing his reaction. Does he ever think about me when he's alone?

No harm in thinking, right? Or in looking?

It's like he always says: Imagination is a beautiful thing.

NOW

NINETEEN

DIANA

I would have liked to hide out in my room all morning but I had to get up and make Ron breakfast. Also, I have to manage to cross-examine a sociopath. Fun all around.

Ron and I don't tend to chat before he goes to work (or anytime, really) and today is no exception. He eats the home-made waffles he requested while I can barely keep down coffee. After he leaves, I start washing up the dishes and that's when I feel a tap on my shoulder.

It's Gavin, his grin wolfish. I have the impulse to tighten the belt on my robe but I resist. I've been trying not to outwardly show fear. I want to look like a worthy opponent.

"Where's Lise?" I ask. Could this be my chance?

"Lise is sleeping in," he says, coming close to me, leaning against the dishwasher. "It's the perfect time for us to catch up."

I start soaping up a bowl, slowly, deliberately. I'm eager to get this over with but Ron's told me many times that you don't want to be the first to speak in a negotiation; silence is power. Gavin came to my home for a reason. There's something he wants.

"I'm not going to be ignored, Di." He enunciates each word

clearly, and I feel myself flinching. He laughs. "You know that line, right? From *Fatal Attraction*? Shame you don't have a bunny for me to boil."

I say nothing, though my hands are starting to shake.

"But seriously, Di, you can't ignore me. I'm here all week and I intend to make the most of our time together."

"What do you want, really?"

"Your blessing. I'm going to marry your daughter." His expression is so broadly innocent that it feels ironic, like he's winking at an imaginary audience.

"I thought I made it clear years ago that I never wanted to see you again. So no, I can't bless this union. What else do you want?"

I'm not looking at him but I can feel his eyes narrowing, the anger radiating off him in waves.

Is that my best move? Should I get him to explode where Lizzie can see? I bet she's never experienced that side of him. They might not be married yet but they're still in the honeymoon phase.

Or maybe she has experienced it, and she stayed with him anyway. What a terrifying thought.

"You really thought you were hot shit back then, didn't you?" He's looming over me, his breath hot on my face and neck. Now I'm definitely flinching; I can't help it.

I feel like I might pass out. It's a muscle memory from years ago when he and I last tangled. He'd won every battle but I thought I'd won the war. Now he's back, with Lise on his side. For all I know, she's his soldier.

"I never thought I was hot shit," I say, trying to sound conciliatory. My hands have stilled on the dish but I still won't turn my head. Looking directly at him would be like looking into the sun.

How he'd love that metaphor. He always wanted to be my sun, and now he's Lizzie's.

"Why are you here, Gavin?" I ask. "I don't understand. Do you really want to marry Lise?"

"Of course I do. I love her."

But I can tell there's more. I turn my head and our eyes meet. His gaze is desirous. Hungry.

I don't want to have to make some sort of trade, my body for Lise's. The thought of being with Gavin ever again is beyond vile, beyond nauseating, just... beyond. But I would if I had to, if there were no other way to foil his plans. Anything for Lise. My life for hers.

"A million," he says. "That's what it's going to take."

"A million *dollars*?" He grins and nods. It's an outlandish sum, far more than I'd expected. "If I give you a million dollars, will you break up with Lise in a way that she will never, ever have you back?"

Even as I say it, I'm not sure it can be done. The way Lise looks at Gavin, it's like he's absolutely golden. She might forgive him any trespass.

The problem is... "I don't have that kind of money," I say. "You know that." Ron has way more than that, but I have no access. It's not like I could just steal it from his accounts.

"You'll have to get it."

"I can't. Not without telling Ron what it's for."

"So tell Ron what it's for." He's smirking. I realize that while he'd enjoy the money, he'd also enjoy knowing I'd destroyed myself and my marriage to get it.

"If Lise tells you everything, then you know the kind of relationship they have. Truthfully, I'm not sure he cares enough about her well-being and future to spend that kind of money." I'm sad to realize that it's not a lie. I really don't know that Ron would part with his fortune to save his daughter.

"Then go to your mother. She's a rich widow, isn't she?"

"Affluent. Not rich." She'd have to liquidate her assets or

possibly even sell her house. He knows that, though. He knows exactly how complicated my situation is with Mother.

That's why he seems to be enjoying this so much.

"This is a you problem, Di. So you're going to need to solve it on your own. I'm done being your sounding board."

Was that how he remembered our relationship? That he'd been my sounding board?

He looks so self-satisfied that I wish I could just pick up that large chef's knife over there and—

"What are you two talking about?"

My heart drops. How much has Lise heard?

TWENTY

LISE

I don't know what I've walked into, why Gavin is standing so close to my mom, why they're talking in such low tones. Urgent tones.

Gavin walks toward me with a big smile. "Good morning, sunshine," he says. He kisses me full on the lips, so clearly unfazed by my appearance that I decide nothing was amiss. They were just talking while Mom did dishes. No big deal.

And yet...

Mom's body language is, once again, bizarre. She's staring down into the sink like it might contain the secrets of the universe. She looks like she can't catch her breath.

She seems terrified. Guilty, too. What kind of conversation would produce that combination?

"What were you talking about?" I repeat. I'm looking at my mom but it's Gavin who answers.

"Your grandmother."

"What about her?"

"Her finances. Whether your mom should wait for an inheritance or try to work out an arrangement sooner. It sounds like a complicated relationship, to say the least." Gavin looks at Mom. "I think that about covers it, doesn't it?"

Mom nods, eyes still averted.

It's a rather unusual conversation but his face is so open, and he and I don't keep secrets from each other.

Well, he doesn't keep any from me.

At some point, I do plan to tell him. I'm just waiting for the right time. Because I don't want to hold on to this forever. It runs counter to our policy of brutal honesty, though if I'm *really* honest, that's more Gavin's policy than mine, and if I'm *really, really* honest, I know that he's violated that policy, too. He's lied by omission. But what kind of couple calls each other out on every little thing?

Gavin and I are over-the-moon happy, and I intend to keep it that way, regardless of any naysayers, which includes my "friends" from last night. And my mother, too.

Gavin kisses me on the forehead and says he's going out for a run.

Now it's just Mom and me. She starts doing the dishes. "How did you sleep?" she asks.

I slip into the space previously occupied by Gavin, leaning against the dishwasher. "Fine. How about you?"

"Not so great," she says.

"Why's that?" Does it have anything to do with what I just walked into, with her trying to get her hands on Grandma's money? I've never thought of my mom as greedy before but I wouldn't blame her for planning an exit route, her soft landing if she leaves Dad. If that's the case, though, why is she talking to Gavin and not to me?

"I'm worried about you." Mom says it just above a whisper, seeming on the verge of tears.

"Well, I'm worried about you. You haven't been yourself since I've been home."

"Are you okay, Lise?"

"Why is everyone asking me that? I'm fine! I'm great!" I'm not quite shouting but I am mad. First Maya, and now Mom. They should worry about their own lives. "Why doesn't anyone want to be happy for me?"

There's a long silence. Mom's never good with big displays of emotion. Finally, she says, "I want you to be happy. I want to be happy for you. But—"

"Why is there a but?"

"You know how anxious I can be, so I'm going to work on that," she says. "I'll try to do better, okay?"

At least she's admitting that Gavin's not the problem; her anxiety is. I give her a smile. "I'd appreciate that."

"I made waffles. Would you like one?"

"Yes, thanks."

As I'm sitting at the kitchen island counter, scrolling on my phone, a text comes in. It's from Denver, saying we hadn't gotten much of a chance to talk last night, could we get together?

It's true, we didn't get to talk much, and I've always liked Denver. I don't think Gavin does but he and I don't control each other. So I text back a quick yes, almost like I don't want time to stop myself.

I'm not looking forward to telling Gavin. But he and I talk all the time about the importance of supporting each other, of never holding the other back from any opportunities, of always being honest.

So why is my chest tightening in fear?

TWENTY-ONE

RON

Of course I recognized Gavin Axelrod. What kind of idiot do these women take me for? What kind of idiot does that man take me for?

Acting like an affable ignoramus gives me the most options. Through the element of surprise, I have all the power.

I need to lull them into a false sense of security. Act like Lizzie's made an excellent choice, like Gavin's a real first-round draft pick. Like I'm going to be a great father-in-law and Gavin's got nothing to worry about.

Diana, though—lulling her will not be an easy feat. She's a bomb. I'm sure Gavin can hear her ticking as loudly as I can. I'll have to decide whether I'm going to cut the red wire or not.

In the meantime, I'll make him good and comfortable. Diana, too.

No one's going to see me coming.

THEN

TWENTY-TWO
DIANA

Gavin and I had been texting. I was venting my fears and then apologizing for venting my fears and finally he wrote: *We should continue this in person. Are you home? Where do you live?*

I was slightly taken aback. But then, wasn't it basically the same thing as meeting in his classroom? We'd sit in the kitchen and drink tea like civilized adults. There was nothing strange about his suggestion, only in my overblown reaction. I was acting like my mother, standing on ceremony, adhering to outdated rules of propriety.

So I texted my address, adding, *If Lizzie gets home and sees you here, she'll freak out.*

Then I realized what I'd done, that I'd just revealed Lizzie's crush on him, but he must have known it already. All the girls were probably wild about him.

Lizzie's working on the school show. She won't be home for at least an hour.

I was surprised he knew her schedule that well but

shouldn't have been. It's a sign of how much she shared with him, and how much he cared. That's why he was the perfect ally.

While I waited, I put the kettle on. I looked around at the house critically. There was no tidying up to do because I kept it pristine. In Ron's mind, that was one of my only jobs. He wasn't entirely wrong. Now that Lizzie was practically grown and avoiding me, I did have a lot of time on my hands.

The knock on the door came quickly. Gavin must have been close by when we were texting. I wondered if he lived in this neighborhood. It seemed doubtful. There weren't many apartment buildings and he was a young, single guy.

Or maybe he wasn't. He very well could have had a girlfriend, or even a wife and he just didn't like to wear a ring. I didn't know anything about his personal life, and that was as it should be.

I opened the door. He seemed taller, somehow, away from the classroom. But just as handsome.

I was blushing already.

"Good to see you," he said.

"You, too. Come on in." I had him follow me inside, and for the first time in I didn't know how long, I considered how my ass might look in jeans. I still worked out five times a week—another of Ron's rules, he wanted to be able to show me off—so my ass was probably holding its own.

Which wouldn't matter to Gavin and certainly shouldn't matter to me. This was a professional visit. He was here about Lizzie.

I showed him the tea selection and he picked one. I took my time pouring the boiling water into the mugs, asking him about milk and sugar. I had to get myself under control. This was no time to act like a schoolgirl.

We sat across from each other at the kitchen table. Now

that he was here, I had no idea what to say. I didn't feel like going on about my various neuroses anymore.

"I noticed Lizzie has a new look," he said.

"What do you think of it?" After I said it, I realized how asinine the question was. "I mean, is it making her more confident or more... forward?" With boys, I meant.

I could tell that he got my drift. "So far, I haven't noticed a change in her behavior."

I let out a sigh of relief. "She really does look great. I've been telling her for forever that she should wear clothes that fit."

"So she finally listened to you. Maybe this is a positive development."

"Do you really think so?" Where Lizzie was concerned, I always felt primed for catastrophe.

"It's hard for you to believe that it's going to turn out well because of what happened to you." I looked at him quizzically. "You told me you got pregnant at sixteen, right? Lizzie's age now. No wonder you're so easily triggered."

I looked away from him. I felt embarrassed by my fragility.

"Everyone's triggered sometimes."

"You are, too?"

"Sure. I'm human, in case you haven't noticed." We both laughed. "I think you really need to work on how to relax, Di. What do you do for fun? What's entirely for you and nobody else?"

My embarrassment increased. I didn't have a ready answer. I deflected, asking about him, and he had loads of answers: playing his guitar, writing songs, reading books, running (which I'd already guessed, based on his physique). I noticed that he didn't mention a girlfriend.

I felt like there was chemistry between us, moments where our eyes just caught and held, but it had to be all in my head. He wouldn't be interested in me. I was somebody's mother. His student's mother.

And I couldn't be interested in him. I wasn't the type to have an affair, no matter how unfulfilling my marriage was.

He told me, with regret, that he had to go. He had an appointment. "But I'm glad I got to see you," he said, extending the gaze.

We never touched but it was like I could feel him all through me.

When had I last been turned on? I couldn't even remember.

Sex had become irrelevant to me. It was just something I did to keep the peace. Every few weeks, Ron wanted it, so I gave it to him.

When did I last do something that was entirely for me and nobody else? Hadn't that been one of Gavin's questions?

The feelings coursing through me had become unfamiliar and yet they were eternal. Primal. Natural as worrying. Natural as breathing.

I headed upstairs to my bedroom. It would be my little secret.

TWENTY-THREE

LIZZIE

I was waiting outside Mr. Axelrod's closed door. I was going to be late for my next class, but it was only art, so who cared? This was Mr. Axelrod's free period, and I intended to make the most of it.

I shifted from one foot to the other impatiently. The hallway was entirely clear now. I'd raced to his room but hadn't been quick enough. Genevieve had beaten me to it.

I felt a little despondent. If Genevieve was after him, then I was cooked. I just couldn't compete with someone that smart and beautiful. She didn't even have to show skin to be desired by every guy. And she was genuinely a good person. I mean, I liked her and I barely liked anyone these days.

There was a window in the door but it was blocked with a poster. What could they be talking about? It wasn't like Genevieve needed extra help. She'd been a straight-A student her entire life. I'd heard about her accomplishments for years, seeing as Mari and Mom were best friends.

I was wearing my new clothes. He'd seen me earlier in the hall and he hadn't said anything directly to me about it because that would be objectifying, but I saw how he looked at me. Not pervy at all, but his expression had been approving. He thought I looked good. I was sure of it.

I heard Mr. Axelrod and Genevieve burst out laughing, and I just wilted. My makeover was so surface. I was still too skinny and pimply, and I'd never even had a serious boyfriend. How had I let myself think that someone like Mr. Axelrod could be interested in me? He was made for the Genevieves of the world, not the Lizzies.

I headed down the hall, blinded by tears. Instead of going to my next class, I walked out the front door. I didn't know where I was going, and I didn't care. About anything.

NOW

TWENTY-FOUR

DIANA

"I've been thinking ahead," I say. "To the wedding gift."

"That's thinking too far ahead." Ron has just gotten into bed, a blob of drying toothpaste beside his mouth, and as usual, he doesn't want to talk. Normally, that's fine by me, but tonight, I have an agenda and I won't be deterred.

I'm facing him; he's facing away as he aggressively pounds a pillow. He's either communicating that I should have already done it for him or that he's in no mood to listen. Both, most likely.

"Sorry," I say, referencing the pillow. "I've had a lot on my mind."

"Have you now." It's a statement, not a question. It contains zero curiosity.

But right now, I need Ron on my side for this fight against Gavin. I have to win. Not for me; for my child. For Lise, I will fight to the death.

Only Ron can't know it's a war.

"I'd prefer that Lise wasn't getting married so young," I say. "But she does seem happy, and this is what she truly wants. So I'd like to give them a significant gift to start their lives." Not "them," him. I need Gavin to take the money and run.

Now I have Ron's attention. He rolls back toward me. "How much is significant?"

"Two hundred thousand, maybe?" Hopefully, the million was just a starting point and Gavin will be willing to negotiate down.

The expression on Ron's face is one of incredulity.

"It could come out of one of your investment funds or company stock that's vested, or whatever," I say. My cheeks flush. I'm embarrassed by how little I understand our finances, but then, that's how Ron likes it. "We have way more than that. We wouldn't even feel it."

"Oh, *we* wouldn't?" Now he's bemused.

"It's not for me. I don't need any more than you provide, Ron, you know that. But Gavin and Lise are building a nest egg."

"You want to buy her love."

"No, that's not it." If anything, I'd be buying her hate. If Lise knew what I was doing, that I'm trying to put a downpayment on her heartbreak, she'd never want to see me again.

But even if I can get Gavin to accept less, once he takes it, how can I make sure he upholds his end of the bargain?

It's not like we'll have a contract that's legally enforceable, and I certainly don't trust him. It's because I have no trust in him, because I think he's an execrable human, that I'm even having this conversation with Ron.

I'm terrified that I'll pay the money and Gavin still won't let Lise go. That he'll never let me go, either.

"If it's not about buying her love, what is it about, Di?" Ron is staring at me with a cold appraisal that makes me quake inside.

"I just think we should do this for her, as her parents. Can't you trust my judgment, for once?"

He shakes his head. "You don't know, Di. You have no idea what I do for you."

With that proclamation, he's truly done. I can tell that this is the final time he's going to roll away, and I won't have access to him until morning. Not that I know what I'll say then. Maybe I do need to go to my mother, though I can't imagine what I'd tell her. If I said the money was for me, to leave Ron and begin a new life, she'd scoff. "Women live longer than men," she'd say. "And Ron's older than you, with a high-stress job. Play the waiting game."

I'm awake pretty much all night, running over potential arguments I could make to my mother or to Ron, hearing Ron's words in my head: *You have no idea what I do for you.* What does that mean? Does he love me more than I've realized? Or less?

The next morning, after Ron's left for work and while Lise is in the shower, I knock on the door of the guest bedroom. My stomach's in painful knots.

"We don't have much time to talk," I say, tilting my head in the direction of the bathroom. "I just wanted to tell you that I'm working on it. On getting the money."

"Well, good morning to you, too, Di!" Gavin gives me a toothy grin.

"I'm trying, but it's not going to be instantaneous. I talked to Ron last night. You know how he is."

"I do." Gavin's expression softens. He likes me hearkening back to our shared past, to his preferred narrative, where he was my confidante and savior.

"To be honest, I'm not sure I can get a million. I tested the water with Ron for two hundred thousand and he basically laughed in my face. But I can keep working on him and hopefully I can have at least that much for you by the time the week is out."

"I can tell when you're lying." He looks deeply into my eyes; I force myself to return the gaze. "You're not lying."

I wait for his answer, praying. Will he accept my lowball offer?

Now he's studying my face fondly. "There are some women you never get over, Di."

My skin is crawling but I can't show it. I have to act like there's still some sweetness between us. That way, I can stay on his good side while I figure out what I'm going to do. How I'll defeat him—this time, for good.

But I guess I'm not fooling him because his face turns stony. "With the way you betrayed me, you're lucky I'm even giving you a chance to pay out. I could destroy you outright if I wanted to. You should be thanking your stars and kissing my feet."

I'm gripped by fear and I have no idea what to say. Should I apologize? Should I—

"The shower's stopped," he says. Then he shuts the door in my face.

TWENTY-FIVE

LISE

"I'm still not used to you with short hair!" I say, as Denver enfolds me in his arms.

We're in the local Starbucks, which is just about the least sexy meet-up spot, in my opinion. Hopefully, that'll put Gavin's mind at ease. He seemed slightly edgy this morning before I left, though he never told me not to go. Our love—our trust—is sacrosanct.

Denver and I stand in line, making small talk, and then once we're at a table, he gives me a big smile. "I can't believe this! Lizzie, back to her old stomping grounds. Now, as Lise. The same but different, huh?"

"More different, I think."

"I liked Lizzie. I always have. But I'm interested in getting to know Lise." He leans forward.

"Fun fact: Lise doesn't like being talked about in the third person," I tease. "Does Denver?"

"Strangely, he does." We both laugh. "So. There's an elephant in the room. The way you ran out the other night."

"I walked, thank you very much." I want to get back to being playful. I'm in no mood to relive that night.

"Maya and Bree were kind of hard on Gavin."

"You saw it, too?" I feel a surge of relief.

"I did. But I also saw how Gavin was acting. He came in with his guard up. Is he always that prickly?"

"No, definitely not. Think of it from his perspective. His history with everyone. How judgmental Maya and Bree were right from the start."

"His history, meaning that half of us had been his students?"

"Yes."

"That *you'd* been one of his students." He's staring at me intently, meaningfully. What is this, an intervention?

Denver never liked Mr. Axelrod, so of course he's not going to like Gavin. This is basically confirmation bias.

"Maybe we should talk about something else," I say.

"I'd love to talk about anything else. Any*one* else." He's shifting uncomfortably in his chair. "I'm just not sure if you know everything about Gavin."

"I know way more than you ever could. He's my best friend, and I'm his."

"But you've heard the rumors, right? Back then, and since?"

I feel angry. I shouldn't have to explain myself or defend my fiancé. "All those teen girls lusting after him—some of them had overactive imaginations. But I saw with my own eyes how he acted. I know who he is. What he would and wouldn't do."

"So you're sure they're just rumors?"

"Positive."

Denver places his hand closer to mine on the table. "I'm sorry, Lise. I don't mean to upset you. If you say your eyes are wide open, then I'm done with the subject."

"I'm happy, Denver." I try to look credible, which shouldn't be hard because it's the truth. "Happier than I've ever been in my entire life. Because of Gavin."

Denver nods. "I've always cared about you and thought you deserved the best. You've got to decide if that's Gavin."

"I've already decided. It is."

"Then enough said." He moves his head as if he's shaking off cobwebs. "Let's talk about you, Lise. I want to hear everything."

It takes me a second to calm down but then we settle into conversation and I remember: this is my old goofy sweet friend Denver, the one who's always tried to appreciate and understand me. We still have a lot in common—even more now—since we're both feeling a bit lost these days in our job searches. We're not entirely sure what we want professionally. We both love the idea of travel, which Gavin hates. He hates it for himself (he's more of a homebody) and he hates the idea of being away from me during work trips. In the ten months we've been together, we've barely spent a night apart.

I love how expansive this conversation feels. It also feels easy. And reassuring, too, to discover that someone as bright and thoughtful as Denver, someone with a degree from Rice University, can also flounder. I'm in good company.

Denver majored in English; I majored in communications. We both love to write. I've been eyeing job openings in marketing and PR but I'm not sure those would ignite my passion. We've both been too paralyzed to even apply for anything, though we realize that having interviews might help crystallize what we do, in fact, want.

In talking so openly to Denver, I realize that I haven't been nearly as open with Gavin lately. I want so much to please him, and if he saw how much I was struggling, he'd give me more input and direction. I don't want to feel like his pupil. I want to be his equal, and I fear that I'm not.

"Hey." Denver looks concerned. "You okay?"

"It's just—it's complicated, isn't it? Scary, even. Thinking about the rest of your life."

"But you already know who you want to spend it with. You're ahead of the game."

I feel like crying and I have no idea why. Denver's right, I'm lucky. I tell myself that all the time. "I wish I knew what I wanted to be. Besides a wife. I mean, don't get me wrong. I do want to be a wife. To be Gavin's wife. But I also want more."

"Of course. You're like me. You want to see the world. Travel is simultaneously inspirational and grounding. It changes people. Who knows who we'll be once we've been everywhere?"

I bite my lip. "How long will that take, though? And how much will I change? Gavin's older, so he's already thinking about kids."

"All the more reason for you to hurry up and get started now. You could find a high-flying job, literally."

"Gavin doesn't want me to be away all the time. He'd miss me too much. And I'd miss him," I add hurriedly. "Also, he worries that if I get on a certain track, it'll be hard to switch to another. A job with a lot of travel might not be very family friendly." Not that I'm 100 percent sure about having kids. Or even 50 percent. But Gavin's sure that I'll get there, and he's right about so many things.

"You need to do what moves you. You can't let Gavin hold you back."

"He's not holding me back. He's just very thoughtful about my future. Our future together."

"Maybe Gavin doesn't want you to outshine him. But, Lise, you are the kind of woman who shines so brightly. I could see you in the dark. You're Day-Glo." He smiles at me.

I couldn't see it back then, how much Denver liked me, *really* liked me, but I'm not blind now. This is probably why Gavin seemed edgy earlier. The intensity of Denver's feelings would be threatening to any fiancé. "I should go."

"Please don't dash off again," Denver says.

But I need to. This hasn't been flirtatious at all but it's been entirely too intimate.

"I love Gavin," I say. "More than I could love anyone else. More than I could love any job. I'd choose him over anything."

"But why do you have to choose?" He looks so innocent asking the question, like he's genuinely puzzled.

I stand up. "Give me a hug, okay? I'm so glad I got to see you again." I mean it and yet...

It felt too good to talk to Denver. And that's threatening. I finally have the man of my dreams, and I'm not going to mess that up.

When I walk into my parents' house, I'm a sweaty mess. I tell myself that's par for the course during a Houston summer. It has nothing to do with Denver.

Gavin's lounging in the living room with a book. Dad's at work, but where's my mom? Sometimes I have the sense that she's trying to avoid me this trip. I would have said that she's trying to avoid Gavin, except I caught her telling him all about Grandma and the inheritance. She doesn't talk to me like that.

So Mom's sharing way too much with Gavin, and I'm sharing way too much with Denver. What's going on here?

Gavin sees that I'm out of sorts. He gets to his feet, almost like he's spoiling for a fight. But not with me; with Denver. "I knew that guy would upset you," he says.

"No, he didn't do anything. I'm fine. I just need a glass of ice water. It's crazy hot out there." When in doubt, blame the Houston weather.

Gavin isn't buying it. "That loser always had the most pathetic crush on you."

So back in high school, had it been that obvious to everyone but me? Or had Mr. Axelrod been paying that much attention to my social life?

I try to tell myself it's flattering. But it bothers me that he sounds so nasty about Denver now. Denver doesn't deserve that.

I'm done with this conversation.

I head for the kitchen, filling a glass with ice from the dispenser in the refrigerator and then adding in water. I press it to my forehead.

"What's going on, Lise?" Gavin's pursued me into the kitchen. "You've been acting strange since we got here. Like the other night, with your friends." He says the word *friends* like there are air quotes around it.

I think the person acting strange is him. He seems so jealous and territorial. "Did something happen between you and Denver at some point?"

"No."

"Then why do you feel the need to insult him? Why are you so threatened?"

Gavin lets out a harsh bark of laughter. "Threatened by *Denver*? You've got to be kidding."

"Then what is it?" This is harder than I usually press. He says he likes assertive women but I'm not sure I've really been one in his presence. I was in awe of him for so long that I tend to just take a lot of his thoughts and opinions without question.

Well, that has to change. I need to stand my ground and trust my gut.

"It's nothing," he says. Is there a note of warning in his tone, like he's telling me to drop this or else?

No, that's not Gavin. Not at all.

"I'm probably going to see him again before we go back to Austin," I say. He's my friend, and I have a right to see my friends.

"If that's the way you want to spend your time..." Gavin trails off dubiously.

"It is."

Gavin turns on his heel and leaves the room without another word.

I'm not used to this behavior from him and it occurs to me

that if my mom is in the house, she might have overheard. I don't know how she would interpret it, if I'd be able to convince her that Gavin and I really never fight.

I think of that expression of fear she wore the first night at the steakhouse. Am I wearing that expression now, too?

If I push, how far will Gavin go?

THEN

TWENTY-SIX
DIANA

I told myself I wasn't doing anything wrong. After all, Gavin and I were spending time together right out in the open, in his classroom, every day after school.

At first we spent most of our time talking about Lizzie. I told him all about what she'd been like as a kid, how close she and I had been. I asked where he thought I'd screwed up. He assured me that I hadn't, that this was just a normal developmental phase. He explained the word *individuation*: Lizzie needed to pull away from me in order to distinguish herself, to become her own person. It was because I was so important and instrumental, because she loved me so much, that she needed that distance.

I loved that explanation, even if I could only believe it when I was in his presence. He was a very persuasive person. Charismatic, too. If I'd been a teenage girl in his class, I would have been as enthralled as Lizzie was.

He started to share more from his own life. He'd grown up in Dallas, whereas I'd grown up here in Houston. We compared notes. I forgot my mother's advice and dropped my guard. As I opened up to him, I was rewarded by feeling truly understood for maybe the first time.

But it wasn't all serious. We laughed a lot. He was clever and I wasn't, though he seemed to find me funny. We weren't flirting, not exactly, but I had to admit we had chemistry. He was the high point of my day, no doubt about that.

I was a person prone to guilt, shame, and self-deprecation, and Gavin wouldn't stand for it. He wouldn't let me put myself down. I expressed embarrassment that I've never lived anywhere else and had barely traveled because Ron didn't like it. He enjoyed "the pleasures of home," so that meant I was stuck.

"No," Gavin told me passionately. He placed his hand on my forearm and the entire limb went up in flames, clear to my shoulder. Honestly? It wasn't that localized. His touch radiated everywhere. "Your destiny isn't set, Di. You have no idea where you'll go or what you're capable of."

I shifted slightly in my seat, wishing he'd remove his hand, wishing he'd pull me closer. I hoped he couldn't see how I felt, what our conversations meant to me. What he meant. This was supposed to be only about Lizzie. He was her teacher, and she had a crush on him, too. "It's too late," I said. "My life is set."

He took his hand away, shaking his head. "If you want to see the world, then see it. If Ron won't go, then take trips with someone else. You have friends, right?"

"You don't know Ron." I wouldn't be allowed that kind of freedom, with his money.

"Tell me about Ron," Gavin said, though we'd always avoided that topic before like it was the third rail. If we didn't talk about my husband directly, then we could pretend that this intimacy wasn't a betrayal.

But the fact was, *husband* was an empty title. Ron wasn't my friend, protector, or lover. He couldn't spare any warmth or affection. On the occasions we had sex, he cared only about himself. And that wasn't just during sex, either. What had he really done to earn my loyalty?

Nothing, and that became clearer the more I revealed to Gavin.

"I get why Lizzie likes talking to you," I said.

"Does that mean you like talking to me?" That intent gaze of his, like he was swallowing me up. "Because I really like being with you, Di."

My face grew hot. Every bit of me did.

I retreated, bringing up Lizzie again. That felt like safer ground. "I followed your suggestion. I was more assertive with her last night. I said, 'You can't just shut me out when I know something's wrong.'"

He beamed like I'd made him proud. We weren't touching but he was still pitched forward, our desks close together. Was it my imagination or every day, did he place the desks closer so that our legs were nearly intertwined?

"It didn't work, though," I said. "She just sat there on her bed, silent, staring at the floor, like I wasn't there. Like I'm nobody."

"Stay the course. She expects you to back down and give up. To give up on her like she's given up on herself. Don't do it. You're a parent, not a friend. You're what's standing between Lizzie and destruction."

"You and me both." My chest had tightened with fear. "We're in this together. Right?"

He smiled. "Right. I'm not going anywhere."

"Thank you." I knew there was no way I could save Lizzie without him. But I'd stayed too long. This was getting too intense. "I should go. It's getting late and I need to start dinner."

"Wait," he said. He put his finger under my chin, forcing me to look at him. "I think about you all the time, Di."

Then it was happening, we were kissing, and it felt not only amazing but inevitable. Meant to be, like I was in my own romance novel. I'd never experienced anything so reciprocal. I never knew I could feel so connected to my own desires while being entirely in sync with someone else's.

But I couldn't do this. I couldn't have an affair with Lizzie's teacher, of all people.

"I have to go." Before he could say anything, I'd pushed past him, and I was running down the hallway, hoping no one would see my smudged makeup and flushed face. That no one would suspect what I'd just been up to.

I'd done the right thing. I stopped it.

But deep down, I knew it was temporary. The hollowest moral victory. Soon I'd be back, in force.

TWENTY-SEVEN

LIZZIE

"She did not," Maya said as we exited the school, passing through the metal detectors in reverse. The door clanged shut behind us. High schools were pretty much prisons, and if it hadn't been for Mr. Axelrod, I'd be all for a jailbreak.

"She really did! It's like she had a personality transplant." I did my impression of In-Your-Face Mom Barbie, pretending to tower over Maya: "I'm your *mother*, not your friend!"

We both cracked up.

Maya was still in her cheerleader uniform and I was in my set-painting smock. As we headed toward the parking lot, I felt a little bit bad for having mocked Mom, the same way I often felt bad for Mom, period, because she was the one truly in a cage, but then the anger followed close on its heels. I shouldn't have had to worry about my fragile bird of a mother. She should have grown a pair by now, not that I liked that sexist phrase.

Wait, wasn't that what Mom was doing when she told me she wasn't my friend?

There probably was no winning for mothers. It's part of why I never wanted to be one myself.

When Mom was being all butch, I kept thinking about Mr.

Axelrod and what he'd told me about finding my own voice and disagreeing when needed, never letting anyone push me around, not even well-meaning adults. Maybe he had a sixth sense about New Mom. If anyone could have superpowers, it was Mr. Axelrod.

Anyway, I knew he'd want me to stand my ground so that's what I did. I wasn't going to tell her my deepest, darkest secrets just because she'd ordered me to.

Besides, Mom was so clueless. What had she even been talking about, saying she knew something was wrong with me? Nothing was wrong. I was coming into my own and I would have thought she'd be supportive of that. I was finally wearing nice clothes and sometimes I'd even catch sight of myself and feel quasi confident, like faking it till you make it wasn't the stupidest advice in the world. In other words, I was doing what Mom had encouraged me to do and she was *still* acting like a total freak.

Case in point, was that her now, bursting out of a side door and hurrying out to her car in the same parking lot where Maya's was?

Yes, that was her, moving like a woman possessed, all flustered and discombobulated and, again, totally freakish. If she expected me to confide in her, she was in for a rude awakening.

But what was she doing here? Who had she been meeting with and why hadn't she told me about it?

I wanted to tell her to stay the hell out of my life and my business but that wasn't exactly our family way. Instead, I glowered in silent rage.

I put out a hand to stop Maya from walking. Then I crouched down behind a car. If Mom saw me, then she'd insist that I ride home with her and the last thing I wanted was to be in a confined space with her when I was this mad. When she insisted on treating me like a child. A defective child.

Fuck her. Nothing was wrong with me.

Mr. Axelrod could see that. Why couldn't she?

You'd think a mother would want to see the best in her child but it seemed like mine was determined to see the worst. Maybe then it gave her something to do. She needed a problem to solve, and she'd decided I was it.

I was trying to figure out why she looked so... not disturbed exactly, but chaotic. Like she'd just been thrown into upheaval.

What had she said? What could she have heard?

I let out a small, involuntary groan. Maya glanced over, an eyebrow cocked. Only I wasn't going to say what I was thinking, wasn't about to express my blind hope that Mom had talked to anyone but him.

If Mom embarrassed me with Mr. Axelrod, I'm going to kill her.

NOW

TWENTY-EIGHT
DIANA

Tonight, I'm serving my blackmailer a classic salmon en croute.

Gavin won't be able to tell that I used the frozen puff pastry dough as a shortcut, my own private measly act of rebellion, though Ron will know immediately when he eats it later. But Ron isn't here, is he? No, he's working late as usual, as if we don't have guests, as if there isn't a monster in our midst who wants to marry our daughter or steal our money or both.

"This is really good, Mom," Lise says,

"Thanks, honey," I say, because even though the name *Lise* has become more ingrained, it'll never roll off my tongue.

Why did my sweet girl have to bring the monster home? But then, I'm the one who fell for him all those years ago and set this in motion. If he'd never victimized me, then he wouldn't be here now, victimizing her.

Or maybe I'm wrong about that. Maybe Gavin and Lise were fated, and we would have arrived at this moment anyway. It could be a gift that I know what he's all about. At least I'll have a fighting chance to protect her.

Right now, though, I'm feeling low and doubtful. I'm

Gavin's marionette, serving him salmon while he plays somme-lier, picking out a French wine from Ron's cellar.

Ron doesn't really care about wine; he just wants to look like a big shot when guests come over. But will he care that we're all drinking what I'm quite sure is one of the most expensive bottles in his absence? I hope he does. I want him bothered. Then he can try to turn the tables on Gavin. He's got a lot more weapons in his arsenal than I have. Millions of them.

But speaking of bothered... something's wrong between Gavin and Lise. In stark contrast to the other times we've all been together, they're not looking at or touching each other. Did they have a fight?

I feel my spirits starting to take off, like the nose of a 747. "So how was your day?" I ask, eyes on Lise's face.

Gavin is the one to answer. "Lise saw an old friend."

"Oh? Which one?" I stubbornly direct the question back to Lise.

"Denver," she says quietly.

"I only met him a few times but he seemed lovely." My gaze is fastened on my daughter. I might need to pay Gavin but I don't need to dignify him. "How is Denver?"

"Fine." Lise is cutting into her salmon. She's not sullen like when she was a teenager but she doesn't seem eager to talk. I have the sense that this dinner is something to be endured, and I feel a certain kinship with her since that's how I feel, too.

Once this is over, once Gavin's out of both our lives, she'll come back and we'll connect for real. I'll finally have my daughter back.

"Is Denver a nickname, since he's from Colorado?" I say.

Gavin emits a laugh that sounds malicious to my ears, but then, I'm definitely biased. "It's his actual name. How stupid must his parents be?"

Lise gives him a sharp look that I'm gratified to see. But then her eyes quickly return to her plate and I realize: she didn't want him to see it.

"What did you and Denver talk about?" I ask Lise. I'm sensing this is a raw spot for Gavin and I want to keep poking it.

"Yeah, what exactly did you talk about?" Gavin adds.

Lise addresses me. "Denver went to Rice and majored in English. He's really smart but he's feeling a little lost. He's kind of an idealist and that makes job hunting tough."

"I can imagine—" I start to say.

"He's entitled, in other words," Gavin cuts in. "He doesn't want to accept that you have to take what you can get, especially when you're just starting out."

"Did you always want to be a teacher?" It's the first thing I've asked Gavin in this conversation. I know the answer he once told me. I want to see if it's the same one he's given Lise. He claimed that being a teacher had been his calling, but that's when he was trying to present himself to me as a benevolent savior.

"No one gets everything." He's ignoring me, talking to Lise. "But some of us have a lot. I never lose sight of that."

I'm surprised by the shift in his inflection, that he's gone from needling her to appealing to her.

He's feeling insecure. He's threatened by Denver.

Duly noted.

"I know we have a lot." Now Lise is looking at him all gooey. She'd picked up on the shift, too. But then, of course she did. Gavin trains his women to be alert to his every nuance, whim, and mood, like those machines measuring the slightest tremors in the earth to warn of a coming quake.

He's taken her hand and is kissing it while she looks charmed. All is well again in their sick little ecosystem.

I scrape my knife and fork loudly across the plate in a pantomime of cutting. But I'm just moving the food around. I can't eat while watching another of their displays.

"Is idealism getting in the way of your job search?" I say to Lise. I need to turn the topic to something decidedly unromantic or I'm not going to be able to power through this dinner.

"I don't think so," she says. She takes a sip of wine and then beams at Gavin. "Good choice, babe!"

He laughs, self-satisfied, as if the wine came from his own vineyard. He's always been so quick to claim credit and rarely sees through an ego stroke.

Duly noted.

Being sensitive to Gavin could actually come in handy. I'm gathering intel, sowing the seeds for his destruction. He'll underestimate me. He always has.

"Do you help with her job search?" I ask him.

"Not really. I don't like to give unsolicited advice." He dabs at his mouth with a linen napkin and I want to laugh out loud. He can't help himself, I'm sure of it. And Lise's expression tells me that I'm right. He's just told a white lie.

How many others has he told? I need to find out. I need to raise Lise's suspicions.

As I continue to press about Lise's future career, I sense that there are unspoken tensions between the two of them. The conversation has the feel of a dental exam where I'm discreetly prodding to see what's inflamed, what hurts. They're not willing to give much away, but my guess? He doesn't want Lise to be ambitious. He won't say it directly but she feels it and adjusts her behavior accordingly. No wonder her job search keeps stretching out while she's still working part-time in retail.

He's in control, and she probably doesn't even know it. Will there be an opportunity for me to point it out?

When dinner is done, we all decline dessert. I say that I'll clean up, assuming that Gavin and Lise will both go off somewhere, but instead, she offers to help.

I'm touched. I would have thought she wanted to escape my company as soon as possible but maybe I've been reading her wrong. If I get very lucky, then Gavin's the one she wants to escape. She just doesn't know how to get out of the engagement. She's always hated admitting she's wrong. How can I reduce the potential shame and give her permission to walk away from this most grievous mistake?

My fear is that even if she does find the courage, he'll keep hanging on until she relents. He'd probably try to blow up our family on the way out the door just for spite.

I can't think too far ahead. All day, I'd been racking my brain, considering different approaches I could take with Ron and with my mother, ways to convince them to hand over hundreds of thousands of dollars. It's sad to realize that I can't be anything close to honest with either of them, that I have so little sway with the people who are supposed to love me.

In this instant, though, it's about persuading Lise. She needs to trust her gut.

Gavin gives her a big, open-mouthed kiss before taking his leave. I avert my eyes, trying not to gag. But I also feel a bit of triumph. That kiss verifies the insecurity that I sensed earlier. He's not entirely on terra firma, and he knows it. This time, maybe Lise can be the earthquake.

She and I bustle around the kitchen. I don't want to speak first. I'm waiting to see if there's anything she wants to bring up, a reason she was hoping to get me alone.

After a few minutes, I decide to break the silence. I can't afford to waste this opportunity. "So Gavin really doesn't like Denver, huh?"

"He doesn't really know him."

"Wasn't Denver one of Gavin's students?"

Lise is loading the dishwasher, so I can't see her face when she says, "Yes, but not in the same class as me. And that was a long time ago."

"Does Denver like Gavin?"

There's a sizable pause. "I'm not sure." I can tell she's lying.

"The thing is, back then, Gavin was Denver's teacher. So Gavin had to like Denver. He gets to have a different opinion now."

"What's your opinion of Denver?" Placing the salmon in a Tupperware container, I pretend not to be too invested in the conversation. If she thinks this is just casual, she might let down her guard.

Another pause. "Denver's really great."

I wonder about that hesitation, if her having a different opinion from Gavin feels to her like disloyalty. I'm sure that's how Gavin subtly frames it.

"Do you get to have your own mind?" I ask.

She whips around, offended. "What do you mean?" What she's really saying is, *Take that back.*

I can't. I have to let it linger there between us. Let it marinate inside her.

"I have my own mind," she says fiercely. "I'm speaking it right now!"

"To me. Not to..." I don't say the name, but he's casting a shadow over this whole conversation. She must be able to feel that. She must know that's not how it should be in a healthy relationship. But then, she's never really seen a healthy relationship. "I'm sorry that I wasn't a better role model. That Dad and I—"

"Gavin's not Dad!" Her eyes are flashing. But she's angry at the wrong person. Gavin's so good at turning people against each other.

"It just seems like there might be things about Gavin that you're overlooking. A red flag or two, maybe?"

"Gavin's not Dad," she repeats.

I get the subtext: I have no business criticizing Lise's relationship given the lousy one that I've been in for over twenty years. I have no standing in this particular court of law.

It hurts, knowing that I lack credibility. She doesn't trust or respect my opinion, and I can't really fault her for that, given what she's seen.

If only I could tell her what I've been through. If only she realized that I'm an absolute authority where Gavin is concerned.

Then he could tell her what I've done, and I'd lose her for good. Depending who else he chose to tell, I could lose everything, including my freedom.

He's the sociopath, but I'm the killer.

TWENTY-NINE

LISE

I'm in the bathroom, washing my face, and Gavin is hovering nearby, sitting on the lip of the bathtub.

"What was your mom saying to you while you were cleaning up?" His tone is conversational, though I feel the underlying agitation that's been present for the past few days. He was himself at that first dinner with Mom at the steakhouse, but ever since, it's like he's channeling someone else. Normally, I feel calm and happy in Gavin's presence, but not this trip.

"Nothing much," I say. "Just chitchat."

"That sounds like her." It's laced with contempt.

I don't know what the deal is with the two of them, why there's this growing distrust and hostility. She thought highly of him when he was my teacher, and he barely knew her back then. But it's almost like they have some unspoken history.

"My mom doesn't seem to like you," I say. "Why do you think that is?"

"I'm not sure you're right about that. She was confiding in me the other morning about your grandmother's money."

"Which was really weird. She's not exactly an open book.

How did that happen?" I'm starting to feel paranoid, and I hate that. I hate everything about this visit, quite frankly.

"I think you might be reading the situation wrong. It's not that she doesn't like me. She doesn't like the new you. The real you."

I dry my face on a towel slowly, stalling while I consider my response. I don't want to let on how much that last remark hurt me. But why am I hiding anything from Gavin? He's the closest person in the world to me.

"Whereas I love the real you. So incredibly much." As he smiles, I know that it's true. Gavin gets and appreciates me on a profound level. Denver is awesome, but he couldn't begin to approach that.

So why do I still feel uneasy? "I love you, too," I say. I mean it, yet somehow it feels perfunctory.

I start smoothing toner over my face with a cotton ball. Gavin remains where he is, watching me in the large vanity mirror. I'm a little self-conscious because even though my skin is clear now, I have a sense memory of the past, when I never wanted to be seen in anything but dim light. Also, my skincare regimen is four steps long, which feels vain but is necessary. I'm phobic when it comes to pimples.

Gavin knows that, and it means that I'm basically a captive audience as he starts to go off on my mother. He's mocking all her questions from dinner, acting like they were both banal and invasive.

But honestly? I think they were just maternal. She wants to know why there's been no movement on my job search and how come I've been so close-lipped. And when we were doing the dishes afterward, I could feel her good intentions. She wants to make sure that my fiancé treats me well.

It's easy for me to be annoyed with Mom since I have a lot of practice. Meanwhile, I don't want to be annoyed by Gavin but his behavior during this visit has been far less explicable.

He seems to have a problem with everyone: my parents, my friends. He's jealous of Denver when he doesn't need to be.

I'm on step three when I interrupt Gavin. "It's been a long day. Maybe we don't need to talk anymore?"

He squints at me suspiciously. I don't know if I've ever seen that expression on his face before. "What's going on here, Lise?"

"Nothing. I'm just tired." He's still staring, which is disconcerting. "I wouldn't lie to you, Gavin. You know that."

His face softens. "I do know that."

And it's true, so long as you don't count that one pesky little secret I'm keeping...

But there's no need to dwell on that. I finalize my last step and then approach Gavin, arms outstretched. I mean to give him a deep hug and a small peck, only he holds on and puts his tongue fully in my mouth.

I don't know what it is, call it the Parent Effect or the Hometown Effect, but I haven't been able to access my sexual side during the visit. Since Gavin's been so sensitive, I just can't reject him right now. So instead, I slide down and undo his zipper. I bet it's the first blow job this house has seen in a long time. Or maybe not. Maybe this is how my mom has survived her marriage.

Ew, there's nothing grosser than having Gavin in my mouth while thinking about *that*. But I get through it, and afterward, Gavin is smiling down at me with this sort of pride of ownership that really perturbs me.

No, that's not ownership. It's love.

This is my fiancé. Marrying him is the most important, adult decision I've ever made. Mom's just being her anxious self and I can't let her derail my life.

I've never been so right about anything.

THEN

THIRTY

DIANA

Gavin wanted me. *Gavin* wanted me. Gavin wanted *me*.

It seemed impossible and yet it was happening, over and over and over and over again in his apartment. And it was so easy, really. On weeknights, Ron didn't get home until at least 8 p.m. and often it was later, which meant he didn't know anything had changed, and Lizzie didn't want to have dinner with me anyway. So I gave up the fight and let her eat by herself. At first, I made up stories to explain where I was going, like that I'd been recruited by Mari to a new charity committee. Then I realized I didn't have to. There was no need to lie because she was entirely uninterested in me or my activities.

For once, how little Lizzie cared was a blessing. It was freedom.

With Gavin, I mattered. He made it his mission to provide the most exquisite excitement, passion, and safety. In his arms, moments of enveloping contentment followed on the heels of the most intense pleasure.

I'd slept with some boys before Ron but it had never been satisfying. They didn't know what they were doing and weren't trying to learn about my body or my mind. In hindsight, I can see that I'd made my choices in reaction to my mother's controlling ways. It hadn't been about the sex at all, which was maybe why I hadn't expected much, or asked for anything.

Until Gavin, I'd never had an orgasm with a man. No one had ever gone down on me. No one solicited or elicited my opinions and desires.

Gavin did all that, and so much more.

I was discovering his body along with my own. For the first time, I was with someone who cared—deeply—about what I experienced, and I felt the same. I loved my effect on him. I'd never been so powerful.

I wanted Lizzie to find her power, too, someday. Years and years from now.

Not that being with Gavin sexually had anything to do with Lizzie. I kept a strict separation, making sure that we never talked about Lizzie once we had our clothes off. Gavin and I agreed that there had to be a clear boundary. In bed, he was my lover, not Lizzie's teacher.

Yes, he remained my go-to person for all my fears about Lizzie; yes, I trusted him to be my eyes and ears, to engage in important conversations with her and be a positive influence on her. Sometimes he had to be the bearer of bad news, that couldn't be helped. I valued his honesty. He handled it as sensitively as possible and then supported me through it. We made plans: what he'd do for Lizzie, what I'd do. We were a team. It was nothing like my marriage.

Then Gavin and I shifted gears, leaving Lizzie behind and moving into the physical realm. It was great to have a focus other than Lizzie, a way to release the stress that she generated.

Intellectually, I knew our relationship had to be wrong. It was adultery and God was against adultery. But hadn't God, in His infinite wisdom, brought Gavin and me together?

When I was with Gavin, my guilt was paused. Sometimes,

after I went back home, I could stave it off by reliving the Gavin moments. But it always came back.

As far as I knew, Ron had been faithful to me. His biggest crime was his work preoccupation, and sure, he was self-involved but that was true of the vast majority of men I knew (not counting Gavin, of course, and Mari's husband). Ron was ambitious because he'd been tapped for greatness early in his life. He'd been a high school football star earning straight A's with a full-ride scholarship to Rice University that he didn't even need since his parents were so wealthy. Then at his company, he'd been marked as CEO material right from the beginning.

He liked things the way he liked them but he wasn't a liar or a cheater. There were far worse husbands. Who was I kidding, there were far worse wives.

I was a liar, a cheater, and a murderer. I deserved a lot worse than an inattentive and callous man for a husband. Recently, I'd felt so much self-loathing over my crime that it was almost a relief when Ron treated me badly. I deserved to be punished. I'd wondered many times if that was why Lizzie hated me, if I had that coming.

But when I was with Gavin, I could forget everything. I could bask in his adoration. I knew it would all dissolve if he knew about the terrible thing I'd done—the most terrible thing anyone could do—but when I was with him, the shadow lifted. I saw myself, briefly, through his eyes. I got a reprieve from all the self-hatred and contempt and just inhabited my skin, happily, for a little while.

I was so grateful for Gavin, and increasingly dependent on him. Which was scary.

It was hard to imagine a time before him and I didn't want to think about a time after him. But he told me I didn't have to.

He said he was never letting me go, no matter what.

THIRTY-ONE

LIZZIE

"Lizzie!" Denver called, racing down the hall toward me.

I had one hand on the doorknob to Mr. Axelrod's classroom. I'd asked Mr. Axelrod a number of times if we could meet after school to talk about the literary magazine and he'd apologized, saying he was unusually busy. Finally, today, he told me he was free.

I reluctantly let go of the knob and turned toward Denver. "Hi." I didn't mean to sound bitchy, but whatever the opposite of impeccable timing was, Denver had it.

"I'm not trying to get in your business but I ran into Maya and she seemed pretty upset," he said, slightly out of breath.

So apparently Maya had even worse timing than Denver. "What's wrong with her?" I asked.

"She's upset with you for ditching her."

"We were just going to her house to hang out. We can do that anytime."

"It's a mistake to alienate your friends." He stepped closer to me and said in a low voice, "Something's a little off about him, isn't it?" He was gesturing toward the classroom.

"Mr. Axelrod is a really good guy," I said.

"He's not supposed to be a guy; he's your teacher."

I felt sorry for Denver. He was so obviously jealous when there was no need to be. Age notwithstanding, Denver and Mr. Axelrod would never be in the same league.

This wasn't about Mr. Axelrod. It was about Denver's insecurities, and I totally got that. I had plenty of my own.

"Thanks for telling me about Maya," I said. "I've really got to go. Mr. Axelrod and I are going to talk about the literary magazine."

"What literary magazine?"

"It's in the embryonic stages." I loved that word, *embryonic*. "I can tell you more later."

"Yeah," he said. "Do that." He smiled almost sadly and then walked away. "See you, brainiac!"

I was smiling when I knocked on Mr. Axelrod's door and he called for me to come in. As soon as I saw him, I knew that what I had just told Denver was 100 percent true. Mr. Axelrod was a really good guy. The best.

He was sitting at his teacher's desk, and I sat in a chair facing him. "I really want to do the literary magazine." *With you.* "What are the first steps? How do we get started?"

"You could try your hand at a short story. Have you ever written fiction?"

"No, not really. I'm more of a confessional poet." I felt slightly deflated. He should have known that by now. Didn't he like my poetry? Why did he think I needed to make things up? Also, I thought the point was for me to work alongside him, selecting and editing other students' writing. He was suggesting I spend more time by myself.

"It's hard to make a living as a poet. It's hard to make a living as any kind of writer, really, but your best bet is novels. You might want to start with short stories." His tone was kind, as ever, but he also seemed slightly rushed, like there was someplace he needed to be.

Why was he so busy all the time? He used to be much more available after school. Had he started seeing someone?

I was his student. I had no right to ask. But it felt unfair and unbalanced, how I told him all about me and I was shut out of his personal life.

"Do you write short stories? Or novels?" I said.

He shook his head. "Unfortunately—or fortunately—my skills lie elsewhere. I'm all about helping other people develop themselves to the fullest."

"Do you really think I'm talented?" After it came out, I wished I could take it back. It was just so raw, and naked. Needy, and who likes needy?

But he broke into a smile. "Of course you are, Lizzie. That's why I'm pushing you."

"I don't feel like you're pushing me. I feel like you're lifting me."

His smile widened. I'd scored a direct hit. "You've got so much strength inside you. I just want to see you bring it forward."

"I am. I'm standing up to people who underestimate me. Like my mom."

"My guess is that she's afraid for you. Because she had you at the same age you are now. That's got to be a mindfuck."

I was surprised that he'd used the word *fuck*. And also surprised that he knew about her being a teen mother. Had I told him that and forgotten?

"Your mom needs to learn that her life and her choices are her own," he said. "Everyone has to figure out their own shit. We all have to make our own mistakes."

"What's one mistake that you've made?"

He laughed. "You mean ever?"

"What's a mistake you make again and again, even though you should know better?"

"Wow, Lizzie." He looked admiring. "That's a great question." I felt myself glowing at the compliment. "I tend to fall for women where there are obstacles. And complications. But that's the definition of every great love story, right? It's about what you've overcome. It's about never letting up, and never letting go. In love, you can't take no for an answer."

Coud it really be? Was he saying what I thought he was saying?

Mr. Axelrod was into me.

He was telling me not to give up on him, that there was hope for us. The complications were what would make us a great love story.

"You are so right," I said, and moved a teensy bit closer.

NOW

THIRTY-TWO

DIANA

Ron surprises me. He says he's going to the office late because he wants the four of us to have breakfast together. He asks me—well, tells me—to make something special.

Could this mean that he's finally concerned about his daughter's welfare? That he's come to think something is amiss with Gavin and wants to take a closer look?

Part of me wants that—to pit Ron against Gavin and let the sparks fly—but I think the safer strategy is to try to convince Ron that Gavin and Lise really are a great couple. Then maybe

he could be persuaded to get on board with the $200K gift. It's possible that Gavin will accept that amount. He hasn't said no, has he? And whenever we're out of Lise's eyeshot, he alternates between giving me meaningfully threatening looks and lascivious ones. I don't know exactly what to make of that but...

I can pull this off. Pay him off, I mean, if only Ron will cooperate.

Except when's the last time Ron cooperated with me? Everything has to be his idea. And it's never Ron's idea to give away a large sum of money.

I don't feel much like going to the supermarket (seeing as I don't feel much like doing anything these days, other than getting Gavin the hell away from my daughter). We already have a bag of organic apples, so I throw together a brown butter apple skillet pie that Ron and Lizzie both love. It feels like a cheat since it smells heavenly and looks impressive without much effort.

While the apples are sautéing, I go to check in with Ron. The goal is to gauge his mood and try to render him as receptive to Gavin as possible. I assume he's in his home office, squeezing in every minute of work that he can. But when I knock on the closed door, there's no answer.

He's got to be ignoring me and what was that line that Gavin quoted?

I will not be ignored.

I'm tired of everyone's disregard. Last night, Lise met my reasonable worries with utter contempt. Yet I'm still here, fighting for her. She's my daughter. I don't have any other choice.

I push the door open, and I see Gavin. I've caught him red-handed, going through Ron's desk drawers.

But instead of being startled or looking alarmed, he smiles.

It's enraging, how bold he is. How untouchable he feels. He figures that he's got this all wrapped up, that I'm entirely at his mercy.

Even though he'd probably mistakenly assumed that Ron's already left for work, he knows that I'm here, in the kitchen cooking, right down the hall. But it's not like he cares what I know or what I see.

"Ron's home," I say. "If he finds you in here, I don't know what he'll do." I gesture to where the gun safe is built right into the wall.

It has the desired effect. Gavin stops smiling.

So he's smart enough to fear Ron. Is that something that I can use? I probably won't be able to convince Ron to give me money, but could I convince Gavin that Ron would do anything to protect his wife and child?

Gavin starts to walk past me, and I involuntarily flinch in the doorway, making myself small. I remember his smell all too well.

He hesitates, our bodies close together. My head is turned away from him. I don't want to look into his eyes, don't want to breathe the same air.

Is this really about the money, or sex, or some other form of vengeance? If it is, then what could he be looking for in Ron's office?

Even if he gets the full million, I don't think he's going to stop. Gavin's insatiable by nature. I ought to know.

He has the ultimate ammunition, and he didn't even have to search for it. I handed it right to him.

A few weeks after I told him what I'd done to my father, Gavin pretended to be soothing, but I know now that he was intentionally amping up my anxiety. A frightened woman is easier to control. Whenever he sensed I was going to pull away, he had all sorts of tricks to pull me back in. But I didn't know that then. I didn't understand anything.

So there he was, stroking my hair, and he said, "It's over and done. You got away with it. If anyone ever suspected, a good lawyer could get you off. Or it'd be negligible homicide, at most. Not that it would ever come to that."

Gavin hasn't threatened to go to the police but we both know that he could detonate that bomb whenever he wants.

I need to stay calm. The police probably wouldn't even investigate such an outrageous accusation. I'm an upstanding citizen and productive member of the community, whereas Gavin had just been passing through, staying only a few years. If questioned, I could say that he'd developed an obsession with me five years ago that had clearly persisted. There's no way the state would dig up my father's body, not when it's Gavin's word against mine.

But this isn't Austin; it's Houston. In this neighborhood full of successful husbands and doting wives, a man's word is worth more than a woman's. Gavin could paint me as some kind of seductress, and for all I know, he's retained evidence to back it up. The police would see that there's nothing upstanding about me at all. I'm a whore masquerading as a respectable wife and mother. In this part of the world, they hate a duplicitous woman more than anything, except maybe a killer. And I could be painted as both.

If there is an investigation, then Gavin's prophecy could come true. Maybe I will be charged. With negligible homicide, or worse?

"You've gone pale," Gavin says. He lifts a hand to touch my cheek.

I push past him. "My apples are burning," I say, dashing down the hall, back to the kitchen.

Thankfully, he doesn't follow me, though his formerly intoxicating, now nauseating scent lingers in my nostrils. I finish cooking and then I let everyone know that breakfast is ready.

Ron comes downstairs, dressed in his business casual. He's followed by Lise in her pajamas and Gavin in his t-shirt and shorts. The two of them are laughing together, and I really don't know how I'm going to survive this breakfast, let alone the rest of the week. I'm just so twisted up with love for her and hatred for him.

I've laid out the food on the kitchen table rather than in the more formal dining room. Lise reaches for the pitcher of orange juice.

"No coffee?" Ron says, and what he really means is, *Get me my coffee.*

"Sorry," I say, getting to my feet. "I forgot. But it's already made. Does anyone else want a cup?"

"I'll get it myself," Lise says. "Gavin's, too. I know how he likes it."

Finally, when we're all settled, I ask Ron, "Do you have any meetings today?"

"A few. I never have less than a few." Ron smiles at Gavin. "You know how it is, right, Gavin? No rest for the wicked."

"I have some staff meetings," Gavin says. "But my job is generally more hands-on."

"Ah, yes. Hands-on." Ron seems on the verge of smirking. Was that a dig about Gavin being inappropriate with his students?

Gavin must think so. He tenses up. Lise puts her hand on his arm and says, "You both have very important jobs."

I wouldn't have guessed that Lizzie would mediate like this. It seems more like something I would do, except that I don't have it in me to turn down the heat.

I'm thinking about that phrase *hands-on*. Maybe Ron's not referencing Gavin and his students; he could be talking about Gavin and me.

If Ron knows about the affair—if he's always known—and now his anger is being reignited, then I could be in big trouble. Even bigger trouble, that is.

Then Gavin and Ron are both threats to me.

Ron essentially called for this meeting, didn't he? He wanted this breakfast, and now he hasn't looked at me once. So is he sending a message to Gavin, or to me, or to both of us?

I feel like crying. All I wanted was freedom, and just a week ago, I'd been on the cusp of it. Now I'm in danger of being shackled forever, as is my daughter.

It's not impossible that my shackles will be literal. I'll have no way to look after Lise from prison. Knowing what Gavin was like as a lover, I don't want to think how toxic he could be as a husband.

"Diana has the most important job," Ron says. "Doesn't she?" He's staring at Gavin, as if daring to be contradicted.

"Absolutely," Gavin says. "I can't wait until Lise and I have kids of our own."

Lise's entire carriage stiffens.

"I'd love to be a grandfather," Ron says. My head snaps toward him. I've never heard that before. Is he just messing with all of us? Because if he means it, then maybe that $200K isn't out of reach. I can say that Lise will want to be a parent if we relieve her financial stress. And it was all Ron's idea!

Gavin smiles. "It sounds like we're in agreement then."

"I guess I should just fall in line," Lise says. She sounds angry, and she should be. Her body, her choice, after all. I'm not sure I've ever felt that way about my own.

"We've got lots of time," Gavin tells her. I remember that tone of his all too well. It used to seem reassuring but now I see that it's just patronizing.

"I might never want kids." I'm not sure if Lise is throwing that in Gavin's face or her father's.

"She'll change her mind," Gavin says confidently, and my blood boils. He believes he can manipulate or overpower Lise in order to get what he wants. If that's how he treats the women in his life, how would he treat a child? The idea of Gavin as a father is revolting and terrifying.

"A woman knows what she wants," I say. "And what she doesn't. It takes a real man to listen."

Gavin turns to me for the first time. "Lise would want to be a mom, except for you, Di. You made it look like no fun at all, always acting so anxious and stressed."

How dare he?

"That's because you *made* me anxious and—" I start to fire back at him and then I stop. I can't let Gavin goad me into giving myself (and my history with him) away. My cheeks are hot as I quickly add, "I meant that Lizzie made me anxious and stressed when she was a teenager."

Lise stares at me as if I've just accused her, which I inadvertently have.

"All teenagers make their mothers anxious," I say. "It just comes with the territory."

I can see Lise isn't going to accept my minimization. "For once, just say what you really mean, Mom."

"I had a lot of problems being the mother to a teenager," I say. "That's all I meant. I love you more than anything."

Lise acts as if she hasn't even heard me. "Gavin's right. A large part of why I'm not sure about kids is because of how you seemed to feel about motherhood. You probably wouldn't have even signed up for it if I hadn't been an accident."

"That's not true!" I stare at her, aghast. "I would have wanted you no matter what! I was happy to be your mother!"

But I can tell she doesn't believe me. I can also tell that Gavin is reveling in this.

"Be a mother if you want," I say. "Don't be a mother if you don't want. You need to honor your gut, okay? Trust your intuition. Use your voice." What I mean is, *See through Gavin; your gut knows something is off. Run.*

"You're hiding something," Lise says. "That's what my intuition is telling me. How about you use your voice and show me how it's done?"

Mom stares down at her plate and for a second, I think she's really considering it. That she might actually be brave and come clean.

But then she just says softly, "You already know everything. Deep in your heart."

"Oh, for fuck's sake!" I explode. I don't need koans from a fortune cookie; I need a mother with some inner fortitude. No chance of that, though. "Gavin! Pantry! Now!"

Gavin follows me into the pantry and shuts the door behind us. I'm fuming. What an absolute shit show.

Why did Dad even stay home? I don't get it. He and Mom are both opaque, in entirely different ways, and I'm sick of it.

"What the hell was that?" I hiss at Gavin. We're surrounded by cans and jars and jumbo-size Costco merchandise, everything meticulously organized and labeled. This is how my mother has spent her life. Pathetic.

Gavin is wearing a mystified expression. "I don't know, babe. She's your mother. She's been spinning out for this entire visit." He's not wrong but...

She was looking right at him when she said, "*You* made me stressed and anxious."

I think of the time that I saw my mother leaving the school in a frenzy. I never did find out who she'd been there to see. I remember hoping it was anyone but Mr. Axelrod.

"How well did you and my mother know each other when I was in high school?" I ask.

"Not well. Or I mean, no better than I knew any of the other parents who felt like their kids were troubled. She's always been a drama queen." He's looking at me as if he thinks I'm the one spinning out. Maybe I am, because I don't like what my intuition is suddenly telling me. "How often did you see her? Was it always at school or...?" I'm having an unwelcome flashback, an image of a car parked in front of our house that looked a lot like Mr. Axelrod's.

"Not often. And only at school. She stopped by my classroom a few times, probably when she was already at the school. Didn't she do PTA kind of stuff?"

"Sometimes."

"Yeah, she seemed like one of those volunteer types." He does a little smile, like we're sharing a private joke. "So she and I talked a few times, always about you. Or she'd text me—"

"She *texted* you? That's not normal, is it?"

"Don't you get it, Lise? She was obsessed with you then and she's obsessed with you now. She wants to run your life. She was a nervous wreck, so I used to tell her to back off, that you'd be just fine, that you'd become an incredible woman. And obviously, I was right. But she still can't see it through her own neuroses."

I nod. He's right; Mom's probably incapable of seeing me as a mature adult.

But I don't think that's all there is to it.

Yes, Mom's neurotic, but her behavior since Gavin arrived

has been over the top. And now that I've learned she was texting my hot English teacher all those years ago…

Is it possible that Mom had a crush on Gavin herself back then? It's not like she would have acted on it, and Gavin definitely wouldn't have encouraged her. If anything more had happened between them, he obviously would have said something.

But maybe she liked indulging in a fantasy life. Since she couldn't have him then, some part of her doesn't want me to have him now. That's why she's searching for any reason to disapprove.

Gavin's always talking about how powerful the subconscious is, and how so many of our actions are motivated by forces we don't recognize or understand. I think Mom's just proved his point. I bet she has no idea why she's been so negative about Gavin and me.

Consciously, Mom would never want to hurt me. She only wants what's best. But what we do subconsciously can still be pretty destructive.

I'm going to have to keep a much closer eye on Mom. For the first time in my life, I just can't trust her.

THEN

THIRTY-FOUR

DIANA

I opened the door and stared at Gavin. It was 2 p.m. on a school day, so he should have been at work. More significantly, he knew better than to stand on my welcome mat.

I glanced at the street beyond. No neighbors were visible but that didn't mean they weren't watching from inside their own houses.

This wasn't the agreement. Gavin and I were supposed to meet at his house at prearranged times. Spontaneity was sloppiness, and I couldn't take any chances with my marriage and family.

I didn't feel comfortable inviting Gavin in, and I didn't want to send him away.

He was grinning, almost like he was enjoying my quandary. No, he was just happy to see me. That's what he said: "I couldn't wait. I got someone to cover my last two periods."

That clinched it. I had no choice.

Once inside, he was on me immediately, his tongue down my throat, and normally, that was where I liked it, but right then, my head was spinning with panicked thoughts. This was Ron's home. Lizzie's home.

In other words, this wasn't right. It wasn't what I'd asked for, or what I wanted.

Tell that to my body, though. It was responding by rote. I pulled him upstairs, steering him to the guest bedroom where he gave me orgasm after orgasm before he collapsed on top of me in a sweaty heap.

"Lizzie's going to be home soon," I said. "You need to go."

"No, she's painting sets. We have another hour, at least."

It felt slightly strange, him knowing my daughter's schedule better than I did, but then I reminded myself that I loved the personal interest he took in her. She needed a trusted adult to keep her on the right path and it was increasingly apparent that I was not that person for her.

But I didn't want to think about that, not when I was naked in bed with my lover. Who should never have been here at all.

"This can't happen again," I said. He looked stricken. "I mean, you can't just show up here."

"I wanted to surprise you." He downshifted from stricken to hurt. "I missed you so much."

"I missed you, too, but there can't be any surprises, okay? We have to be really careful. I've told you that Ron has a punitive streak. This is playing with fire."

"I love our fire." He smiled at me and twirled a lock of my hair around his finger. "Let's light it again."

"No." It came out forceful enough that we were both startled. "I'm sorry. But this is my home, with my family. I can't jeopardize that."

"So this is your real life. I'm just your sidepiece. I get it." He pulled away and started to get out of bed. I grabbed his arm.

"You mean so much to me. You know that. But I have to protect my family. You'll understand someday when you have your own."

He pulled his arm free and then started putting his clothes on. "Maybe you're the one who doesn't understand. You're my family, Di. But I see that I don't make the cut for you. That I'm less than, and I always will be."

"No!" I felt panicked. "If anything, you're too much! I mean, you're too good for me. I can't even believe you want to spend time with me."

He spun around, the smile back on his face. It was jarring, how quickly he was changing from one emotion to the next. I'd never seen him as this type of volatile weather system before. He'd always been nothing but blue skies.

He knelt down beside the bed and took my hand. "I'm in love with you, Di."

"Oh." I hadn't seen that coming, and I wasn't sure that was the best descriptor for what I felt for him. But in that moment, he was just so vulnerable, like a butterfly that I could crush in my hand. "I love you, too."

Now he had tears in his eyes as he climbed back into the bed. He hugged me so tight that it was almost suffocating. We were lying like that for a while when I heard the front door open.

I stared at him, my eyes wide with fear. "I think that's Lizzie," I whispered. I raced over to shut and lock the door. How could I have been so careless? How could he have put me in this position?

"Should I hide in here? You can come back and tell me when the coast is clear."

I didn't have any better ideas—he couldn't climb out a second-story window—so I nodded miserably. "No one ever uses this room," I said, "but normally the door is open."

"I'll lock it. She won't get in."

"But she could ask questions."

"You'll have to come up with answers. She's just a kid." He gave me a reassuring smile. "It's not what you say, it's how you say it. Sell the lie."

I threw on my clothes and then hurried out of the room. I

went down the hall to my own en suite bathroom, washing my face and brushing my hair. Did I smell like sex? Would Lizzie know what sex smelled like anyway?

I took a quick shower and put on fresh clothes just in case. Fortunately, Lizzie never sought me out. She liked to go straight to her room to shut and lock her own door. Once she did, I'd get Gavin out of here.

Oh God, what if she saw him? How would I explain any of this? She was a kid, but a smart one.

I crept out into the hall, listening. I couldn't tell if Lizzie had already gone into her room because the door was closed all the time, whether she was home or not, even though I would never go through her things. I would not turn into my mother.

I went downstairs, worried about every step. Was it possible that Lizzie had heard the whispered conversation between Gavin and me while we plotted strategy?

She was perched on a stool at the kitchen island, eating an apple with peanut butter on it. She'd tossed her shoes and her backpack in the middle of the floor, even though I'd asked her a thousand times to leave them in the front closet. But I definitely wasn't going to pick a fight with her. I needed this to be as quick, clean, and painless as possible. Get her to her room so Gavin could flee the scene.

If Lizzie found Gavin here, she would freak out. But what form that would take, I didn't know.

Something I would never tell anyone was that I didn't fear only what could happen to Lizzie (like someone attacking her at a party); I feared what she would be capable of, seeing as she was my daughter. People surprise themselves, sometimes in terrible ways.

I never would have imagined that I could kill my own father. So who knew what Lizzie would do in extreme circumstances?

"Is someone here?" she asked. Her tone was unconcerned but my heart nearly stopped at the question.

"No, why?"

"Because there's a car parked right outside. But I didn't think it was someone who'd come here. Your friends never have cars like that. My teacher has a car like that."

I was too terrified to speak.

"You know, Mr. Axelrod?"

THIRTY-FIVE

LIZZIE

"Oh?" Mom asked. "Your English teacher?"

Why were her hands shaking on the handle of the refrigerator? Was she having a conniption?

"Yeah, my teacher," I said. "Did you go see him at school the other day? I saw you leaving the building."

"No, I wasn't there to see him."

"So who were you there to see?"

She was staring into the refrigerator like it contained the secret to the universe. Normally, she didn't believe in between-meal snacks.

"Are you okay?" I said, more irritated than worried.

"I just haven't been feeling well today. I'm a little out of sorts." She finally took out a can of bubbly water.

She was flushed and had beads of sweat breaking out on her face. "Do you have a fever?"

"I don't know. I haven't taken my temperature. Maybe." She seemed grateful for my question. It probably had been a long time since I'd appeared to give a shit about her, which made me feel guilty. But it also made me feel even more annoyed.

Why hadn't she just stayed upstairs? Then we wouldn't

have to go through this embarrassing and futile exercise; we wouldn't be reminded that we have absolutely nothing in common. If we weren't related, we would never speak.

There was a thump from upstairs. Mom looked terrified, of course. She's scared of her own shadow.

"Do you want me to check that out for you?" I said. "See if there's a burglar?" I was just teasing because it was the middle of the day and everyone around here had security systems. It was appallingly safe, really.

"No! I'll handle it. I mean, I'm sure it's nothing."

"Well, obviously." I rolled my eyes as she left the room.

She was acting bizarre. If I hadn't known for a fact that she was the most boring, predictable person alive, I really might have thought she had something to hide.

I glanced outside at the car again, then found myself smiling. Mr. Axelrod, in my house?

I wished.

NOW

THIRTY-SIX

DIANA

At 2 a.m., I inch downstairs. But before I go, I make sure there's no light coming from under the guest bedroom door. I'm presuming Lise and Gavin are both asleep.

Gavin's always slept like a baby. No matter what he does, he manages to feel justified. It's a good trick, one I wish I could pull off more frequently myself.

I stay quiet and keep the lights dim as I microwave a mug of chamomile tea. I stare out at the pool that's gotten no use this visit, though Lise suggested we have a pool day tomorrow. The thought of having to be in a swimsuit in front of Gavin is part of why I don't have a prayer of getting to sleep.

But suddenly he's here, next to me. I shouldn't be surprised that he's an excellent creeper.

"Alone at last," he says, practically salivating.

Then he's on me, grabbing my face roughly and kissing me. I'm struggling against him but he's holding fast. What would happen if I screamed?

I'm not prepared to find out. Instead, I put both hands against his chest and shove as hard as I can. He stumbles backward. I think he's going to be angry but instead he's looking at me like my efforts to resist are simply adorable. As if we both know how this is destined to end.

He turns seductive. Cajoling. "Come on, Di," he says. "Why not? Just for old time's sake? We always fit together so well."

"My daughter—your fiancée—is upstairs sleeping."

"So what's the risk? You don't want me with her anyway." He moves toward me. "You and I deserve a few stolen moments."

"I never want to be with you again, and if I had my way"—*you'd be dead*—"I never would have set eyes on you in the first place." It's not a smart or strategic thing to say, but I've reached my limit.

"Who says I care what you want?"

It's true; he never did. I just didn't realize that until I was in far too deep. But I got out once, and I can do it again. So will Lise.

"Keep me happy, Di, or I just might tell Lise the truth. I could go upstairs and do it right now."

"If you do that, your relationship with her will be over."

"Depends which truth I tell. There's what you did with me, and what you did to your own father. When he called you out for stealing, you murdered him."

I go pale in the moonlight. "You know that's not what happened."

"I only know what you told me and we're both well aware of what a liar you are. So what did you do with the money you stole?"

"I didn't steal!" I don't sound entirely convinced, though, or convincing. The fifty thousand has always felt ill-gotten. Tainted.

"I guess we can agree to disagree about the theft," he says magnanimously. "But you still have it, right?"

I say nothing.

"You said it'll take time to pull together the whole million but I'm going to need a $50K downpayment. I just don't know if you're good for the rest, honestly."

I shake my head, disgusted. "If Lise knew what you're really like—"

"You've been living in an awfully big glass house since before you met me." He looks around in an exaggerated pantomime. "I wouldn't throw stones if I were you."

I get what he means instantly. I killed my father before Gavin and I ever met. That wasn't his influence; I did that all on my own.

"If you tell Lise, if you hurt her like that," I say, "it'll prove that you don't care about her at all."

"Or maybe I'd be setting her free."

No, that's not why he'd do it. He's malicious, and malignant. Incapable of love. Lise and I are both just pawns in his sick game.

But for now, I have to play, too.

I propel myself forward. "It's hard for me, having you here," I say, making my voice soft and inviting. "Despite everything, there's still a part of me that..." I don't continue, because I can't, not without gagging, but hopefully his arrogant mind will fill in the blanks.

I see that I'm having the desired effect. He's susceptible to manipulation, too, and I can't let myself forget that.

"I knew it," he says. "If you can't have me, then no one can, not even your daughter."

"Have you ever thought about it?" I force myself to lightly trail a fingertip down his face in the way he likes, even though my own skin is crawling. "Have you fantasized about us being together again?"

"I'm here now, aren't I? I've been napping on your couch every night waiting for you to come downstairs and make yourself a cup of tea."

"I can't be with you with my husband and daughter upstairs," I say. "I'd feel too anxious. Too inhibited."

"What do you want to do? Get a hotel room?"

Perish the thought. "Let's get everything wrapped up with Lise and then we can talk again. Or do more than talk."

He nods slowly. "I still want my money, though. After what you did to me, I deserve reparations."

"I understand. But I need time. I invested the $50K and I've taken some losses. Plus, if I pull it out of the market suddenly, I might have to pay penalties and—"

"Not my problem."

"It's just not as simple as you might think. But I'm working on it. I really am." I try to give him my best damsel-in-distress expression.

Now he's running his fingers over my face like it's Braille and he's hoping to find some secret message. Is he deciding whether he can trust me, or is he just turning himself on?

"Please," I say. "Just give me a little more time."

"This gets done before I leave Houston. So you've got, what, three days? That should be plenty. Then on that last night, you and me, we're going to celebrate."

THIRTY-SEVEN

LISE

I roll over and see that Gavin's side of the bed is empty. He's usually such a sound sleeper, but this trip, everything's been off. About him, about my mother. About me, too, maybe? It all feels topsy-turvy.

I can't wait to get back to Austin but I don't intend to cut this short. That would be like an admission of... guilt? Weakness? Fallibility? I don't know; I just don't want to give the wrong impression. The impression that Gavin is the wrong guy for me, that is.

Before we arrived, I had a vision that it would go so well that Dad would want to spring for a dream wedding (a destination wedding, somewhere with white beaches and sapphire water) and Mom would want to help plan it with me. Hers had been thrown together hastily because she didn't have much time before her pregnancy would start to show. I thought that this could almost be like a do-over for her, or a sort of wish fulfillment. She'd be providing for me what she never had herself, which has always been her stated goal.

How sad, when you think about it: your most cherished goal

as a mother is for your child's life to turn out differently than your own.

I'm not supposed to know this, but Gavin's been married before. I snooped in his apartment one time, back before I'd moved in, and made the discovery in a box of sentimental objects. I found his first wedding ring.

I thought of confronting him but then I'd be confessing that I'd gone through his things, which would be like confessing that I didn't trust him. But I did trust him when I first started going through his closet. I'd just been bored and mildly curious. He was practically my first boyfriend and inexperienced people make dumb mistakes, okay? But I couldn't let that dumb mistake jeopardize such a beautiful relationship. So it had to become a secret, though I know how he feels about secrets, which is that they shouldn't exist in a beautiful relationship. Except that he's been keeping his own secret about having been previously married.

Like Mr. Axelrod once said, great love stories have complications.

And like I said, it was relatively early days, and now we've grown much closer, tighter, and stronger. But I still hesitate to admit what I did. I keep hoping that he'll tell me about his first wife, though given what I learned about the way it ended, I can understand why he wouldn't want to talk about it. Maybe some boxes should never be opened. Just ask Pandora.

I actually went to look for the box again not too long ago but it was gone. I took that as a positive sign. We're engaged now and he wants a truly fresh start. He's not hanging on to the past.

I would like to know more about her, though, through his eyes. Why her, back then? And now, why me? Why have I been chosen?

All I know is, Gavin and I are in this for eternity. No other woman will ever come between us.

THEN

THIRTY-EIGHT

DIANA

It happened in bed, of course. I'd shed my clothes and my inhibitions and then I was ready to go all the way.

It wasn't until I'd taken the full plunge and told Gavin everything, start to finish, that I realized the enormity of what I'd done.

I'd just confessed to a crime. The biggest crime there was. In doing so, I'd given Gavin Axelrod all the power. I'd hoped that he'd set me free from my own conscience but what if he sent me to prison instead?

It was a huge risk, one that I shouldn't have taken. Not when I had a daughter to consider. But somehow, I'd managed to forget all about Lizzie.

Here's what I told him, my voice barely above a whisper:

It had occurred more than two years ago. Lizzie had just celebrated her fourteenth birthday. My father had Stage IV prostate cancer and treatments had failed him. All modern medicine could do was keep him comfortable. He was slated to die, and soon.

Not that it excused my actions but it was context. Daddy had made his wishes known: He was to take his last breath at home, not in a facility, even though Mother had made her objections known. I could tell she was horrified by the idea of doing things like sponge-bathing him. It was just so unseemly. Not ladylike in the slightest. Mother didn't like to acknowledge that any of us even had bodies, let alone that they would someday break down and require the most intimate tending by others.

Usually, my father gave in on all domestic matters, and one could argue this was very much domestic in nature. It was her home we were talking about, where he'd spent very little time over the years because he'd been working such long hours.

"But it's my life," he said quietly, "and I want to be here when it ends."

So that was that. It was decided. Mother was to be his nursemaid, with the help of hospice workers who would stop by at regular intervals. She expected me to "make myself available." I agreed, without hesitation. I'd never had such access to my father.

It was supposed to be several months but no longer. Daddy wouldn't actually die in his own bed because a special one—the kind you see in hospitals—was delivered to the guest room. Mother continued to sleep in their bedroom next door with a baby monitor so that she could hear if he needed anything.

Mother unraveled quickly. She was tense and irritable and, I imagined, prone to private crying jags (her eyes were often red, though she'd never cry in front of others). It was evident that she hated caring for my father, and I could hear how short she was every time she spoke to him. It was painful to listen to their interactions. He sounded pleading and she sounded irate.

My initial distaste at the idea of seeing my father naked paled in comparison to my horror at how he was being treated. I asked Mother to notice her sharp tongue but she just lashed me with it next.

I started to take over. I spent more and more time at their house meeting my father's needs. I fed him, bathed him, and made sure he got his pain medications on time. I grew to know and appreciate the hospice workers and their commitment to what they called "a good death."

Daddy and I had never spent very much time together, and even when he was around, he was taciturn and reserved by nature. But now that he was spying the end, he was much more talkative. He was grateful for my company, even if we were just sitting in companionable silence. He loved when I read him books; he regretted that he'd had so little time for reading. "I regret a lot of things," he told me, and I had the sense that included not getting to know me better. That was amplified when he added, "You have such a beautiful voice, Di." Then he closed his eyes.

He often drifted off to sleep in the middle of a chapter. I'd close the book and sit in the chair beside his bed for a while longer. Sometimes minutes, sometimes hours. I felt needed. And loved.

My father finally loved me. Or maybe he always had, in his own undemonstrated way. But now he was showing it.

It was a precious time, that month. Daddy was tired but his vitals were steady. He had all his faculties and was in fine spirits. The nurses gave me a lot of credit for that. One told me in private that death can ultimately be a matter of will, that it matters when people are ready to loosen their grasp on life. "Your father wants to live because of you," she told me.

Daddy had never been unkind to me; he'd just been uninvolved. Otherwise occupied by work. He let me know that he was sorry about that. "I missed a lot," he said. Then he reached out a bony hand toward me. "I'm just so glad you're here now, Di."

"There's nowhere I'd rather be," I said.

It was true. I liked ministering to him. My favorite times were when I brushed his hair (he didn't have much but he loved the feeling, and at his request, I'd do it for a half hour or even a full hour at a time). That's when we'd exchange confidences. He never insulted my mother but he said, "You get out of marriage what you put in, and I never put in enough." It was probably also a veiled reference to how little time my mother spent in the guest room with him, that she had basically outsourced him to me and the hospice nurses. He didn't seem upset about this arrangement because whenever my mother joined us, she would bustle around and look for things she could do. She'd dust or plump pillows and her energy set Daddy and me on edge. We were glad when she'd say, "Well, that's that," and then leave.

I told my father the truth about Ron and me. "I never loved him," I said.

Daddy didn't look remotely surprised. "I wouldn't love him, either," he said, and I had to laugh. "Ron's got an ego the size of Texas."

"I used to think he was like you because you both worked so much. But really, you're nothing alike."

"I sure hope not."

"How come you never told me how you felt about Ron?" I asked.

"It wasn't my business." He looked away and sighed. "That's a cop-out, though, isn't it? I should have done more for you, Di."

"You did your best."

"I had a narrow conception of my best." Another sigh. "You don't love him, he treats you like a servant. Maybe it's time to leave him."

"I couldn't do that. I mean, I've never had a job, and we have a prenup that's very much in Ron's favor. Besides, there's Lizzie to think about."

"Lizzie would adjust. It would do her good to see you happy. I wish I were going to be around to see that but..." He trailed off, then looked me in the face. "I've got a rainy-day fund. Did you know that?"

I shook my head.

"It's got about fifty thousand dollars in it. Your mother doesn't know about it. You know how she is about money."

"She likes to control all of it." She liked to control everything.

"I was never planning on going anywhere, so I'm not sure why I even opened that account. But now I see. It was always meant for you, even if I didn't realize it."

He insisted on putting the account in my name. We called the bank together and figured out how it could be done when he wasn't well enough to take a trip to the bank. It was a rigorous process because the bank wanted to make sure that I wasn't committing some sort of financial elder abuse, but in the end, Daddy got his wish. The money was mine.

I let him think that I would be leaving Ron imminently, even though I knew I couldn't. I didn't want to worry Daddy in his final months by explaining how punitive and vengeful I feared Ron could be. I needed to let the funds grow and then make my escape once Lizzie was older.

It meant a lot to me: not just the money itself but that my father wanted me to have it.

Daddy started to worsen physically and mentally. He was often irritable, just like Mother, but paranoia was setting in, too. Sometimes he eyed me suspiciously; on one occasion, he didn't recognize me at all.

Those were the saddest days for me. He'd endure my reading but the tender conversations stopped. Often he didn't seem to want me there at all.

One time, I tried to brush his hair and he pushed me off with a surprising amount of violence. It didn't hurt, he had almost no strength, but it was the hostility behind it. I was stunned and wounded. I felt like our closeness had been a mirage. I would log into the bank account just to remind myself that had really happened. He had loved me, briefly.

But the next time I saw him, he stared at me with hatred in his eyes. "You stole from me," he said.

I was shocked at the accusation. "What are you talking about?"

"My rainy-day fund. You tricked me into giving it to you."

"That's not what happened." Could Mother have gotten wind of it and distorted the whole situation? "Did you talk to Mother?"

"About what?" His eyes were cold. "You know she has no use for me. And you only care about money."

"That's not true at all." I was starting to cry.

"Save your crocodile tears," he said harshly. "I'm not falling for them ever again. You've always been a manipulator, Diana. You saw your chance and you leapt at it."

"No, I'm not like that!"

"You got yourself knocked up by a man who was going places, didn't you? You trapped him and then you want to whine about it. You've never had to work a day in your life."

"He trapped me," I said. I was devastated. It was like everything I had shared was being turned around, wielded as a weapon.

I told myself that Daddy wasn't in his right mind. He must have been delirious. But he sounded so sane and sure.

"You stole from me," he repeated.

"You wanted me to have that money. You said that you'd never needed it, that it was always meant for me."

"That's what you tried to make me believe. And I have to admit, you're good. It worked for a while. But now I'm seeing you clearly for the gold digger that you are." He leveled me with a contemptuous stare. "So here's what you're going to do. Get the bank on the phone and put that account back in my name."

"What are you going to do with that money now?"

"That's none of your business, Diana. I'm not going to be scammed by my own daughter."

I couldn't give him back the money. Not only because of what it meant for my escape but because of what it represented. When Daddy and I spent all that time cutting through red tape together so I could have my own rainy-day fund, my father had loved me.

"Call the bank, or I'll tell your mother what you've done," he said.

I felt like he'd driven a stake through my heart. The betrayal was that acute. For the past month and a half, Daddy and I had created our own little world, and my mother had largely been persona non grata. But now I was the unwelcome one. After everything I'd done, he was acting like she was his protector.

"This is all bullshit," I said, my voice rising in anger.

"Don't test me, Diana. Because your mother will know what to do with an ungrateful bitch like you."

My nails were digging into my palms, deep enough to draw blood.

"You've always been good for one thing, and one thing only," he said. "Shaking your ass all over the place, tempting men to go against their better natures."

"What are you even talking about?" I didn't want to think he really meant any of what he was saying but he sounded plenty lucid. It was as if he were letting me into his deepest, darkest mind. Into his truest and ugliest self.

"Get out. I'm tired of looking at you." He leaned back against the pillow, clearly spent. "Tired of everything."

I fled from the room, shutting the door behind me and leaning against it. I had to regain my composure. I'd need to go tell my mother that I was leaving and that she should turn on the baby monitor. He was all hers now.

I was nearly hyperventilating from hurt and fury, and I

could hear that my father was struggling to catch his breath, too. It was like we were strangely intertwined in that moment.

Then Daddy became louder and louder, raspy and jagged. I could tell that he was in severe distress.

Hadn't he said he was tired of everything? Hadn't the hospice nurses said that in a way, he was the one who'd decide when he was ready to go? He'd sent me away, so who was I to stand in the way?

It wasn't like he was calling out for help. He never said my name. This was his choice, not mine.

I squeezed my eyes shut until the house went silent.

Then I called 911 and reported an emergency. By the time the paramedics showed up, it was too late to save him.

I tried to tell myself that his last words ("tired of everything") were like a suicide note. By not getting him help, I'd helped him. He no longer had a reason to live, so I let him die.

But I knew the truth. The hospice nurses had taught me CPR. It wasn't only that I waited to call 911 but that I never opened the door. I'd cared for his body all those weeks, yet I couldn't fathom breathing into his mouth. I didn't want to give him my air after what he'd said to me.

By not even trying to save his life, I'd taken it.

That hadn't been to relieve his suffering or to grant him personal agency. I did it because I wasn't going to let any man take anything away from me ever again.

I murdered my own father, and I'd hated myself for it ever since.

At the end of my recitation to Gavin, I felt as spent as I imagined my father had in his last moments. I wanted to wilt against the pillow but Gavin wouldn't let me.

He insisted on staring into my eyes. "You are the most amazing woman I have ever known," he said fiercely.

I stared back, astonished. It almost seemed like he loved me more now, like he was proud of me.

"You just can't let the bastards win, can you?" Now his admiration was undeniable. "Remind me not to get on your bad side."

"Oh my God, do you think I could kill you?"

"Sorry, no, I didn't mean that. I just meant... That story about your dad, it wasn't about his will to live; it was about yours. You were born again in that moment. Don't ever forget what you've got inside you."

That was what terrified me. What did I have inside? What was I capable of?

"You did what you had to do," Gavin said.

"No, you don't understand," I said. "I could have saved my father—"

"Best-case scenario, he might have lived another week or two. It's not like he was ever going to get out of that bed again. His life was over already. Why should you have gone down with the ship? You needed that money to get away from Ron." Gavin smiled. "I'm glad to know you've got it. Think how much fun we'll have someday, when you're free."

Gavin was telling me exactly what I'd wanted to hear. He'd absolved me completely. And I hadn't lost his good opinion; if anything, I'd risen in his estimation.

I'm getting everything I want, so why doesn't it feel better? I've just come clean, so how come I feel so dirty?

THIRTY-NINE

LIZZIE

I wasn't sure that there would ever be a literary magazine but at least Mr. Axelrod was meeting with me to talk about the short stories I'd started writing.

I watched anxiously as he scanned another page. While I loved this opportunity to study his face, it was also excruciating, waiting for him to render a verdict.

He set down the stack of papers. "I admire you, Lizzie. You're willing to take a risk and do something new rather than stay in your comfort zone."

"In other words, that story sucked."

He laughed. "I wouldn't say that. You just can't be afraid to fail."

"Well, I can, but I'm not letting the fear stop me." I knew it was the kind of answer he'd like, and I was right. He rewarded me with a smile.

"It's almost Christmas break," he said. "I'm going to miss you."

"Really?" I felt dazed. It was just so exactly what I wanted to hear. "I'm definitely going to miss you!"

"You have any interesting plans?"

"I might get together with Denver." I figured that Denver was the kind of person Mr. Axelrod would approve of.

Instead, Mr. Axelrod got this little pucker between his eyebrows. "You know, I'm always struck by the differences in maturity between males and females at this age. There's just nothing a girl like you can learn from a guy her own age. They're under seasoned, you know? They lack insight." I wasn't sure exactly how to respond to that, so I just nodded.

"Maybe you and I can meet up at a café at some point. I'll text you."

Was I hallucinating, or had Mr. Axelrod just asked me out? "Sounds great." I tried not to smile too wide. Play it a little bit cool. When he texted, I'd have to keep it to myself. I'd tell Mom I was meeting Maya or Denver.

Holy shit, this was really happening. Maybe I was finally due for a happy New Year.

NOW

FORTY

DIANA

"Change of plans," Lise tells me when I come down the stairs in the morning. She's never the first one down. I wonder where Gavin is.

"Oh?" I don't know whether to feel upset or relieved. I'm all dolled up—or rather, the opposite of dolled up—for the pool day that Lise requested. I've done my best to show my age. My face is devoid of makeup and I'm wearing a generously proportioned swimsuit cover-up, a very un-MILF-like muumuu. My intent is to keep it on, considering Gavin's attempted kiss/mauling last night. "What did you want to do instead?"

"Gavin decided he really wants to meet Grandmother. I'd been planning to spare him this trip, but he said no, he thinks he should get to know more of my family."

Okay, now I know what to feel. Terror.

I hadn't gotten any sleep after what Gavin said last night. He has so many avenues to destroy me and now there's a ticking clock. A countdown. I've got three days to save my family.

If I pay him, I've got no guarantees. He might keep the money and keep Lise, too. He'd tell her that I was trying to blackmail him into leaving, but he couldn't do it, not with how much he loves her. He'd convince her that I'm the villain and I deserve to rot in prison while they spend all that cash.

That's just one potential yarn he could spin. Who knows what he'd say? Who knows what he'd do?

And now he wants to meet my *mother*? If that's not a threat...

I just have to hope he doesn't mention anything suspicious about money since I haven't asked her for it yet. I've been biding my time, praying I wouldn't have to go there.

Would he dare to say anything about my father? More specifically, about my father's death?

Lise is staring at me blankly. She hasn't even said sorry about her rudeness. I mean, the pool day had been her idea. Now, she's canceling at the last minute with no expression on her face. Has Gavin already told her something that's turned her cold?

My intention for the pool day had been to play nice and try to woo her back to my side, even if that meant being grossly indulgent and over-the-top supportive of her engagement. Because I haven't forgotten what she said over breakfast either: that she doesn't want to have kids since I made motherhood look so unappealing, and that I have no right to question her relationship given my own marriage. Gavin was right about one thing. I do live in a glass mansion. Time's running out before it shatters.

Now I have the morning free, and I need to make the most of it. While I'm losing valuable time to rebuild trust with Lise, the relief is setting in. Now I don't have to pretend to smile and be charmed as I watch Gavin laying it on thick, dousing Lise in lavish adoration and compliments. I remember all those lines, all too well.

Does he want me to recognize them, or is it possible that he doesn't even know he's recycling them? I read somewhere that some sociopaths mean everything they say, at the time. They're so convincing because they've convinced themselves.

I've also read about cults and their tactic of love bombing. I know why I fell into the cult of Gavin, but why did Lise? Why was she such an easy mark? I did my best to raise her differently than my parents raised me, to tell her that her feelings and desires and opinions are truly important, and yet, the outcome is the same.

No, the outcome hasn't happened yet. This match is still in progress.

I tell Lise, "Have fun!" and dash back upstairs to change out of my muumuu. The clock is ticking all right. Time for me to go on offense.

I don't want to tell Lise what Gavin did to me, but what has he done to others? What's he hiding? And what kind of trouble is he in right now that he needs money so badly?

I've already done a little sleuthing, calling the high school where he works. The Austin school district let out for the summer the previous week (one week earlier than Houston's), so there weren't many people around to question. I was able to learn that Gavin is still employed but no more than that. For all I know, he could be on thin ice, under investigation for his conduct with his students (or their parents).

To save Lizzie's future, I have to go back to the past.

I drive to the high school that I've avoided ever since Lizzie graduated, even avoiding routes that take me past it because the memories of Gavin are too visceral. I can still see his classroom in my mind's eye, where it all began, when I mistook him for a protector when he was really a destroyer.

Since it's the last week of school, there's a certain lazy energy that I can feel as I walk through the hallway to the main office. Everyone's done mentally, though their bodies have to be present for a few more days.

I don't recognize the admin at the front desk. She's perky, probably in her early thirties, with a blonde ponytail, wearing a t-shirt and shorts. Lizzie was never in trouble, so she didn't spend time in the office and neither did I.

I introduce myself, saying, "I'm sure you don't remember me, or my daughter Lizzie—"

"Of course I remember Lizzie! She was the sweetest." I'm surprised just how effusive she is and hope it can work to my benefit. "How is she?"

"Well, that's a complicated answer. She's engaged."

"Congratul—"

"To Gavin Axelrod."

"Oh." At his name, her face has instantly shifted to an expression that's, well, more complicated. She knows something, I can feel it.

"Confidentially, can I ask you about him? I know he left a few years ago, that he lives in Austin now, but I'm wondering about the circumstances. Do you know what happened?"

The admin stiffens, though she does seem compassionate toward me. "I'm not really at liberty to talk about that."

So there is something in particular to be discussed? My hopes rise. "Is the principal here?" Maybe she's at liberty.

"Let me check." The admin's polite smile doesn't give me much hope.

She opens the principal's door, enters, and then closes it behind her. After a few minutes, I'm told to go on in.

The principal gives off the air of a seasoned professional, her manner briskly pleasant. She's probably not far from retirement. She leads with, "This shouldn't take long as I can't talk to you about my former teachers."

"I probably should have come to talk to you about Gavin Axelrod six years ago when he was my daughter Lizzie's current teacher. Now he's her fiancé. Which is problematic, to say the least."

"I wish you and Lizzie all the best." But she can't get involved, that's what she's saying.

"Lizzie goes by Lise now. She wants to think she's all grown up, but it's clear to me that she was very impacted by Mr. Axelrod's actions when she was his student. I underestimated how much."

"If you're here to make an allegation, there's a protocol for that. I can refer you to the correct person. Are you aware that he's no longer employed by this district?"

Hmm, that has a certain cover-your-ass quality to it. "Gavin Axelrod is a bad man. I suspect you know that. You wouldn't want him marrying your daughter, would you?"

"I'm sorry, I can't comment on a former employee." She looks like she really does feel sorry—for me.

"I wouldn't quote you directly. I'm here for information but I wouldn't tell Lise how I got it."

"I really can't tell you anything."

"But there is something to tell?" She doesn't answer, though she does hold my gaze. I think that's a yes. "Lise is head over heels and she won't listen to any of my concerns. But if I had a kernel of something from a third party, that might give her pause. Maybe then she'd do some digging, and she could change her own mind."

"I understand what you're asking, and I wish I could be of assistance. But I can't." Her moral quandary is evident. It's a button that needs pushing.

"You're an educator. You care about kids. You care about people. Maybe you even have children of your own?" I stare at her, hopefully mother to mother. "You could save my daughter's life."

She appears torn. Finally, she says, "I'm so sorry. I can't tell you anything."

"Thank you for your time," I say. I write down my phone number and slide it across the desk. "Just in case."

As I leave the principal's office, I make sure to close the door firmly behind me. Then I walk over to the admin, on her side of the desk, and whisper, "I get that no one from the school is allowed to talk to me about Gavin but can you please direct me to someone who might be able to talk, off the record? For my daughter's sake?"

The admin hesitates and does a quick glance at the door behind her. "You didn't hear this from me, but if I were you, I'd talk to your old friend Mari."

My old friend Mari? More like my old enemy.

Because I'd taken Gavin's side over hers. Because all these years, I'd done my best not to think of Mari and Genevieve at all (it's just too painful). I've wanted to believe that Mari and Genevieve were lying, and while Gavin might be a lot of things, he could never be a child abuser.

I walk out to my car on wobbly legs. I should drive straight to Mari's. This is a lead and I need to follow it. Anything for Lise, right?

Sitting in the driver's seat, the air conditioning on full blast, I'm still sweating. I take out my phone to see the string of bullying texts from Gavin.

I'm here with your mother, Di. We're having a lovely time.

I've got a funny feeling you haven't even asked her for money yet. What are you waiting for?

You need me to light a fire under your ass? Okay, here goes. You succeed, then you and I get to party. You fail, and Lise and I aren't going back to Austin. We head to Vegas.

I'm either going to be rich in money or in love. You pick.

Don't get any ideas. Don't go thinking you're smarter than me. You're good at a lot of things, believe me, I still have fantasies, but thinking isn't one of them.

One of my fantasies? Telling your mother the truth right now. She'd have the body exhumed, I'm sure. It's not like she loves you or anything.

He's using my every fear and insecurity against me. I don't think it's just about beating me into submission and compliance. He wants me to suffer.

That's okay. I can withstand it. Every day, I have to live with what I did to my father. But I'll make sure that Lise doesn't have to live with Gavin Axelrod.

FORTY-ONE

LISE

"Hi, Dad." I approach the table where he's already seated. It's in a bustling deli. I was right on time, but he couldn't wait for me?

"I already ordered for us," he says. "I don't have a ton of time."

I took an Uber inside the loop, all the way to this downtown lunch spot near his office, and he's already letting me know that I'd better make it quick?

It's my own fault. I shouldn't have dropped everything when he texted me this morning with the last-minute invite. But it had been so unexpected and intriguing. He never wants alone time with me.

I got his text while Gavin and I were at my grandmother's house. Whenever I'm with her, I can't help but feel sorry for Mom. What must it have been like to be raised by a person that buttoned up, that imperious?

Gavin was getting on my nerves, too. He was just so phony with my grandmother, acting like such a perfect gentleman, and sure, a little bit of that is warranted with elders, but did he have to be *that* phony?

It bugged me that he wanted to visit my grandmother at all. I mean, he knows I don't like her, so it wasn't for my benefit. What was he trying to prove? And to whom?

I'm starting to wonder how phony Gavin is with me, how often he skirts or embellishes the truth.

I could use some space. That's why I was kind of happy when Dad texted me: *Come alone.*

But now I'm stuck with some hummus and red pepper sandwich, while Dad's biting into what looks like pastrami. I'm not saying I like or want pastrami, just that I would have liked the choice.

How long ago did he arrive, if our order is already up?

The server asks what I'd like to drink. I tell him a gin and tonic. He says they don't serve alcohol.

"A Coke," I say, in resignation.

When the server's gone, Dad launches in. "There's a perception that really bothers me. The perception that your mother is the only one who cares about you. I want you to know I care very much."

"Oh. Well, thanks."

"Timing's a funny thing. How one marriage comes together as another is falling apart." He's got a mouth full of pastrami. It's disgusting. Why doesn't he think he needs to use table manners around me? Does he treat all his subordinates this way?

I wait for him to continue. It's not like he's looking for my input.

"I'm on the verge of becoming the CEO and I'm not sure I want to reach that pinnacle, the highest peak of my or anyone's professional life, with someone as disloyal as your mother by my side."

"Disloyal how?"

He doesn't answer, juts chomps through a pickle with startling alacrity.

"Didn't Mom help you get there?"

"She probably thinks so. One could make the counterargument that if it hadn't been for her, I would have gotten there sooner."

Disloyal how?

"Finding the right partner is the most important decision of your entire life," he says. "Don't make it in haste."

"I'm not."

"You just finished college. You seem clueless as to your future career. And you've been with this guy for, what, a year?"

"A little less," I admit. My Coke is placed in front of me and I suck it down greedily. I'm not touching that hummus sandwich in protest. I mean, hasn't he noticed I'm not a vegetarian anymore? That I'd suggested meeting at a steakhouse for that first dinner, the one he hadn't even bothered to attend?

"How well do you really know Gavin Axelrod?"

Annoying, how Dad can't seem to get my new name right but is saying Gavin's full one. "I know everything I need to know."

"You're equivocating, Lizzie. We're talking about marriage here. You need to be certain."

"I am certain," I say tightly. "What's this all about? You've never really said what you think of Gavin." I wait for him to answer the implied question but he doesn't. He's going to make me ask, which feels humiliating in a way I can't quite explain. "What do you think of him?"

"I don't."

Now that's humiliating in a way I can explain. He's telling me that my fiancé is undeserving of true thought, that he's unworthy of contemplation. What does that say about my value in my father's eyes?

"Gavin's an amazing person," I say. "You'd know that if you gave him a chance."

"I never said I didn't like him."

"What are you saying then?"

He shakes his head as if I'm hopeless, like he can't believe he has to spell it out. "Haven't you noticed anything odd about the way your fiancé interacts with your mother? Isn't there something awfully... familiar about the two of them?"

"I guess Mom used to act overly familiar with him when he was my teacher. She used to text him. She wanted to talk about me."

"Do you really think that's all it was?"

I don't like what he's intimating. "Gavin wouldn't lie to me. He also wouldn't do something as disgusting as what you're suggesting."

"I'm just making observations."

He's so infuriating. "What have you actually seen, though? They haven't touched each other."

"But sometimes they're standing close together, aren't they? Talking in low tones? And they stop talking when you walk into the room?" He tilts his head. "Come on, Lizzie. Use your head."

"I don't need my head. I know Gavin, and I know Mom!" I say hotly.

"If that's what you need to believe." His tone is mild.

"It's what's true! Gavin wouldn't lie. We have a relationship." *Not like yours and Mom's.*

"So Gavin and your mother used to text, and that's all. But can I ask, when did you learn about their *texting*?" He makes the word *texting* sound positively filthy. "Was it since you got here? Was it a way to explain away your doubts?"

He's the last person in the world who I want to be right. About anything. But he's not right about this. He can't be. "Maybe Mom had feelings for Gavin back in the day. Maybe she's a little jealous now. But that's all it is."

"You tell yourself that, Lizzie."

"My name is fucking Lise!" It comes out loud and other patrons turn to stare.

Dad stands up, tossing some bills on the table. "Tread lightly, Lise." He walks out, not looking back.

He's telling me that Mom and Gavin have both betrayed me, but since when is Dad someone to be trusted? He's been emotionally MIA my whole life. He's never given a shit about me, but I'm supposed to take his fatherly advice now?

It can't be true. Dad's either lying or reading the situation all wrong. He's looking for a way out of his marriage, so he's seeing things that aren't there.

Gavin doesn't want Mom. He never did. He wants me. He's always wanted me, even when he knew that he couldn't have me.

That's my (love) story, and I'm sticking to it.

Or is that Gavin's story, and I'm a fool to believe it?

THEN

FORTY-TWO

DIANA

"And that's when I said, 'You're damn right it isn't!'" Ron concluded his story to loud laughter. I forced myself to join in. Ron was in entertainer mood, his audience receptively tipsy. Every year, he loved Mari's Christmas party far more than I did.

As usual, the house was done up like an elaborately wrapped present, with red, green, and silver wherever the eye happened to land. The tree had to be fifteen feet tall with a staggering number and array of ornaments. Servers circulated with canapés and glasses of champagne.

I scanned the room for Lizzie. She was nowhere to be seen but then, the kids often went upstairs to one of the twins' bedrooms. I should probably stop calling them kids, seeing as all the assembled guests had teenagers by now.

Having fun?

I didn't appreciate the intrusion. I hadn't explicitly told Gavin not to contact me tonight, but he knew I was paranoid whenever Ron's around. And if Ron saw me texting, he'd probably wonder about the recipient, given that all my friends were ostensibly in this room.

I decided not to respond right away. I'd wait until later, during a trip to the restroom. Gavin had to understand that I couldn't—wouldn't—be at his beck and call every second.

So far, the Christmas break had been hard for him, just as he'd predicted it would be. I empathized with his feelings but he was too reckless for my taste, texting me at all hours of the day and night, trying to get me to sneak out and meet him. Now I had to keep my phone on silent whenever Lizzie and Ron were around. Gavin and I almost had our first fight yesterday when I made it clear that I wasn't going to take unnecessary risks. "You and I have very different definitions about what's necessary," he said. We eventually had to agree to disagree or we would have wasted our precious time squabbling.

So he could be needy sometimes. That just went to show how much he loved me. As he said often, he couldn't live without me.

I grabbed another champagne flute and looked around to see which group of revelers I'd most like to join.

I shrugged off the momentary tension from Gavin's text since overall, I was feeling so much better this year than I had in years past. Lighter. It must have been the effect of telling Gavin my secret.

When I first came out with it, I hadn't felt the relief I expected. I'd been almost perturbed by how instantly Gavin had absolved me. And for the next few days, I was on alert, sure that he would realize the truly terrible nature of my crime and what it said about my own nature. We're talking about patricide, after all. I thought Gavin's feelings for me would have to change, and they had. He admired me even more. He said I was the strongest woman he'd ever met.

It had never occurred to me to see what I'd done as my declaration of independence, a refusal to be gaslit or controlled by the man who was supposed to love me most. "Your father gave you that money and then he called you a thief," Gavin pointed out. "But it was the other way around. He was trying to steal from you, to take back what was yours, and you wouldn't let him."

"But I stole the rest of his life," I said.

"Which would have been what, a few lousy weeks? And I mean lousy. He was clearly out of his mind. He would only have done more harm to himself and the people around him."

Gavin seemed so confident, as if he'd drawn the only sensible conclusion, and I'd started to believe his interpretation. I wasn't bogged down by guilt anymore.

That was what love could do.

I only wished I could love Gavin so unreservedly. I mean, I did love him; I was almost sure of it. It was just hard to give myself over fully after witnessing my parents' corseted marriage and then experiencing my own loveless one.

It wasn't like I was lying when I said those three words. My feelings for Gavin were undeniably intense, and if he preferred that I term it "love," then I could do that. I would do anything for him, and if that wasn't love, then what was?

I drained my champagne flute and surveyed the room, flooded by warmth. The party always had a great turnout since Mari's the unofficial mayor of our planned community. For once, I felt like I really did have something to celebrate, even if I had to keep him a secret.

Maybe I liked it that way. I got to carry Gavin with me all the time in a place no one else could see or touch. He was all mine.

He told me that often: that he was all mine, and I was all his. He said that Ron didn't matter, and on an emotional level that was true. But I was entirely financially dependent on Ron, and that wasn't the only source of control my husband exercised. I was realizing through my conversations with Gavin that

I did a lot just to avoid Ron's scathing remarks. Then there was his penchant for slow-burning vengeance.

When people crossed Ron at work, he seemed to enjoy biding his time, sometimes for years. He nursed a grudge with a tenderness that should have been reserved for the people he loved. Instead, he relished the building of a trap and eventually catching his unsuspecting victim. He'd cut out many of his professional rivals this way, untraceably. When the CEO retired, Ron was supposed to be a shoo-in for his replacement. But if that didn't happen, then woe to the new CEO. He'd be contending with an invisible enemy.

I looked over at Ron and then down toward the phone vibrating in my purse. It had to be another text from Gavin.

That's when Mari swooped in, saying with mock horror, "I can't just let my best friend stand here all alone in the middle of my soiree! Why aren't you mingling? Are you feeling all right?"

"Everything's great." I smiled at her fondly.

She gave me a long once-over. "You," she pronounced, "are glowing."

"Thanks. I spent ages getting ready." I'd learned from my mother that you always want to deflect. When women compliment the outcome, stress the effort. They'll like you better that way.

"It's not just tonight, though." Now Mari studied my face. "What's the secret?"

I laughed a little uncomfortably. "Just clean living, I guess!"

"You mean you're on a new diet?" I didn't think she quite believed me but she was being kind. We were best friends, after all. She'd said it herself just a minute ago.

I decided to take the out she'd just offered. "Yes, it's a sort of paleo thing. I forget the name of the cookbook. I'll text you the cover tomorrow."

"It's Texas, we're all paleo. Meat morning, noon, and night." She gave me a slightly lascivious look, and I laughed again.

"Well, I'm glad you're finding your mojo. We're more than just moms, you know."

Oh, I knew. During this Christmas vacation, I'd been feeling the call of the wild a lot but hadn't been able to answer it much. Lizzie was home practically all the time—she'd gone to meet up with Denver once but that was it—and I was afraid to lie to her after that close call in the kitchen a few weeks back. I'd nearly had a heart attack when she seemed to recognize Gavin's car out front. My acting job had been atrocious. From what I could tell, I'd gotten away with it, but barely.

"You okay?" Mari said, sensing the shift in my mood.

"Of course!" I gave her what I hoped was a brilliant smile. An untroubled smile. "Do you remember when we used to walk these streets pushing our strollers?"

"Well, that was random."

"Sometimes I just get nostalgic. I remember when it actually felt rewarding to be a stay-home mom." Back when Lizzie really loved me. Now she was off somewhere with the other teenagers and she'd refuse to answer any questions about it later. "So what about you? How are the twins?"

"Oh, we don't need to get into that." Mari waved a hand, trying to seem casual but it felt evasive instead.

"Mari, you know you can trust me. What is it?"

She hesitated and looked around, making sure we wouldn't be overheard. Then she said, "Genevieve hasn't been herself lately. And she won't talk about it, which is also unlike her. It reminds me of... Well, you know what it reminds me of."

I was one of the only people who did know. "You can't jump to conclusions."

"I haven't jumped anywhere. But I don't like it when things are hidden. If you're doing right, then who needs privacy?" Her eyes bore down on mine. Were we still talking about Genevieve?

I was probably just being paranoid. That was the downside of keeping a secret. "Just know that I'm here for you," I said.

"I appreciate that." She patted my arm as if I'd just been the one confiding in her. Then she looked over my shoulder, spying a new arrival, and excused herself for the greeting.

I slipped away to the powder room and saw that Gavin had been texting me throughout my conversation with Mari.

Why aren't you answering me?

Aren't you thinking about me at all?

What's going on in there, Di?

I hurriedly texted back about how boring the party was and that, of course, I'd rather be with him. I tossed in a dozen emojis, hoping that he'd be sated.

I'm outside.

Oh shit.

Don't worry. I'm not in Mari's grand circular drive. I'm just up the street.

What are you doing here? What I wanted to write was, *How dare you?* All my friends were at this party. My husband was down the hall and my daughter was... somewhere. For all I knew, she could look out the window and recognize Gavin's car again. I didn't like the risk he was taking with my life.

Come outside, Di.

I can't.

You can't or you don't want to?

I can't.

Because you don't want to.

I didn't want to fight with him but I couldn't just let him breach the boundaries I set. *You're right,* I typed. *I don't want to.*

There was a long pause, and then he wrote: *Come outside now, or I'm coming in to get you.*

My chest seized with fear. He'd never threatened me before. *I'm coming out!*

It felt like I had no choice, like it was a hostage situation, but at least I knew this house well enough to take precautions. I was able to leave through the side garage door. Then I searched the street for Gavin's car. He made it easier for me by turning his headlights on and off, like a signal. I had to hope that none of the guests noticed. I dashed over to the car—parked across the street and up a little ways, like he said—and yanked open the passenger-side door. From here, he had a clear view into the party.

If he could see, then couldn't he also be seen?

Lizzie was most likely on the second floor, where the blinds and curtains were all closed and drawn. At the moment, no one was peering out. On the ground floor, all the adults were caught up in their laughter and conversations. I spotted Ron in one of the clusters.

How long had Gavin been out here, spying on me? "Hi," I said, with frost in my voice.

"Don't be mad," he said. His manner was imploring, almost servile, in direct contrast to that text where he'd summoned me. "I needed to see you."

"Well, now you're seeing me." I sunk low in the seat and kept watch on Mari's house.

He ran his hand under my dress, up my thigh. I felt like slapping it away but I didn't dare.

"I needed to feel you."

"This isn't the time or the place."

He laughed. "You sound like your mother. Just how you've described her."

My anger intensified. What kind of person would force me into his car and then laugh at my discomfort?

"You've been pulling away, Di. I can feel that I'm losing you." Now he'd turned, pleading again. "I can't let that happen."

"How many times do I have to explain this? It's the holiday break. My family's around."

This was exasperating. My eyes were glued to the house to be safe, but also, I didn't want to look at him.

"I knew it. You don't love me anymore."

"That's not true. But I can't sit here and reassure you. I'm supposed to be inside at my best friend's party. With my family." Now I was the one pleading for understanding.

"I saw you laughing with Ron. You never told me how funny he is." Gavin sounds accusing.

"I have to laugh at his jokes. The same as I had to come out to this car."

"You're not actually comparing me to Ron, are you?"

"I live with a controlling asshole. I don't want to date one." I was shocked to realize I'd said it out loud.

Gavin turned to me, astonished. And newly furious. "You're the one who controls me! I can't eat or sleep or think about anything or anyone but you."

"That's not my fault."

"Maybe it is, maybe it isn't. But regardless, you're the one driving this car. You're the one making all the rules."

Was that true? I was in no state to evaluate. My head was aching, and I'd had too much champagne. "I don't want to drive. I just want to go back inside and get this party over with."

"So you're not having fun?"

I didn't like how hopeful he sounded. Shouldn't he have wanted me to be having fun? Weren't we supposed to want the best for each other?

I'd forgotten his hand was on my thigh but then it started migrating north. "I have to be with you tonight, Di. Please, just let me inside you."

I shook my head. "I don't want to. Not like this." Not when he seemed to have no concern or regard for my feelings or my situation. Lizzie was in that house. Didn't he even care if she found out about us?

"I need you to abandon yourself to the moment," he said. "It can't be roses every time. Where's your urgency? Don't you have any passion for me anymore?"

The idea of having sex in a car parked across the street from my best friend's house during a Christmas party being attended by my family didn't strike me as remotely appealing. Gavin might have been feeling passionate but I felt dirty and debased. Coerced. Like I was there to fulfill his needs and the hell with my own.

That was the story of my marriage. It wasn't supposed to be the story of my affair.

My affair. No wonder this felt tawdry. I'd been elevating it in my mind, but really, it was just two people sneaking around and fucking. Like Mari said, if it's right, you shouldn't have to hide.

No, this was love. It had to be.

I met Gavin's eyes, and I could see that it was. For him. So I had to do my part. He needed this.

"In the backseat," I said. Once we were lying down, people from the party wouldn't be able to see us. I just had to hope no one would be out walking their dogs at this time of night.

Gavin was eager, and my body quickly responded to his fingers. I yanked at him, pretending it was about lust and not expediency. "Faster, faster," I said. Then I faked an orgasm for the first time in my life. (I'd never needed to with Ron since he didn't care, and prior to this, Gavin had always reliably made me come.)

When it was over, I grabbed tissues out of my purse to clean up as best I could. I felt cheap and filthy. As I rearranged my dress, I lied. "That felt good, baby. I love you so much. I just need to get back inside before anyone realizes I was gone."

"It's not like any of them miss you the way I do." He snuggled up against me like we had all the time in the world.

There was a satisfied expression on his face that seemed to go beyond the sex itself. It was almost like this whole thing had been a power trip, or a test. He'd been gauging how far I'd go for him, whether I'd choose him over my family.

No, he wasn't like that. He was just a man desperately in love with me.

I'd hated the encounter and what it said about me and about us; I hated pretending that it had been some sort of bonding moment before sneaking back into the party. During the walk toward the house, my knees were shaking. I prayed no one saw.

I went back in through the same side door I'd exited. Then I stole down the hall to the same powder room where I'd answered Gavin's texts earlier. I was disgusted by the stickiness in my underwear so I took it off and stuffed it into the trash can under the sink. I urinated and then I wet some toilet paper and wiped myself down, wanting to expel and erase all traces of him.

I was full of shame and fear. What if someone could smell the sex on me? What if Ron could?

I took a brush and lipstick from my purse, trying to fix the damage. That was when I got another text: *Thanks, baby. Man, I needed that. Love you so much.*

I gritted my teeth: *Love you more!*

I felt defiled by Gavin, but he had also become the most important person in the world to me outside of Lizzie. So I wasn't going to focus on what had just happened; I needed to forget as quickly as possible.

I returned to the party, mingling while staying far away from the groups that contained Ron or Mari. I only wanted to be around more distant acquaintances. I said little, holding a glass of champagne like a prop while I provided a laugh track.

I hadn't even realized that Mari was watching me until she pulled me aside. "What's wrong?" she asked. "What happened?"

"Nothing." I tried to sound airy. Drunk and airy. "It's all great."

Unlucky for me, she didn't seem drunk at all. She waited a few scrutinizing beats. Then her gaze softened. "It's all great until it isn't."

Was she seeing through me? Or had she seen me going to Gavin's car?

My lower lip trembled. I felt raw and vulnerable. The bad kind, where you're just exposed, even though Gavin acted like all intimacy was innately good.

But then, we didn't have to agree on everything, did we?

Though I did spend a lot of time agreeing with him, didn't I?

Not tonight, though. This was the most assertive I'd ever been with anyone, and even then, it had ended up with me having sex that I didn't want.

Gavin and I also spent a lot of time with him telling me what he thought, which seemed an awful lot like what I was supposed to think.

This was all Ron's fault. He'd never wanted to hear my

opinions and now I was bringing that baggage into my new relationship. I just needed to get better at speaking up and challenging Gavin. He wanted a strong, self-assured woman who stood up for herself. Consider how he'd reacted to the story about my father. Gavin thought patricide was sexy.

So I needed to assert myself right now, with Mari. "I think you might be misunderstanding me," I said. "Excuse me."

As I turned away from her, I ran right into Ron. Or rather, he made a point of running into me.

"Lizzie was looking for you a little while ago," he said. Was he staring at me harder than usual, or was I just being paranoid?

"That's good news, I guess. She never looks for me."

"She's not having much fun upstairs. She wants to know how soon we can leave." He drank the last of his whiskey. "We should go soon."

I tried not to show how relieved I felt. "Sure, we can go."

"You look beautiful tonight," he said. He didn't sound happy.

"Thank you."

"You've looked beautiful a lot lately." There was something in his inflection that made the bottom drop out of my stomach. Because it didn't seem like a compliment.

It felt more like a threat.

FORTY-THREE

LIZZIE

The adults must have known we were upstairs getting drunk. We'd done it last year, too, which was when Mari's son, Alec, had absconded with multiple bottles of premium champagne. At least, I assumed they were top shelf since Mari's parties were legendary in her own mind.

This year, he'd brought more of an assortment. There were still a few bottles of Veuve Clicquot, but there was also vodka, rum, whiskey, and various juices and mixers. The makeshift bar was in his bedroom.

As a result, everyone was in there while Genevieve's was empty. After I'd taken some shots, I was ready for some solitude.

I would have preferred to go home and I went downstairs a while ago to find my parents and tell them that. Mom was off somewhere but it wouldn't have mattered what she said; it all came down to Dad. And he was having a fine time boring people with work stories where he was always surrounded by idiots and he was the hero saving the day through quick thinking and decisive action.

I hated being surrounded by drunk adults, especially at that time in the evening when they all started flirting with each other's spouses. If their kids hadn't been upstairs, it might have turned into some big swingers event.

It wasn't the worst thing, being in Genevieve's room. She had a bookshelf and good taste, so I'd spent a good part of the night curled up in an overstuffed chair reading a borrowed novel.

Needless to say, I'd never liked Alec. He was so full of himself, always taking up inordinate amounts of space in every academic and social environment. He was a self-absorbed dick, constantly cheating on his girlfriends. But I liked Genevieve, because how could you not? She was sweet, as well as smart and beautiful. She had a quiet confidence that I'd always envied. It was impossible to hate her, as much as you might want to.

So many guys were into Genevieve, but other than a few short-lived relationships, she'd spent high school single. She said guys were low on her priority list, that she had other things she needed to do with her time. She was in all AP classes and a dozen extracurriculars and had a bunch of close female friends.

I wasn't one of them, though she'd always been nice to me. And she was still nice to me when she came in her room and found me thumbing through her closet.

"Sorry," I said, embarrassed.

"You want to borrow something?" she asked. "We kind of dress alike these days."

I was startled to realize that was true. Since my makeover, I had been dressing like Genevieve. "No, thanks," I said, my face like an inferno.

How truly mortifying. She must have thought I was a total stalker, copying her style and now pawing through her closet.

But she didn't seem like she was thinking about me at all. She'd basically wilted onto her bed.

I noticed that she had dark circles under her eyes and a few pimples around her hairline. She wasn't wearing any makeup, even though it was a party and she was normally perfectly put together.

"Are you okay?" I said.

"Just stressed." It didn't feel like the most honest answer. Genevieve had been going 110 miles her entire life, so she was pretty used to stress. This seemed like something else.

Especially since she wasn't smiling, when Genevieve was practically always smiling. Come to think of it, she'd seemed downcast all night. I'd barely heard her say a word in Alec's room. She picked at her cuticles, which I noticed were already bloody.

I thought of sitting down on the bed next to her but we weren't really close enough for that. I sat on the rug instead. It was plush and Persian and obviously expensive, like everything in this room and in this house.

"You can talk to me if something's bothering you," I said. "I wouldn't tell anyone."

"Anyone, like who?" Genevieve looked slightly alarmed.

"I wouldn't tell Denver or Maya or Kristina." I gave her a smile to show we're all friends here. "It would stay between us."

Genevieve smiled back, but she was looking down, so it was really like she was smiling at her own hands. Sadly. "You wouldn't understand."

There was nothing sharp in her tone but it still stung. It made me feel like a little kid, like I wasn't good enough to know her adult business.

I thought of the day when I was standing outside Mr. Axelrod's classroom and she was the one on the inside. There had been something in the way they'd laughed, something that had made me wonder if they were more than just teacher and student. But I was just being paranoid. I'd never seen or heard anything else that had raised my suspicions.

I wanted to bring up his name, find out for sure, but the

words wouldn't come out. Maybe I didn't really want to know. Because if Genevieve was my competition, I'd lose for sure.

This whole week, I'd been moping around and checking my phone obsessively for his text. But I'd been stupid for even hoping. Of course he had better things to do with his break than hang out with me.

Genevieve and I sat in silence. I wondered if she was waiting for me to leave but was too polite to kick me out. I also wondered how long I'd have to stay at this party, when my mom would come looking for me. Where had she been earlier anyway?

A text came in and when I saw what it was—who it was from—I felt like jumping to my feet and shoving my phone in Genevieve's face. It was like we had some sort of psychic connection, how he'd texted just when I was thinking about him. Not that I hadn't been thinking about him all week, but the point was, he wasn't texting Genevieve; he was texting me.

Mr. Axelrod wanted me.

NOW

FORTY-FOUR

DIANA

"I need you downstairs. Now." Lise looks frenzied and she didn't even knock on my bedroom door, just threw it wide open.

I'm in the overstuffed chair in the corner, overlooking the pool. I've camped out here because I want to keep an eye on Gavin, who's been doing laps for the past half hour. If he's coming back inside, I need to be ready.

He knows that I'm watching. Every so often, he lifts himself out of the pool by his forearms and does some stretches while looking pointedly up toward this window. His ego is boundless. I bet he actually thinks he's turning me on.

"What are you doing, staring at my fiancé?" Lise demands.

"I get how it looks, but I wasn't—"

"Yes, you were! I saw it with my own eyes."

It's not untrue but it's also not what she thinks. I don't see how I can defend myself, though. Not without giving myself away. This whole trip has been full of those sorts of minefields.

"Downstairs," Lise practically growls. "Now."

I follow her mutely to the stairs. I'm not sure what to say since I have no idea what brought this on. Could someone have told her about my visit to the school? Or to Mari's house afterward? It's hard to imagine Lise has spies all over our neighborhood. Besides, Mari wasn't home.

I'll just have to try again later. I can't call or text because I'm undoubtedly blocked and a conversation of this magnitude needs to occur face-to-face.

"Wait here," Lise says, once we've reached the kitchen. Then she storms outside and I can tell by her body language that she's just ordered Gavin out of the pool. He looks as bewildered as I feel, which is not reassuring in the slightest. Whatever this is, Gavin and I are in it together, and that's the last place I ever want to be.

Gavin towels off quickly as he trails Lise across the yard. Before they enter the kitchen, he knots the towel around his waist. His muscular stomach and upper body are exposed, and I try not to look at them.

Lise sees me averting my eyes and she glares. Then she turns her glare on him, in a more promising development. It seems like she's about to let him have it, too.

"What the fuck went on between you?" she says. "When I was in high school."

I glance at Gavin, feeling like he should be the first to answer. He has the most sway with Lise.

"Don't look at him!" she snaps. "Look at me."

"Where were you?" I ask. "Why are you coming back in such a rage—"

"I'm asking the questions here." Lise has turned her gaze on Gavin. "You said that my mother used to text you but that's not all that happened, is it?"

Gavin takes a step toward her. "I've already told you everything."

"Have you, really?" Her tone is icily dubious, which should be great for me. Maybe their relationship will explode before my eyes. "Because I feel like there's a lot more to it. Why did you wait to tell me about the texting until we were here, in this house?"

"It just wasn't a big deal, Lise. You know what your mom's like. She's a neurotic mess. Always has been, always will be. She was afraid of you growing up and becoming your own person. She was seeking reassurance wherever she could get it."

"And exactly how did you reassure her?" Lise hasn't thawed, despite the fact that Gavin is moving steadily closer to her. He wants to box me out of this conversation.

"I told her what she wanted to hear," he says. "But I was also telling her the truth. That you'd turn out fine. Better than fine."

"Is that what he said to you?" Lise is looking at me now, and I can feel that underneath her anger is a thread of hope. She wants me to corroborate Gavin's story.

Of course she does. She doesn't want to think that Gavin and I were having an affair, even if that's what her gut is telling her.

Or did someone else tell her? Who's she been talking to?

"He tried to reassure me," I say. "I believed him at the time and then my anxiety would ramp back up. So I'd text in order to hear it again. He's right, I was a mess. A needy mess, and he took pity on me. That's all it was."

I hate being on the same side as Gavin, but for the moment, it's my best move. Until I can get the goods on him from Mari, until I can prove to Lise what kind of man he really is, I have to protect my own credibility, which means protecting his.

Lise is scanning Gavin and me, searching for clues. I'm hoping that I can stand up to the scrutiny, but my heart is pounding out of my chest.

"You know me," Gavin says. "I'm always going to tell you the truth." She nods, but without conviction.

"I need to get out of here," she finally says.

"Let me get dressed. I'll come with you." Gavin starts to

walk past me, toward the stairs. I feel my body go rigid at his proximity.

"No," Lise says. "I want to go alone."

Gavin's eyes narrow almost imperceptibly. He was willing to put up with Lise's accusation, but once he's issued his denial, he fully expects to be believed. She's not supposed to go thinking for herself.

"What did your dad say to you at lunch?" he asks.

I turn to Lise in astonished horror. "You and your father just had lunch?" Behind my back?

"It was just a normal father-daughter conversation," she says, but I can tell she's lying. "Dad thought we should spend a little time together."

My wheels are spinning. There's nothing normal about this. Ron invited Lise for lunch and then she came back suspecting that Gavin and I had an affair. Which means that Ron knows Gavin and I had an affair.

Which means I'm dead.

FORTY-FIVE

LISE

I'm nearly hyperventilating as I slam the car door. I just had to get away from both of them.

Gavin and Mom looked so earnest, so aligned, a real united front, and I want to believe them so badly. I'm just not sure that I can.

I consider texting Denver. He'd be happy to meet up and I could really use a friend right now, but is he really the best choice? Even in high school, he was suspicious of Gavin. And it's not like he's objective. I'm pretty sure that he had romantic feelings for me then and that he still does now.

I'm debating whether I should even be leaving the two of them alone in the house when Mom stumbles out to her car. She looks a little bit sick. Sick with guilt?

For a second, I actually consider following her, which is a sign of just how crazy this has all gotten. I don't even know whose life I'm living anymore.

Gavin is texting, asking where I'm going and when I'll be home, and I start the engine and peel out. I don't even care about the destination. I just need to be moving. I want to put some distance between Gavin and me, which is an awful feeling. You shouldn't have to run away from your fiancé.

I end up driving to the mall, then wandering it aimlessly. I know I should be thinking but instead I'm trying not to think. My system is overloaded, my circuits blown. It's just all too much.

I'm hoping for anonymity, not to recognize or be recognized, and it's all going okay until up ahead, walking toward me, is a girl who looks eerily familiar.

Oh my God, it's Genevieve, or at least a ghost of her. She's got greasy hair pulled back in a tight bun and pale skin with a ring of pimples around her mouth (it's the summer, when normally she would have been sporting a golden tan). She's wearing a sweatshirt even though it's ninety degrees outside. Isn't that what cutters do when they're trying to hide their arms?

Now I can see why that first night at the bar, everyone had gotten a little quiet when Maya said Genevieve's name, as if in memoriam.

Our eyes meet, and Genevieve's expression goes through a series of rapid changes. She finally settles on one that I've never seen before from her. It's contempt.

"Lizzie," she says, as we come to a stop a few feet away from each other. It feels like some sort of showdown.

"I go by Lise now." I smile, hoping to ease this inexplicable tension. "Hi, Genevieve."

"What are you doing in Houston?" It's not a friendly question.

I don't know what this is about. I always liked Genevieve and I'd never picked up any enmity from her when we were in high school together. Sure, we tended to steer clear of each other after our moms had their falling out. I never knew the reason but is that why Genevieve is hating on me now? It doesn't quite make sense, but what else could it be?

"I'm just visiting," I say.

She nods slowly, as if she's evaluating my answer.

"I graduated from UT Austin early this month. How about you?"

"How about me?" she responds sharply. It's like she thinks I'm somehow baiting or mocking her.

"Where did you graduate from? Did you wind up going to Harvard or—"

"I went there for a year. Then I came back. I live at home and go to community college. Is that what you want to hear?"

I'm stunned by her vitriol. Sure, sometimes I was envious and even a little threatened, like that time I heard her and Mr. Axelrod laughing in his classroom, but I've never had any ill will toward Genevieve. This is heartbreaking. I mean, she had more promise than anyone.

"I'm sorry you're having a hard time," I say.

"*You* might be," she allows, "but do you think your fiancé feels the same way?"

"Oh." I pale. "You heard that I'm engaged?" Of course she did. The news must have spread through this community like wildfire.

Is Genevieve the one who's jealous of me now? Is that what this has been about?

"A lot of us had crushes on Mr. Axelrod back then," I say. "I really never thought that I'd be the one who'd get this lucky."

She lets out a harsh laugh. I've never seen such a nasty expression before on Genevieve's formerly beautiful face. Never thought she could look washed up by twenty-two. It's just so sad, really. I shouldn't even take it personally.

"Lucky," she repeats. Her face softens. "Yeah, good luck with that. You're going to need it."

Before I can think of an adequate response, she's gone.

THEN

FORTY-SIX
DIANA

It had given me pause, what happened at Mari's Christmas party, how Gavin treated me, but a week later, my faith in him had been restored.

It was when Lizzie had come home at almost 2 a.m. She hadn't responded to any of my texts and when I finally called Maya, I woke her up. Meaning, Lizzie had lied. She wasn't with Maya.

I'd woken Ron up but he shrugged me off. "Lizzie's probably fine," he said, rolling back over, "and if she's not, well, she'll have learned her lesson. She'll know not to lie to us and take stupid risks again."

I went out to the backyard and called Gavin, sobbing. It was too soon to call the police, I knew that, so what could I do? "She could be out there somewhere, in danger," I said. "Anyone could take advantage of her. She could have overdosed. She could be sex-trafficked."

Gavin managed to talk me down without making me feel foolish. As he did, he drove up and down the streets of the neighborhood, keeping an eye out for Lizzie.

"She could be hurt," I said. "Or what if she hurt someone

else?" I had never seen that side of her but that didn't mean it wasn't there. After all, no one—including me—would have guessed what I was capable of, with enough provocation.

Gavin was by my side and in my ear for the next hour until Lizzie finally stumbled in. She was disheveled and obviously drunk or high, clothes askew, lipstick smeared (since when did Lizzie wear lipstick?).

I could tell immediately that it had been a messy night rather than a fun one. Or maybe it had been fun and turned bad. Like Mari said, it's all great until it isn't. Most rapes were committed by people you knew.

"Oh, Jesus, Mom!" Lizzie sounded scathing. "I was at a party. Being a normal teenager. Do you even know what it is to be normal?"

"This isn't you," I said. "You're not yourself."

"You don't know my self!"

But Gavin did, and he'd been warning me that this was where it was heading: Lizzie engaging in some reckless behavior, probably with boys. Boys who didn't give a shit about her, who'd just use her and throw her away. My smart, beautiful, sensitive girl meant nothing to them. What if one of them got her pregnant and ruined her life?

In the days since, I'd been leaning on Gavin more than ever, and he'd been more than happy to provide the emotional support that my husband wouldn't.

When I worried that I was useless to her, that I had nothing to offer, he'd remind me how strong I was. "Show her your strength," he said. "Make her listen. Lock her in the house if you need to."

"But she'll hate me."

"Only for a little while. You can do this. Remember that song I played for you, 'Tupelo Honey'? That's what you are to me."

He really loved Van Morrison, and I'd started to, also. I

listened to that album all the time and it was like having Gavin right there, soothing me.

But when he opened the door to his apartment, he was the one who needed soothing. He walked away—stalked away—without a greeting.

He had a real bachelor pad, and I wasn't critical of it because it served its function. It was made for clandestine couplings. He had a black leather couch and a matching ottoman with a bamboo tray on top as a coffee table stand-in, and right then, he was pacing the room frenetically.

"What's wrong?" I asked, taking a seat on said leather couch. I'd seen him upset before—usually when I kept him waiting or if he felt insecure, like he loved me more than I loved him—but this was a new level of agitation.

"Your friend Mari is a class-A fucking bitch."

"Whoa," I said. "What are you talking about?"

He stopped pacing to stare me down. "Mari's daughter, Genevieve, came on to me and obviously I turned her down. These girls, they pull this shit all the time. I don't know what it is with this generation, why they need to validate themselves by fucking an authority figure, but I'm not here for it."

"Of course you're not." Genevieve, though? That didn't sound like her. Not at all.

"You don't believe me?"

"I didn't say that. I just... That's not the Genevieve I know."

"Well, how well do you really know her? You've seen the good-girl act she puts on for her mother's friends, and you've heard the stories Mari tells. Genevieve's probably got Mari snowed, same as Lizzie snows you."

I was too taken aback to respond. He just sounded so brutish.

"Genevieve obviously isn't used to hearing the word *no*. Her overachiever brain couldn't handle rejection. It went haywire. She told her mother that I was the one who tried to kiss her and not the other way around. Those fucking bitches."

I wanted to ask him to stop talking like that. It made him sound like some kind of misogynist, when I knew he was the furthest thing from that. He loved strong women. He'd been trying to build me up for the past few months, same as he'd been building up Lizzie.

"Now Mari is threatening to go to the administration with this bogus story. She wants to ruin my career so her daughter can save face. And you know what? Genevieve doesn't even want Mari to tell anyone because she knows it's bullshit."

"So Genevieve is asking Mari not to go to the administration and Mari's doing it anyway?"

He glared at me. "You know how women like Mari are. They get their way, regardless of the truth."

Mari could be very persuasive. But then, so could he. "I'm sorry this is happening to you. I'm sure it'll work out fine, though."

He came and sat down next to me, roughly grabbing my hand. "Di, I need you."

"You need me to what?" I asked, a little fearfully. If I had to take a side, I'd take his, but I'd prefer not to be involved. Hopefully, Genevieve would tell the school what really happened and it would all go away.

"Mari must have some skeletons in her closet. As her best friend, you must know what they are. There has to be something you can threaten her with."

I looked down at my hands—our clasped hands—as my face clouded over.

"You've got something, I can see it."

I couldn't confront Mari, not with that. It would be too cruel. Mari had been a good friend to me. She'd have kept my secrets, if I'd ever shared them with her.

Or maybe she wouldn't have. She might have loved to

betray me, if she'd had the ammunition. Just think what she was threatening to do to Gavin. She was trying to ruin him.

"There has to be another way," I said. "Could you talk to Mari again?"

"You can't reason with a woman that entitled." He looked at me fervently. "It has to be you, Di. You're the linchpin. Think of this as an opportunity. It's your chance to prove that you really do love me more than anything. Except for Lizzie, of course, and I accept that she has to come first in certain ways."

"You want me to prove my love by threatening my best friend?"

He nodded with even greater urgency. "You believe me, right? You know there's no way I'd abuse anyone, ever."

I did believe him, 100 percent. I'd heard how he talked about his students; I knew the way he was with Lizzie. He realized these were children who needed guidance, even if they swanned around in crop tops with their thongs peeking out of the waist of their jeans.

"There has to be another option," I said.

"I've been over this again and again. There really isn't. If you truly love me, you have to do this."

I didn't answer. My thoughts were a jumble as I searched for a loophole.

"How many hours have I spent listening to you go on and on about Lizzie?"

"Many," I said unhappily. "But—"

"If the tables were turned, I'd do it for you. I wouldn't even hesitate. I'd do anything to protect you and Lizzie."

"Mari's my best friend."

"So what am I, just some guy you're fucking so that he'll keep tabs on your daughter?"

"No! Of course not."

But Gavin wasn't listening anymore. "You and I both know you're not the innocent you pretend to be. I mean, Jesus, you're capable of killing when it's for your own interest, to make sure you hang on to some money, but what are you willing to do for the man you love?"

Was that really what he thought about me, that I'd killed Daddy for the $50K? It had been so much more complicated than that, and I thought that Gavin understood.

He was watching me closely, and I realized that he hadn't deployed this ammunition lightly. He'd been keeping this in reserve, just in case I resisted. It was a veiled threat: he was willing to use my secret against me in order to get what he wanted.

If my secret wasn't safe, then neither was I.

I caved because I had to; it wasn't about love. The spell that Gavin had on me was broken. I could see him clearly for the first time.

"I'll go see Mari tomorrow," I said. I needed the extra time to see if there was some way out of this.

"No. You need to go now. Right now." His chin was set stubbornly. "My whole life is in jeopardy. Don't you get that?"

He really had taken good care of me—and of Lizzie—all these weeks. Even if our relationship wasn't going to survive, I still owed him something. And I knew in my heart that he hadn't hit on Genevieve. For one thing, he was too obsessed with me. When would he have found the time or the energy to get involved with some sixteen-year-old?

Regardless of whether Gavin and I had a future, I couldn't let Mari make a mistake like this and destroy his life.

Slowly, I nodded.

"Call me when you're done," he said, and I felt sick. He made it sound like a mob hit.

I drove to Mari's house, my hands shaking on the steering wheel. I prayed that she wouldn't be home but no such luck. She answered the door and gave me a big hug.

"I'm glad to see you," she said. "It has been such a rotten day."

I couldn't let her tell me about it. I was a woman on a mission, and I couldn't allow for any distractions.

Mari took in the expression on my face and turned serious. "Looks like you've had a rotten day yourself."

"I have." My eyes brimmed with tears. I had to remain on the doorstep, as I knew I'd never be welcome in that house again after this. "I'm so sorry, Mari."

"For what?"

"What I'm about to say. I know about Genevieve and Mr. Axelrod. I mean, I know that she's made some accusations. But I also know that they're not true. You can't go to the school."

"I already did. I just got back a little while ago." She stared at me. "Who told you?'

"You said that Genevieve had been molested as a child by her gymnastics coach. At the time, I had no reason to doubt it. But was that a false accusation, too?"

Mari's face frosted over. "Stop talking. Now."

"I wish I could." The tears were flowing down my cheeks. I felt awful but I had to continue. "I can't let you destroy a good teacher—a good man—with a false allegation when we both know that Genevieve has had a, what do you call it, a propensity for inappropriate relationships with trusted adults."

Mari looked like she wanted to haul off and slug me. "Have you lost your goddamned mind?"

"Doesn't it seem strange to you that one girl would be victimized by two separate people?"

"No, it does not. Because the world is fucked up. It's full of predators, and children are children. Even teenagers are still children and need to be protected. Are you really standing here defending a predator?"

"He's not a predator. I know that for a fact."

"Oh, you do?" Her eyes narrowed. "Just how do you understand the inner workings of Gavin Axelrod so well, Di?"

My voice faltered as I said, "He looks after Lizzie. He's the kindest teacher she's ever had."

"Well, maybe he's not attracted to Lizzie. Or maybe he's grooming her, too, and just hasn't made his move yet."

"He wouldn't abuse any child."

"Let's get real, Di. You're not taking his side because he's involved with your daughter. It's because he's involved with you."

"That's not it." Even to my own ears, I sounded less than convincing. "I just know he wouldn't have done what Genevieve's accused him of. If you've already made some kind of complaint, then you need to rescind it."

"Or what? What if I don't, Di?"

I took a deep breath. "The school has a right to know Genevieve's relevant history."

"I just want to make sure I'm understanding you correctly." She squared up like she might punch me. "You're saying that you would spread my daughter's past abuse in order to protect a current pedophile?"

"Don't call him that." My temper flared. Gavin would love if he could overhear this; he'd know that my loyalty to him was real. "Whatever you think you know, you don't. So keep your fucking mouth shut."

"Or you'll drive my daughter to another suicide attempt." Mari shook her head in disgust. "Didn't know you had it in you. How do you sleep at night, Di?"

She didn't wait for an answer, just slammed the door in my face.

Had Gavin turned me into a monster, or had I been one all along?

FORTY-SEVEN

LIZZIE

I straightened my skirt before knocking on Mr. Axelrod's classroom door. It felt like all the momentum between us had stalled in the weeks since coming back from Christmas break. Today I was determined to get things moving again.

Why wasn't he answering? I confirmed earlier that we were finally going to have another meeting of the literary magazine. I wanted to have him all to myself.

Over break, I really thought we'd made some progress. He'd picked me up near my house and driven thirty minutes to a café inside the loop where no one would see us. And while he hadn't done anything especially flirtatious or touched me, we sat close and talked for hours. He told me all about the movies and TV shows he was watching, the books he was reading, and the music he was listening to.

I spent the rest of my break following his recommendations. I came back to school bursting with thoughts about *The Wire* and *The Sopranos*, two shows I never would have thought to watch except that he'd gotten me to recognize their greatness.

You know what's funny? I'd caught my mom watching *The Wire*, too, but she turned it off when I came into the room.

Maybe we could have bonded over it, but more likely, she would have told me to stop watching, that it was too mature for me.

She also would have thought Mr. Axelrod was too mature, but she'd be wrong.

She was still pissed off that I'd come home late. It was because I'd taken his advice, trying out a guy my own age just for practice. She actually grounded me. He'd warned me that could happen, that I might have to fight for independence since a person as anxious as my mother wouldn't want me to grow up.

The best part had been the confidence building. I went into a party, decided on someone, and made it happen.

Now I just needed to keep that streak going with Mr. Axelrod.

He wasn't making it easy, though. For the past week, he'd seemed really crabby. He had us spend two different classes doing silent reading and writing, like he couldn't be bothered to teach. When he did facilitate class discussion, he had little patience. At times, he was scathing. Not with me, but with the people saying stupid things. Maybe they deserved it.

I knocked again. Still nothing.

He hadn't canceled our meeting, so he should have been waiting for me. But instead, it seemed like he'd forgotten all about it. I hated that, being so forgettable.

Well, I'd walk away now, but I wasn't giving up.

One way or another, Mr. Axelrod was going to remember me. I'd make sure of it.

NOW

FORTY-EIGHT

DIANA

I've always felt horribly guilty about what I did to Mari. When I confronted her five years ago at Gavin's insistence, I knew that she was doing what she thought was right. She believed her daughter had been abused. By making an allegation to the school, Mari's intention was to look out for Genevieve and all Mr. Axelrod's other potential victims.

I never thought Mari was lying. But at the time, I really thought Genevieve was. That's how I could rationalize what I did.

In the years since, despite everything that transpired between Gavin and me, I continued to believe there were lines he would never cross. I didn't want to think that my former lover—a teacher who had regular access to impressionable young people—would ever abuse a child. But now I'm thinking there's nothing he wouldn't do.

When Mari opens her door, I expect her to have hatred in her eyes. And she does. But there's a glint of something else, too. A kind of satisfaction, or triumph.

She knows that Gavin and Lise are engaged. Of course she does. Mari has always been the epicenter of gossip.

But as far as I know, she never told anyone the truth about what happened between the two of us when our kids were in high school, about how I showed up on this very doorstep to threaten her. That's probably because it would have meant exposing Genevieve's secrets, too. She knew I had the ammo and she couldn't risk me using it.

I'm guessing that's the reason she never told people about my affair with Gavin. Or maybe she had, and word finally traveled back to Ron.

I deserve that, though. That and a lot more, considering the horrible thing I did to her and the even more horrible thing I did to my own father. Maybe Gavin coming back into my life is just karma. Only I don't believe that Lizzie should be destroyed because of my bad karma. The buck needs to stop with me.

"Could I come in, please?" I say. "I'd really appreciate if I could talk to you."

"Let me guess. You want to talk about Gavin Axelrod."

"Yes, and I owe you a massive apology."

She shook her head, lips pursed in a tight, humorless smile. "How convenient. Now that your daughter's the one in danger, you've grown a conscience."

"I swear, I didn't think Genevieve was in danger back then. I thought Gavin was, that he was innocent and you were making a mistake that would destroy his career. He was good at getting me to believe whatever he wanted."

"Oh, so you were a victim, too?" She crosses her arms over her chest, indicating there's no compassion to be found here.

That's okay, I don't deserve any. "If I can make him pay, it'll be for me, for Lise, for you, for Genevieve. We can all get our revenge in one fell swoop."

She continues to stare me down.

"Please, Mari. With your help, we can stop him. He's in Austin now, still teaching. He's engaged to Lise, as you know. He thinks he's on the cusp of a beautiful life. Let's blow it up."

She pulls the door open wider and walks inside. I shut the door behind me and then follow her into the atrium. It's as sun-drenched and gorgeous as ever. At a glance, you'd think nothing had changed for her. She's still dressed to the nines and perfectly made up. She and her husband are still together. I've seen them out a few times and before I dashed away in shame, I got the impression that they still adore each other.

But up close, in the brightness, I see the lines around her eyes and mouth. And I've heard through the grapevine that it didn't work out for Genevieve at Harvard. That's probably Gavin's fault. And mine, for helping to cover up his crime.

She sits back in her chair, her gaze as unforgiving as the light. She doesn't offer me anything to eat or drink, making it apparent that she's not hosting. I'm a very unwelcome guest.

But she let me in, so my proposition is at least a little bit intriguing. Or she wants to see me grovel and then kick me while I'm down.

"I really am sorry," I say. "I've always been sorry because I knew that you thought you were looking out for your daughter—"

"Correction: I was looking out for my daughter. And for all the other girls that he hadn't yet victimized. How many more do you think there've been in Austin and wherever else he's taught? You made sure he walked free."

"Just so you know," my mouth is painfully dry, "I don't think you should forgive me. When I threatened you, I was a grown woman. I'm responsible for my actions."

"And for the damage it caused."

I'm flooded with shame. She's right, I enabled an abuser. I have to face that, finally.

I don't want to think what he did to Genevieve, and what he might have really done with Lizzie way back when. They're both claiming nothing happened when she was a teenager, but he's a lying manipulator and she's entirely in his thrall.

"Yes, I'm complicit." I force myself to look into Mari's eyes. "But Lise isn't a grown woman, not really. She's twenty-two, and Gavin Axelrod is a sociopath. He's using every trick in his arsenal. I'm watching him do to her what he did to me. It's the same playbook."

Mari's face softens slightly. "I bet he was grooming both of them. Lizzie and Genevieve, and who knows how many more. Hedging his bets, seeing which horse would come in."

"So the power he has over her now is because he laid the groundwork then." It makes a lot of sense. I should have realized it myself sooner. If I told Lise, though, could she possibly see it?

"Of course. That's how serial predators work. I tried to bring him to justice and you tied my hands." She regards me coolly. "Ironic, isn't it? If you'd helped me stop him then, your daughter wouldn't need saving now."

I can see how much she wants to continue to hate me, but it doesn't come easily to her. She's not taking any pleasure in this.

Mari's a good person, and I hurt her, terribly. I hurt her through her child, which is the very worst way to hurt a person. But I didn't want to. I was operating under the influence.

"I am so sorry, Mari," I say. "You are an incredible mother, the kind I wish I'd had. The kind I'm trying to be. You go to bat for your kids, hard. I wish I'd taken your side—and Genevieve's side—instead of Gavin's." I'm crying now. "I should have helped you stop him then, but all I can do is try to stop him now. If I tell Lise what Genevieve went through—"

"You want me to trust you with my daughter's story?" Mari's eyes widen. "After the way you threatened me years ago?"

"Yes, that's what I want. I would never repeat it to anyone other than Lise."

"But Lise could just go back and tell Gavin. You said yourself he's a sociopath. I can't risk him coming after Genevieve.

Me, sure. But he doesn't go for the strong ones. He goes for the weak."

It's a jab, but she's right. I was weak even back then.

"I'll tell you his MO, but if you repeat it, I will come after you with everything I have. Do you understand?" I nod. "He could see how deeply Genevieve cared about her grades and about pleasing authority figures. He kept lowballing her with B minuses, which is like waving a red flag in front of a bull. She went to him after class, of course, asking how she could improve. He said that her writing was 'technically good but lacked passion.'" Mari looked like she was trying to contain her fury. "He said he didn't give grades based on what was on the page but on what could be on the page—as in, his curve was based on potential. And he believed that Genevieve wasn't working up to her potential."

I'm nauseated but I owe it to Mari to keep listening. To validate her outrage.

"Genevieve was so upset, and she told me about it, and I said, 'Well, you're up to the challenge.' You don't know how much I regret that response." Mari closes her eyes, which means she's trying not to cry.

"It's not your fault. You didn't know what he was really like."

She opens her eyes. "He offered to tutor her during her lunch, which happened to be his free period. From what I found out later, he was often putting her down while extolling her potential, urging her to 'do more.' And eventually, 'doing more' meant sucking his dick."

I'm shocked by her coarseness, just as she clearly intends me to be.

"Genevieve was tormented, I could see that, but she didn't tell me what was really going on for a long time. She was all turned around, just like she was supposed to be. That's the effect of his grooming. He got her thinking that giving him what he wanted was what she wanted."

"Yes, I'm familiar with that experience. But I didn't think... I mean, that's not how Gavin grooms people."

"Not people like you or Lizzie. You needed him to build you up, so you'd feel like you were on his level. But with Genevieve, he had to knock her down a peg."

It's an insult, but it's not untrue. After what I did to her, I'm lucky she's even speaking to me.

"Mr. Axelrod knew how to play the long game. Apparently, he liked a challenge, and he kept at Genevieve. Eventually, she started sleeping with him."

So Gavin was sleeping with Genevieve—his sixteen-year-old student—at the same time he was sleeping with me. Then when he got caught, he sent me—his lover and the mother of another of his students—to my best friend's house to blackmail her out of reporting him.

It's official. He really is the lowest of the low. He's a pedophile. He's engaged to Lise, but he could still be having sex with his students.

"Genevieve was conflicted and distraught," Mari continues. "As her grade went back up to an A in English, she started struggling in other classes. She was missing her extracurriculars and ignoring her friends. In other words, her life was going off the rails. I could see it, but she wouldn't talk to me."

"I'm so sorry, Mar. I know how awful that is."

Mari shakes her head, resisting my comfort. We'll never be friends again; she's making that clear. This is a one-off.

"Gen thought it was her fault," Mari says, "that she brought these situations on herself because otherwise, how could it be happening again? First the coach, now her teacher. She thought —she still thinks—she's damaged goods. That she's a terrible person."

I want to extend sympathy, but I bite my tongue. She doesn't want it from me.

"Gen's never recovered from what Mr. Axelrod put her through. Their affair, if you could call it that, was short lived. It ended soon after Christmas break of her junior year. He told her that he'd had an attack of conscience. She wound up in a psychiatric hospital a few days later."

Christmas break of her junior year. So when he'd browbeat me into leaving Mari's house during the Christmas party, had he also been there to see Genevieve?

"When I learned the full story, I went into the school guns blazing, and who knows what would have happened if I hadn't been threatened into withdrawing my complaint? If my alleged best friend hadn't forced me to go back to the school, tail between my legs, and say, 'Whoops, never mind!'"

Silence descends. There's no point in my apologizing again. I can't take any of it back. I've done grievous harm, and I have no idea how to begin to make amends.

"What eats me up is knowing how much she suffered, entirely alone, because of course the first thing a predator does is isolate a victim," Mari says. "He kept stressing the need for secrecy. It tore her up, but he didn't care. In his eyes, she was just an object to be used."

"That's how he sees women. And, apparently, girls, too."

"For years, I've been trying to figure out how to get vengeance on that man. I've considered suing Gavin Axelrod and the school district, seeing as the school failed to protect her. But that would mean publicizing everything Genevieve has been through. She couldn't handle that. She can barely handle community college. She's in therapy three times a week."

"Was she the only one, do you think?"

"Of course not. How do you think he wound up teaching in Austin? Houston passed the trash."

"What do you mean?"

As I sit stupefied, she explains the practice of "passing the trash," which is widespread and commonplace (it's only illegal in a few states). When a school finds out they have a perpetrator in their midst, they frequently decide to take care of it internally. A secret deal is cut between a school administrator or superintendent, the teachers' union officials, and the teacher who's been caught. No one complies with their legal responsibility to report child sexual abuse to law enforcement or child protective services. They don't inform the victims' parents nor do they provide counseling or compensation to the victims themselves. No disciplinary action is taken; nothing is recorded in the teacher's personnel file. The teacher agrees to voluntarily resign in exchange for a positive letter of reference. The trash is passed to the next school.

My mouth is hanging open. "How is this happening all across the country? How could I not know?"

"It's a dirty secret. Until your kid's in the club, you don't even know it exists." Mari looks as if she still can't believe that this is where she's found herself. "There's a certain lawlessness in school culture, you know? People like Gavin Axelrod feel like they're above the law; they're sure that none of their colleagues will report them. And the schools are afraid of the lawsuits that can be initiated by the unions. They protect their public image rather than the students."

"How do they sleep at night?"

"How did you sleep at night, Diana?" She doesn't wait for my answer. "People can justify all sorts of things. The truth is rarely an impediment."

"Sometimes you can't even see it."

"I'm not sure anything would have happened even if I hadn't withdrawn my complaint. The schools do their own investigation rather than hiring someone independent from the outside. Gavin would have known how to cover his tracks and how to make her look unstable. I mean, she was unstable when he got through with her."

"No wonder Gavin was so fearless." He went right for me, didn't he? At the same time he was pursuing Genevieve. No, not pursuing. Abusing.

"An absence of consequences emboldens predators. Why worry about getting caught, when it's catch and release?"

"I can't believe that they're just throwing these kids to the wolves."

"Evil prevails when good people ignore it." Mari doesn't exactly shrug, but I can tell that she's already experienced enough impotent outrage to last a lifetime. "School personnel don't get much training in how to spot and report abusers. Unions aren't set up to find and eject the bad apples. Districts aren't legally required to release information to the public about incidence rates. There's just an overall lack of transparency, and predators love the dark."

Mari's learned so much and yet Gavin's gotten away with everything. What would I have done if I'd discovered back then that he was grooming Lizzie? If someone like Mari failed to hold him accountable, I wouldn't have stood a chance.

But then, I took care of Mari for him.

I'm full of rage. He weaponized me against my best friend. He's left a trail of shattered girls and women behind him.

That ends now.

"Gavin Axelrod is the trash that's been passed all over Texas," Mari says glumly.

"I couldn't see it and I was an adult," I say. "How can any teenagers be expected to?"

"You've always been a sixteen-year-old girl, Diana. It's like you were frozen in time at the age when you got pregnant and were forced to marry a man you don't love, who doesn't love you."

"Wow." That was harsh.

"I'm not here to shield you from the real world." She leans in. "Teen girls are sexualized by society, and they're told that their sexuality is power. You know, all these grown men acting like they're made weak and crazy by youth and beauty, like they can't be expected to control themselves near some young hottie. Teen girls play their parts. They pretend to be sophisticated but they're still minor children who need protection."

"I agree."

"When a teacher manipulates and coerces a child—it's not always girls, you know, boys get groomed, too—their development as people suffers. They're in the process of figuring out who they are and these older teachers—not always men—start to shape their tastes and preferences. These children get molded. It's like they've been stunted, you know? Hijacked at a crucial developmental moment. They can be twenty, twenty-five, thirty, and they still don't know who they are."

"It sounds like you've done a lot of research."

"It's not just reading. I've made it a point to meet survivors. I've talked to their parents. And you know what a lot of those mothers feel? Now this is going to be very relevant to you, Di." I like that she's calling me Di again. "A lot of mothers, especially in a place like Houston, feel like they sort of pre-groomed their daughters."

"What do you mean?"

"As females, we're taught certain messages that we then pass along knowingly and unknowingly to our girls. Messages about being polite and deferring to men, about needing to be pretty and pleasing—that's like catnip for predators. It plays right into their hands."

I feel like I've been punched in the stomach. Was Lizzie an easy mark because I made her one? Was I an easy mark because of my mother's conditioning? And what about my mother's mother? It's overwhelming, imagining the intergenerational cycle.

If Lise has kids of her own, what'll happen to them?

Nothing. This ends now.

"I've been angry with you for so long that it's strange to sit here across from you," Mari says. "I always used to feel sorry for you, being married to Ron. Lizzie grew up watching you defer to him."

"She says that she and Gavin are nothing like Ron and me. She says that she's a woman of agency."

"Yeah, right."

"I've been a terrible role model, haven't I?"

"Not in every way." That's as much kindness as she's prepared to offer right now, but it's definitely something.

I fit the victim profile—isolated, with low self-esteem, obviously vulnerable and needy—and I raised a daughter who also fit. Gavin's exploited us both.

Maybe my life is ruined but Lise has so much ahead of her. So whatever it takes, I'm going to be a woman of agency.

Gavin Axelrod is trash, and he's going to be disposed of, once and for all.

Dad's arrived home at 8 p.m. on the dot, cheerfully blasé. It's as if our lunch never happened, like he hadn't thrown a grenade at his wife and my fiancé.

Now he's sitting by the pool, waiting for his dinner. I have the impression that he texted Mom earlier to tell her when, what, and where he wanted to be served. She seemed unsurprised when he showed up, though you can tell that she's jumping out of her skin.

I don't know what to do with this quartet anymore. I've been eager just to get back to Austin, back to normal, but now I'm not sure there's any such thing. One way or another, this trip will be transformative.

"Gavin, you can go on outside," Mom says in her silky hostess voice. "The wine's already chilling. Ron asked for a chablis." So I was right, Dad has orchestrated this meal. The Last Supper is what it feels like. "Lise, could you please help me with the pork tenderloin?"

I'm about to glance at Gavin to see if he has some objection to me staying behind with my mother but then I realize: We're not like that anymore. The power has shifted. For too long, without my conscious awareness, I've been deferring to him. It's going to be different now. He's the one who ought to be looking to me anxiously, wondering where he stands.

I've come to the necessary conclusion that there was no affair. But Gavin and Mom did conceal vital information, and they have been acting strangely. I get why Dad has his suspicions.

"Yes," I say to Gavin, "go on." Shoo.

He hesitates. "You're sure you don't want my help?" he asks Mom.

"Thanks for the offer, but Lise and I will be fine." Now Mom is doing her practiced hostess smile.

"I miss you already," he says to me, with a smile that I can't fully manage to return.

After he's exited through the patio doors, Mom crosses the kitchen and stands close to me, speaking in a low and urgent voice.

She tells me that she visited my high school. No one would speak on the record, they're bound by some sort of confidentiality, but she'd been referred to a parent who once made allegations against Mr. Axelrod. She learned that he'd been seducing teenage girls in his classes. "It's called grooming," she says, "when an adult—"

"I know what grooming is. Do you hear yourself, Mom? This is crazy, what you're accusing Gavin of!"

"No, it's not." She shakes her head solemnly. "The parent I spoke to wasn't able to get Gavin out but someone was, eventually. That's how he wound up teaching in Austin." She's speaking rapidly, her pupils flitting between the patio doors and my face.

All these years I've been waiting for my mom to speak up and use her voice and this is what comes out?

"Houston passed the trash," she says.

"Are you really calling my fiancé trash?"

"That's the actual term for it, when a teacher abuses a student and then walks away without any consequences. He's just transferred to a new school, where he can do it again. Google the phrase *passing the trash* and you won't believe—"

"I don't believe you. How can you sink this low?" I stare at her in amazement. "I know you don't want me to marry Gavin for whatever reason but you're basically calling him a pedophile."

Gavin had moved to Austin because he was sick of Houston. We had that in common.

And I know that he wouldn't be sexually involved with his students because he'd never crossed any lines with me despite how tempted he must have been. He was in love with me, even then.

"I don't want you to marry Gavin because he's not a good person," she says. "He's an abuser. I just want to protect you, Lizzie."

"I am not Lizzie! When will you get that through your thick skull?"

I'm glaring at her, full of self-righteous indignation, and then I flash on an image of Genevieve. How she looked. Her peculiar behavior. The way she told me that I wasn't lucky; no, on the contrary, I'd need luck.

Could Mari be the parent who Mom's talking about? That would mean that Genevieve—

No, there's no way. Or Mari is just telling stories. She's always been the neighborhood gossip.

"You're wrong about Gavin," I say. She has to be. "I love him."

"I know you do, and I wish just loving someone automatically made them good. But it doesn't work that way." Mom's face is full of compassion, like she's been there before.

But Gavin is not Dad. And I am definitely not Mom.

"I know Gavin through and through," I say. "He would never hurt someone the way Genevieve's obviously been hurt."

"I never said anything about Genevieve." It's a gotcha moment but nothing in Mom seems remotely triumphant. I can tell that she hates this. She's doing it for me. "Was there a rumor? Did you hear something from Denver or one of your friends?"

"No." It's true, no one has made any outright accusations. But it's been implied, hasn't it? Numerous times. Denver never trusted Mr. Axelrod, and now he doesn't trust Gavin.

"I love you, Lise," she says. "I love you so much that it's killing me. I have to tell you what I'd want to know if it were my fiancé. I'd want to know before it's too late."

"No, you wouldn't," I say scathingly. "You've always been afraid of the truth. You bury your head in the sand and—"

"You're right, I have done that. I've made so many mistakes but I'm still your mother. No one cares about you the way I do."

My anger dissipates but my resolve remains. "I believe you didn't sleep with Gavin but that doesn't mean you didn't want to. And I believe that you're trying to protect me but that doesn't mean I can trust your judgment."

For whatever reason, Mom has turned against Gavin and now she's ready to believe any negative story about him to justify her feelings.

I love Gavin and he loves me. We're getting married. These are all lies made up by people who want to bring him down. Or maybe they want to bring me down because they can't stand other people's happiness.

Mari and Genevieve and whoever else—they're all just jealous. They wish they had their own Gavins, but he's one of a kind, and he's mine. I've won.

So why do I feel like crying?

FIFTY

GAVIN

I'm not going anywhere. That's what they don't seem to realize —Lise, Diana, Ron, the eagle-eyed old crone from this morning —and the fact that they don't realize it is half the fun. In their own ways, they're each fighting me, which keeps it spicy.

This is my favorite family so far.

I told Lizzie years ago that great love stories are about obstacles and complications. Well, those are essential ingredients for thrillers, too. And I want it all. The passion and the danger. I can't stand to be bored.

Before we got here, Lise was starting to seem a little one-note. How much simple adoration can one man take? But now she's running hot and cold, which is enlivening. I do my best work when my back is up against the wall.

And Ron—what a curveball he threw today. I'd thought we were getting along this trip, that he might really be waving the white flag and welcoming me to the family, but then he summons Lise to lunch and... whammo! He decides to tell her about my affair with Diana, which might be more about his hatred of her than of me, but regardless. All of a sudden, Diana and I are in cahoots, lying to Lise together. Talk about strange bedfellows.

I'm a romantic. I love love. And money. And a challenge. Really, this family's got it all.

I'm genuinely attracted to both mother and daughter, and I know they feel the same. Diana's trying to resist, pretending that she doesn't want me anymore, but I'll break her down. I installed the buttons years back and I can push them again.

I'll get Diana to pay me off—hopefully she has to debase herself to that battle-ax of a mother for the funds—and then I'll stick around. Our agreement was hardly a binding contract. What'll she do, go to Lise crying and say, "Your fiancé broke our deal"?

The fact that she's a killer doesn't scare me. It titillates me. I like to make it sound like I'd go to the police, but really, I want to keep Diana free and accessible. I'm not turned on by orange polyester jumpsuits.

Besides, if she were in prison, who'd watch the grandchildren? Ron's not exactly the doting type.

But he is the type to consider his legacy, always more invested in the next generation than the current. Or maybe he does really care about Lise and that's why he tried to warn her this afternoon at lunch. I'm not quite sure of his motives, yet he's got me intrigued, I'll give him that.

See why I love this family? Never a dull moment.

I suspect that the big money will come through the grandkids. Once I've fathered Lise's children, I'll have maximum leverage. I'm going to enjoy spending the next however many years torturing Diana. Fucking her in every way imaginable. And today Lise showed that she might be formidable herself. I'm on my heels at the moment but that just means I need to get creative.

I've finally found my people, and I'm not about to let them go.

THEN

FIFTY-ONE
DIANA

Gavin wouldn't stop crowing about my success. "You did it, babe! Mari withdrew the complaint!"

I felt no pride in what I'd done. On the contrary, I was overwhelmed with shame. But at the very least, I would have thought it would prove my allegiance to Gavin. Somehow, though, he seemed to trust me even less. He was constantly monitoring my whereabouts, asking me to account for myself and my feelings.

Tell me you love me, he demanded by text, multiple times a day.

"Tell me you love me," he demanded in person.

No matter what I said, it was never enough. He accused me of lying, and you know what? I probably was. I didn't even know what love was anymore.

At his insistence, I'd gone Mafia on my best friend, and he must have been able to see that I was shattered by it. But he kept making references to what I'd done, rubbing my nose in it. I'd already chosen him over Mari, but it still wasn't enough. I was starting to think nothing ever would be.

All of a sudden, he didn't have much to say about Lizzie. He told me that she was fine, there was nothing to worry about. "You have to stop making yourself crazy," he said.

It was obvious that he was placating me so that I'd just shut up. He'd had enough of my anxious venting. One day, he blew up: "I'm your lover, Di, not your undercover agent!"

Really? Was that what I'd asked of him all this time? I thought it was what he'd offered. He used to tell me all the time that he wanted to be there for Lizzie and me. But either he felt differently now or he'd been lying the whole time.

He'd definitely been steering me wrong, and I wasn't sure it was accidental, either. He'd told me, "Being a parent isn't a popularity contest. You have to do hard things." And I trusted him. I cracked down on Lizzie and it drove her further and further away until she couldn't stand the sight of me. He must have known that because he'd been talking to her throughout. She didn't trust me anymore, but she trusted him.

No, there were no accidents with Gavin Axelrod.

He was a master manipulator and I needed to break free. But in the big picture, he didn't even matter. Only Lizzie did. I had to keep her safe, which meant that I had to know the truth.

Before I could stop myself, I barged into her room. I went through every single dresser drawer, peered under her bed, scavenged in the top and bottom of her closet. I was looking for her diary. She had to have one. Gavin told me she did.

Deep into my frenzied search, I caught sight of myself in the mirror over her bureau. My hair was wild, matching my expression. I looked like a madwoman. Mad as in insane, and mad as in angry. I was furious that Lizzie was so withholding that I had to search her room.

No, I didn't have to; I chose to.

This was a choice that I swore I would never make. I was never going to violate Lizzie's privacy in the way my own mother had routinely violated mine.

I was suddenly grateful that I hadn't found the diary

because if I had, I probably would have read it. Regardless of what I discovered, it wouldn't have been worth crossing that point of no return. I didn't want to be that person.

I was still looking at myself in the mirror, thinking, *This is the woman who Gavin loves. This is the woman he made. A woman who threatens her best friend's family and ransacks her daughter's room.*

I could hear his voice adding mockingly: *A woman who killed her own father. I didn't even know you when you did that. So who are you going to blame?*

I was responsible for every action and every choice.

The only question was, what was I going to do next?

FIFTY-TWO

LIZZIE

This time when I knocked on Mr. Axelrod's door, he opened it. But he didn't seem happy to see me.

As his eyes flickered past me, up and down the hallway, I caught a whiff of paranoia. "I'm in the middle of something, Lizzie," he said.

"Are you okay, Mr. Axelrod?"

He stared at me coldly. I'd never gotten that kind of look from him before. Had I done something to upset him? Or was he in the middle of something really bad?

"You can talk to me if you want," I said. "I can be a good listener. We don't always just have to talk about my problems."

He shook his head and let out a small, angry laugh.

"Are we okay?" I asked, my heart starting to race. And not in the way that it usually did around Mr. Axelrod.

"We're not a 'we.' I'm your teacher, Lizzie."

I stared at him, hurt and confused. "I just... I thought, over Christmas break... And what about the literary magazine?"

"The literary magazine is dead." He wasn't even making eye contact with me. It was like he didn't even realize how sharp he sounded, or he didn't care.

This was my own fault. I'd built our relationship up in my mind, read way too much into one hangout over Christmas break. Like he said, he was my teacher. A man like him would never be interested in a girl like me.

To my mortification, there were tears in my eyes. Equally mortifying, though? He didn't even seem to notice.

I should have just walked away but I needed him to see me. To remember. "That's a shame about the magazine," I said. "I guess I'll just miss our time together."

"I can't have you skulking around my classroom anymore, all right? There are people who'd love—" He cut himself off and seemed to pull himself together. "I just really think it's best if you focus on people your own age."

The door shut in my face.

NOW

FIFTY-THREE

DIANA

The sun hasn't gone down but the temperature has cooled to where it's just barely tolerable. I've lit candles in anticipation of the dark, which will descend suddenly. I can tell that tonight's sunset will be quick and dramatic. Will this dinner be the same way?

The pork's overcooked and the salad's wilting. No one's dared to break the silence yet, though Ron seems the most comfortable. He's smacking his lips with satisfaction as he polishes off a glass of the chablis that he requested ahead of time via text, like I'm the help.

He hasn't been looking at me. No one has. But then, I'm not trying to make eye contact with anyone, either.

For now, Lise is still standing by her man. But there were two positive takeaways from our talk. She's clearly harboring some suspicions when it comes to Gavin's history with Genevieve, and he's not in control as much as I feared. He's doing damage control, putting on a submissive act.

I'm assuming Gavin's angry at Ron, given the allegations that were made at lunch. But Gavin's body language is pretty submissive there, too.

Can Ron tell that his plan didn't work, that Lise doesn't believe there was an affair? If he hasn't realized it yet, he will soon, and that's a scary prospect. It's hard to imagine he's going to let me off so lightly for betraying and humiliating him. So what's his next move?

The air is heavy with humidity and tension. It's hurricane season all right.

I'm hypervigilant, on high alert. All my senses are way too acute. The sound of cutlery scraping against plates is deafening, and I don't know that I can stand it much longer. I finish my glass of wine but it's nowhere near strong enough. My nerves vibrate like a tuning fork.

That's it, I'm the first to crack. "So you and Lise met up for lunch?" I ask Ron, my tone the sweeter side of neutral.

He doesn't answer, just shifts in his chair to regard me.

"I think it's great," I say. "You and Lise having some private time."

"Can we just cut the shit, please? For once?" He rolls his eyes. "It's tedious, your little airs and graces. You can drop the act." He turns to Gavin. "You, too, loverboy."

"Sir, with all due respect—" Gavin begins.

"What do you know about respect?" Ron's eyes are blazing. "I thought we had an understanding. You were never to darken my doorstep again."

I stare at Ron, shocked. Does this mean that years ago, Ron and Gavin had some sort of confrontation? What kind of *understanding?* I feel like cattle that's been bartered.

Gavin went away and left me alone so that I could keep on serving my husband. That's until he had no use for me anymore.

Meanwhile, Lise is staring at Gavin. "What's he talking about?" she says.

"I have no idea." Gavin looks convincing in his bewilderment. "Sir, all I can tell you is, I'm entirely devoted to your daughter. Her happiness will be my number one priority for the rest of my life."

Ron nods slowly. Can he really be buying this? He looks at me. "What do you think, Di? You think he can be trusted?"

I wish I knew what answer he wanted. Was there any way for me to prove my loyalty now when he already knew the truth? When he'd known it for years?

"The cat's got Mom's tongue," Ron drawls to Lise. She clearly doesn't share his amusement and is instead watching me. What can I say that will get us out of this, unscathed?

And I don't just mean Lise and me. Since talking to Mari, I've become aware of my obligation to the others: the ones who Gavin's already damaged like Genevieve, the ones he has yet to meet.

I don't want to just pass the trash. I want to stop Gavin once and for all.

But it's not going to be easy. I'm now fighting a war on two fronts—against my husband and my ex-lover. What if they're somehow in cahoots, though? What understanding did they have then, and what do they have now?

"I think that Lise needs to listen to her gut," I say, "and then as her parents, we have to trust her."

"Lise has already made her choice," Gavin says. "Haven't you?"

She nods mutely, eyes on her still-full plate.

"I'm just not sure that we need a big wedding." Gavin is broadcasting to Ron and me. "There might be better uses for that money." His eyes linger on mine when he says the word *money*. He wants me to know that despite all the action today, he hasn't forgotten. I still owe him, and he intends to collect.

Gavin puts his arm around Lise and pulls her close, planting a kiss on top of her head. She's humoring him, and if I can tell that, he can, too.

I'm afraid for her. I know how dangerous he can be when he feels his possessions slipping out of his grasp.

"What would you use it for instead?" I say. "The money." I hope he'll give me something I can use, show his hand at least a little.

I need more information. I need more time. I need my daughter to see what's right in front of her nose.

"Growing our family." He's still holding on to Lise, whose eyes remain averted. It's like a hostage situation. "To me, family is everything. I'm so glad you're all going to be mine."

FIFTY-FOUR

LISE

I've withdrawn deep into myself, a turtle inside its shell. I'm not even here at this dinner anymore. I've disappeared.

The crazy thing is, all around me, Gavin, Ron, and Mom have started making small talk about the fucking peach crumble. Small talk is Mom's native tongue but what about Dad and Gavin? Seriously, who are these people? Are they all insane? Am I?

I don't know if I can trust any of them. For the past half hour, there have been so many allusions and insinuations, all those references to conversations that have seemingly gone on behind my back. I can't keep up. I don't even know how to poke holes in anyone's stories at this point. It's too convoluted.

I only really need to trust one of them, though. Two of them were assigned to me at birth, and one I chose.

If Gavin is who I always thought, then he and I can take off and never see my parents again. It'll hurt at first, but over time, they'll become a distant memory. Gavin will be my family, and like he said, family is everything to him.

But I'll need to test him. That means that when we're alone,

I'll be taking drastic action. It's the only way I can know for sure.

I came here to rebuild bridges but it looks like I might have to blow them up instead.

THEN

FIFTY-FIVE
DIANA

I just need a little time. Time to get my head on straight.

I was lying. I needed time to figure out how to loosen Gavin's grasping fingers and get myself out of this mess.

The worst thing I'd ever done was take a human life; the second-worst thing was bullying my best friend. Gavin was in full support—in awe, really—of the former, and had instigated and insisted upon the latter. Oh, and then the third was ransacking my daughter's room for her diary, a diary that she probably hid because she sensed how untrustworthy I'd become.

With Gavin's "help," my relationship with Lizzie had disintegrated. She wasn't merely surly anymore; she was contemptuous. When I got within five feet of her, she basically ordered me to stay back.

I could see something was wrong with her, but I couldn't reach her. She was lost. We both were, by Gavin's design.

Now he was hammering at me. *How much time? One day? Two? A week? A week's too long.*

I'll freak the fuck out, Di. I love you like I've never loved anyone.

You can't just leave me hanging. Is this really how you treat someone you love? After all I've done for you. I've treated you like gold.

I asked again for space. Instead, I got three days of nonstop harassment. I had to turn my phone off to escape the barrage of texts and voicemails. Sometimes Gavin was plaintive and pleading. At other times, he was furious at my audacity. "You're killing me," he said, in anguish and in rage. *You're killing me, Di.*

What a hypocrite he was. He only wanted a strong woman when she agreed with him.

How dare I put myself first? How dare I tell him what I wanted, if it weren't him?

There was no point in trying to tell him the truth because he'd only try to convince me of his truth. What I knew was that I didn't like myself anymore. I wasn't a good role model to Lizzie. I wasn't a good person, period. I couldn't change what I'd done in the past but I could change my future.

When I didn't cave under pressure, he started threatening to talk to Lizzie about his heartbreak. "She should know what your love is really worth," he said.

I realized then that he wasn't merely misguided or delusional or addled by obsession. No, he was evil. He was willing to treat Lizzie—a vulnerable sixteen-year-old girl, his student—as a human sacrifice. He didn't care about anyone but himself, and how had it taken me so long to figure that out? How had I been so blind?

He threatened to tell Ron, too. My knees buckled at the thought, but I refused to give in. This was an existential crisis, a moment of reckoning. I couldn't let Gavin control me ever again, no matter the cost.

A pattern emerged. After every ugly recrimination and failed threat, for every time I exhibited determination, there would be an equal and opposite reaction where Gavin would prostrate himself. He'd cry and try to take it all back, saying how sorry he was, that he hadn't meant any of those things, he'd never do any of them. He was just so desperate, so in love. For Gavin, love was the ultimate "get out of jail free" card.

Though I didn't respond, I read and listened to them all just to keep tabs on him. I wanted to know how unhinged he'd become. Occasionally he threatened to kill himself. Was he going to threaten to kill me or my family next? If he crossed that line, I'd have no choice but to go to the police. I preferred not to, because my part of Houston was its own small town. Mari knew about every domestic violence charge and restraining order. Surely this would get out, too.

I'd strung Gavin along, hoping that he'd realize on his own that it was over and he should move on. But he needed me to say it outright.

I can't do this anymore, I texted. *I wish you well. Please don't contact me again, and please don't hold this against Lizzie. She's just an innocent kid who looks up to you.*

I was out. I was done. And maybe now that Gavin was no longer living in hope, I could live in peace. He could go find someone new who'd appreciate his kind of love.

Either that or he'd go ahead and kill himself. I'd made my choice, and he'd make his.

As I blocked his number, my conscience was clear. In a peculiar way, Gavin had made me a stronger person. What's that expression, "the strongest steel is forged by the fires of hell"?

But then the devil came banging on my front door. He was shouting, "I know you're in there!" I drew all the blinds and crouched down on the floor, my hands over my ears. No matter what, I would not answer. If the neighbors called the police, so be it. I feared that he'd break down the door, he was kicking it so hard, but finally he went away.

In the coming days, he must have missed a lot of work. He sat outside my house for hours. He was waiting for me to leave, so I didn't. I had the groceries delivered. One time, I snuck out through the backyard, pulling myself over the back fence just to take a walk and see the sun.

It was stalking, plain and simple, and every day I considered going to the police and then didn't for fear of the affair getting back to Ron and Lizzie. Sure, Gavin was making me a prisoner in my own home but he wouldn't be able to keep it up long-term, not without risking his job.

He and I were in a game of chicken, and I would not swerve.

He started pushing notes through the mail slot in my front door. He wrote things like *You'll never get away from me. You're mine, Di,* and *I'll just tell Ron and let him deal with you, you fucking bitch,* and *I didn't mean what I wrote about Ron. I just love you so much it's eating me alive. I can't sleep. I can't think. My body is shutting down.* There was a long pornographic letter with all his sexual fantasies, what he wanted to do with me and to me. I raced to the bathroom and vomited.

One day, I decided I had to face it—face him—head-on. I went outside and got into the passenger seat of his car. He was unshaven and unkempt. He smelled rancid.

"You need to let me go," I said. "I'm never going to be with you again."

"Why?" He managed to look genuinely mystified. That's when I knew that he was untethered from reality.

So I spoke slowly and gently. "I don't want to be with you. You've been terrorizing me, Gavin."

He shook his head. "I'm sorry you see it that way but a man

wants what he wants. If he stays the course, eventually he'll get her."

So much for all of Gavin's pseudo-feminist bullshit. It had all been a pose. Of course it was fake, like everything about him. The Gavin I'd thought I loved was pure fiction. No, pure propaganda.

"You can't force someone to love you," I said.

He stared out the front windshield. Was it that he couldn't face me, or couldn't face what he'd done?

I wanted to think he was capable of shame.

"I can force it," he said. "I've done it before."

I was electrified by fear. Gavin believed he should possess me, that I had no right to autonomy. In his mind, I didn't get to say no.

"Remember my ace in the hole," he added. "There's always Lizzie."

I assumed he meant that he would make good on his threat and tell her about the affair. But it felt even more ominous than that, in a way that I couldn't even articulate to myself.

I sprang out of the car and ran back into my house. I bolted the door behind me and set the alarm. But I knew it wasn't enough.

He was so much more dangerous than I'd realized, operating without the guardrail of a conscience. If he couldn't get to me, he could still get to Lizzie.

My heart was beating so hard that I thought I might be able to see it coming out of my chest, the same way when I was pregnant I could sometimes see the imprint of a hand or a foot on my belly as Lizzie punched and kicked. I used to tell Ron, laughing, "She wants out, now!" She'd been so feisty in utero.

To save us both, I'd need to be the feisty one now.

FIFTY-SIX

LIZZIE

Mr. Axelrod was not well.

He hadn't been at school for days and now that he was back, he still wasn't there, if you know what I mean. He seemed vacant and hollow-eyed. Traumatized. He told us to spend the class period doing silent reading.

My first thought? Someone must have died. His mom, maybe?

My second thought: that he'd had a girlfriend this whole time and she'd just broken up with him. He seemed like the portrait of heartbreak.

I felt like a total idiot. He'd probably never been interested in me at all. He was in love with someone else and he felt sorry for me. I was a skinny, pimply poet. Even if he'd ever go for a student, it wouldn't have been me. It would have been someone like Genevieve.

But I wanted to stay behind after class and say something. He was so clearly suffering, which meant I suffered, too. There was no denying the truth: I really did love him. Would that mean anything to him?

The bell rang. I was lingering behind, packing up my books

extra slowly. He finally looked up and said, "Lizzie." That was all, just my name, and it suddenly felt like I was levitating.

I approached his desk. He was looking down and he didn't speak until the room had fully cleared. Then he said, "I need to see you."

"I'm right here." I smiled awkwardly. Why wouldn't he look up?

This close, I saw just how much of a toll something—someone?—was taking on him. His hooded eyes, his pallor, the uneven beard growth. He didn't look good, but I didn't care. That was how much I loved him.

"This Saturday, are you free?" His eyes were still averted. Maybe he was embarrassed at seeming so wrecked. "I want to take you somewhere. Show you something."

"Yeah, I can be free." I wouldn't tell my parents where I was really going. Mom might not even ask any questions. For days, she'd seemed jumpy and depressed at once, even though I would have thought those were incompatible.

He smiled a little to himself but there was no happiness in it. No life, if that even made sense. It kind of gave me the chills.

But I'd never say no to Mr. Axelrod.

NOW

FIFTY-SEVEN

DIANA

I have no good options, but I'm not done fighting.

I can't get through to Lise and I'm in deep shit with Ron. So I'm going to need that money and there's only one place left to get it. That's why I'm sitting outside my parents' house at ten o'clock at night.

I've visited as rarely as possible since Daddy died, always offering to take Mother out for a meal rather than have her cook. She's gone along, probably more because she dislikes cooking than out of any sensitivity to my grief. I'm not sure about the contour of her own grief. Really, she's seemed largely unfazed by Daddy's death. She dabbed delicately and prettily at her eyes during the funeral, and that's the last time I saw her cry.

Mother is displeased that I've shown up without calling, and she wants me to know it. She's in her nightgown and robe with curlers on her head. Normally, she'll be seen only in full hair and makeup, even by me.

"Thanks for opening up," I say. It occurs to me just then how strange it is that I don't have a key to her house.

"It's not like you gave me a choice," she says. "You wouldn't stop knocking and screaming."

"I wanted you to know it was me at the door and not some burglar."

"Do burglars usually knock?" Her look is withering but she steps aside to permit me entry.

It's the same house I grew up in but it's been extensively renovated. It's much smaller and the ceilings are lower than mine but it's got that same immaculate and sterile hotel feel. There are flower paintings on many of the walls, and fresh flowers feature prominently in every room. Flowers are her one true love.

Mother starts making tea. "Would you like any pastries? I have some left over from when Lise and her young man were here."

"No, thanks. I don't want you to go to any trouble." Oh, fuck it. I don't have the energy for sugarcoating. "I need a million dollars."

Mother spins around to show me an artfully raised eyebrow.

"If I want Lise's young man to go away—and I very much do —then I have to make it worth his while."

She comes and sits down across from me. Her landing is heavy, though she's still bird-thin. I can see her age and it's not just about the lack of makeup. She's rickety. Tired.

Right now, it feels like I'm playing with house money because when it comes to my relationship with my mother, there's really nothing to lose. Gavin's probably right, she never loved me. But this isn't about her love for me; it's about my love for Lise.

"Lise can't marry Gavin," I say.

"I hate having to call her Lise. It's so pretentious, isn't it? I know kids today enjoy renaming themselves but you can't just turn yourself French. She's a Texan, whether she likes it or not." Mother studies her manicure in a very affected way.

I know she finds hard conversations to be gauche but this

could be something else. I've barely seen her in the last year. Maybe she's in cognitive decline.

That's all right by me, so long as she writes the check.

"I need you to trust me," I say. "Gavin is unsuitable for reasons that you wouldn't like hearing. You really don't want to let him in our family."

"I didn't care for him," she says, "but you need to let your children make their own mistakes."

That's never been her parenting philosophy. She married me off to Ron when I was sixteen and has made her opinions known about every major (and minor) decision at every step of the way.

"Not when it's a mistake this colossal," I say, trying to keep my cool.

The kettle boils and she busies herself with the tea while I think of my next argument. I have it by the time she returns to the table with our porcelain cups.

"I'm happy to use my entire inheritance to save my daughter," I say. "Give it to me now and cut me out of your will. I can't go into why, but I promise you, I'm right about this. I have to get her away from that man."

"It's an interesting proposition." Mother levels me with a penetrating stare. She's trying to see through me, which at least represents a change. She typically cares only about the surface appearance of things and never what's underneath. Since when does she want to know what I'm really thinking and feeling?

While I don't think she's ever held me in particularly high regard, I've always felt compelled to preserve whatever regard she did have. And since Daddy died, there's been an additional financial incentive to playing nice. She inherited his entire estate, and while I imagine they had an understanding that she would then leave it to me, nothing's guaranteed. When I annoy her, she likes to hint/threaten that "there are so many worthy charities."

I don't know where I stand with her, seeing as we've barely had a real conversation. I've inadvertently continued that with my own daughter, haven't I?

Well, it's time to break with tradition.

"When Lizzie was in high school, I had an affair with Gavin," I say. "He manipulated and abused me. I suspect he's doing the same with her now, and I'm terrified about how much worse it could get once they're married and he sees her as officially being his property. He is a truly vile man, Mother. I need you to believe me."

Why doesn't she seem more surprised? "I knew there was something I didn't like about him," she murmurs.

I'd almost smile except that I'm nearly paralyzed with fear. Mother and I are in uncharted territory, having gone from sharing zero confidences to sharing one this extreme. We've left social graces far behind.

"Daddy could be manipulative, too."

I stare at her in shock. Are we actually *trading* confidences? "Excuse me?"

"When Daddy was dying, you spent so much time with him. And I've always wondered about the end. Were you giving him what you thought he deserved or putting him out of his misery? I suppose it could be both. Killing two birds with one stone, so to speak." She's not looking at me, is instead focused on putting sugar in her teacup.

"How long have you suspected?" I whisper.

"I didn't suspect at first; it was something the social worker said when she came out one last time. Something about how sometimes family just needs the end to come and it's not uncommon for a family member to freeze up and not do CPR or to freeze up before calling 911. She also made it clear that in her profession, she sees all kinds of things. Women in a field like that, they know how to keep their mouths shut."

"But why didn't you ever ask me? Didn't you want to know

for sure? I mean, he was going to die soon, but essentially, I killed him. I killed your husband." Is she really so unfeeling that she doesn't care about that?

"Your father and I were together a very long time. There were things I overlooked and I probably shouldn't have. Like when you were a little girl and he used to go into your room late at night."

"What?" I have no idea what she's getting at.

"Was he just watching you sleep, Diana? Or was there something more? These are other questions I should have asked then but I guess..." I can see shame pass over her face, just for a second, and then it's gone. She's never been one to linger in negative emotion.

"I don't remember anything strange." But could there have been more and I've blocked it out? I've heard that happens to victims. To survivors.

"What I've come to believe is that you did the right thing. You put your father out of his misery." Her tone is final.

I'm speechless, my mind whirring.

"That money is yours, Diana. Use it however you see fit." I know I need to thank her but I can't seem to form words. "Just know that whatever you do from now on, you have my full support."

It's almost like she can see inside my head right to my plan. Like she knows that I don't intend to give that money to Gavin; I'm going to give it to someone who'll take care of him once and for all. Or someone who can cover my tracks when I do it myself.

I have my mother's blessing to become a murderer, twice over.

FIFTY-EIGHT

LISE

Gavin and I are lying in bed. He's reading a book, and I'm pretending to do the same. I know that I need to take extreme action—smash the piñata, see what falls out—but I find myself hesitating.

Do I really need to do this? I mean, I know the man I'm going to marry. Don't I?

Gavin would never have abused one of his students; I'm sure of that in my heart. So whatever Mom heard at the school was just a mean-spirited, unfounded rumor.

But then I think of Genevieve from high school, how sweet and beautiful she was, and I contrast that with the angry, bitter girl I saw at the mall today. The one telling me, "Good luck with that." *That* being Gavin.

Now I'm inundated with memories from my junior year. I was so taken with Mr. Axelrod and while nothing sexual happened, let's face it: Something was happening. He was more than a teacher to me. He must have been able to see that and he encouraged it. Until one day, he didn't.

Was it because Genevieve came along and stole his interest? Or was there someone else, like Mom? Or had he gotten caught in a compromising situation and needed to clean up his act, fast?

No, no, and no. Gavin's an innocent man who's being dragged through the mud. He wasn't going around grooming teenage girls. I have to believe that.

Only...

I've always prided myself on being opinionated, nothing like Mom. But as I look at the book in my hands and think of the TV shows I watch and the music I listen to, there is a common denominator.

They're all things Gavin likes, too. What he likes most? Turning me onto his preferences.

He did that when I was in high school, sliding recommendations into conversation. Infusing me with aspects of his personality, letting me know what traits he appreciated. He even told me what style of dress he liked. Sometimes he talked about his "dream girl." And gradually, I became her.

I've always thought one of the strengths of our relationship is just how much we have in common. But now I'm thinking that it might be a one-way street. I mean, how often does Gavin really let me influence him?

He says he loves a strong woman. It's time to challenge that. To challenge him.

"I need to know something," I say, setting my book aside. He does the same, turning toward me with a pleasantly expectant expression. It looks calculated somehow, like he's playing the role of the perfect fiancé. "I know you were married before." Screw the preamble. "Why didn't you tell me?"

"Where did you hear that?" His face hasn't shifted; he hasn't assumed a defensive posture. But he's answering my question with a question, which feels evasive.

"Is it true? Were you married before?"

He shifts away from me slightly. "If I wanted to talk about that, I would have told you myself already."

"So it is true."

"It's a tragedy, is what it is."

Yes, it was. She was young and she killed herself. But you would have thought that something from their past life together would have come up during all our hours of conversation. Also, it must have affected him. It's not healthy to keep it bottled up inside. "Why didn't you want me to know? Don't you trust me?"

"It's not about trust. I just didn't want to relive it. And sometimes you don't know when to let something go. You're always so fucking curious."

"There's no need to curse at me." His anger feels damning. I'm on his side; I want him to prove all my fears are unfounded, but so far, that's not happening.

"I'm sorry. I just didn't think I'd have to revisit the worst time of my life. As if this trip hasn't been bad enough."

"No, I'm the one who's sorry." He's right; this trip has been a shit show. "I shouldn't have gone through your things."

"Wait, when did you go through my things?" He looks confused. "What things?"

"We hadn't been together long and there was that box in your apartment. But by the time I moved in, it wasn't there anymore."

He stares at me with mounting ferocity and I feel myself starting to squirm. "Maybe this isn't about whether I trust you. It's about you not trusting me since the beginning."

Could that be true? Mom's been saying that I should listen to my gut.

Gavin and I had been so happy then. There wasn't a single cloud on the horizon. Yet I'd been going through his apartment.

"I guess I came into the relationship with trust issues," I say. "Dad issues, you know?"

Gavin doesn't nod, doesn't move a muscle. He's giving me nothing, letting me hang myself. Punishing me. Which is exactly what my father would do.

I'm not marrying my father. And I'm not apologizing again. "I must have sensed that you were keeping something from me, and I was right." There's an edge to my tone.

"You've known this for months and you're just telling me now?" He's started flexing his hands on top of the duvet cover and even though there's never been even an intimation of violence between us, I suddenly feel afraid.

"If I hadn't brought it up, you probably never would have told me."

"You don't know that."

"What were you waiting for, huh?" My voice has gotten louder. The stress and strain of the last days is too much. I can't —I won't—contain myself anymore. If he's a monster, he needs to show his claws. I have to know who I'm dealing with.

"It's my business, Lise. It's my life."

"We have a life together. Why didn't you want me to know about Hannah?"

"I don't like to talk about her. That's not the same as hiding, or lying." He shakes his head, more disappointed than annoyed. "I thought you understood me, Lise. I thought we got each other. But it turns out you're going through my stuff. Do you check my phone, too? Dig through my trash?"

At the word *trash*, I have an involuntary reaction, sort of a flinch. Is Gavin trash that's been passed all around this state? Between women, one of whom is dead?

"What the hell is going on here, Lise?"

"I don't like when you curse at me."

"Don't act like you're some Southern belle. You're not your fucking mother. I would never be with someone like that."

"Stop cursing!" I'm close to yelling. Are my parents asleep, or can they hear me? If this gets ugly, will they come running? "I don't know why we're even talking about me. You're the one who was keeping a secret first, a big one. My snooping was a lot less of a violation than you concealing vital information."

"Oh, is that right? You're the judge and jury now?"

"I just want you to take responsibility for what you did. You lied by omission." Maybe he's lied in other ways, too. "You never take responsibility for anything."

"I apologize to you all the time. It's practically all I do."

"But there's nothing behind it." I hadn't realized it until just then, that he apologized way too easily, like a means to an end, a way to placate me or terminate uncomfortable conversations. Had I ever seen genuine remorse?

"You're acting like you know everything about me." His disappointment is back.

"I know I don't." I look away from him, toward the door. This whole week in Houston, I've been defending Gavin: to Maya and her girlfriend; to Denver; to my dad; to my mom, most of all. But what if they're right, and I'm wrong?

Gavin does a big exhale, visibly calming himself. Then he turns toward me and moves to take my hand. I feel myself shrinking back.

"Hey," he says softly. "What's happening to us?"

"We have been moving fast. Maybe we really don't know each other well enough to be married."

That's when he starts crying and apologizing with what looks like true feeling—a suspicious amount of feeling—and saying how much he loves me and how scared he is to lose me. But is it real?

I've never felt this way before, like I'm watching him from a distance.

I think of how urgent my mother's warnings have been, how terrified she's seemed, right from the first second she saw Gavin at the steakhouse. Dad's right, there is something intimate about it all.

I have a sudden flash. A noise from the guest room. Mr. Axelrod's car parked outside. Mom in the kitchen looking like she was about to have a legit heart attack.

"Tell me the truth," I say. "Is this the first time you've ever been in this guest room? Or did you used to have sex with my mom in here?"

He looks deeply into my eyes. "I swear, Lise, I never had sex with your mother. Not here, not anywhere else."

I want to believe.

But I don't. My gut has spoken. "You're a liar," I say, more sad than angry or disgusted or anything else.

He inhales deeply and I think he's going to double down but then he surprises me. He looks... remorseful. Genuinely. "I am lying," he says. "Because I had to. Because I couldn't lose you."

"You're saying that you did have an affair with my mother when I was in your class?"

"Yes." He stares down at the duvet cover with palpable shame. "You and I weren't together back then because we couldn't be. You were too young, and a student. I couldn't cross that line. So I guess I just took the next best thing."

"You were with her because you couldn't have me?" It's so gross and yet, it's also a little flattering. I wasn't second best; I was unattainable.

"I was in love with you but I couldn't act on it. No matter how incredible you were. How incredible you are." Now he's staring at me with angst and adoration in equal measure.

I feel the dinner rushing up through my esophagus and I race to the bathroom, slamming the door. I can't look at him right now.

He loved me back then, yes, but he was also having sex with my mother.

"I'm so sorry," he's saying through the door. "I should never have done it. But she was just so needy. And it wasn't that deep, Lise. She wanted me as a security blanket. Mostly what we did was talk. About you. You remember what a nervous wreck she was. She was so scared that you'd get pregnant and wind up like her."

I sit on the edge of the bathtub, trying to regain my equilibrium. Because what I feel most is destabilized, like I came here with one reality and I'm leaving with another. How does a person begin to process something like this?

"She was just using me to get intel about you," he continues. "You talked to me and you never talked to her, for obvious reasons. She wanted to keep me close to her, and close to you. It's something I only realized fully in hindsight, just how sneaky and manipulative she is. You've told me yourself. You can never see the real her."

She might have showed her true colors earlier tonight, when she passed along those rumors and tried to destroy my relationship with the man I love. Maybe because he's the man she still loves?

"I'll do anything to fix this, Lise. If I lost you, I'd die. I swear I would." He sounds so sincere, choking back tears. And I know what I've experienced over the past ten months, the connection we've shared. I know what I've felt. "Lise? Could you please open the door?"

"Not yet. I just need a minute."

"Let's leave tonight. We can run away together. We'll go to Vegas and get married. I'd marry you right now if I could just teleport a judge in." He waits. Does he think I'm capable of laughter? "Please, you have to forgive me. Marry me."

I don't know what to do. I can't think. And I'm feeling way too much. It's overwhelming. Every limb, every cell, is tingling. Am I having a panic attack, or a heart attack?

"I'm not letting you go, Lise. You're too important to me." He's still talking through the door but it's like he's whispering right in my ear. "I will never, ever let you go."

FIFTY-NINE
RON

Diana left the house after dinner and she's not back yet. Is she planning to stay out all night just to avoid being alone with me?

Soon she'll have to face up to what she's done. She got a five-year reprieve, wasn't that enough?

I never thought I'd find myself back in this particular triangle. Or I guess it's a rectangle, if you count Lizzie. She should never have been involved at all. I should have taken care of Diana and Gavin years ago.

It was Mari who tipped me off back in the day at her Christmas party. She'd seen Diana climbing out of Gavin Axelrod's car, pulling her dress down. Mari told me, "I can't let her make a fool out of you."

Honestly, I was surprised she cared. Mari and I had never been particularly close, and I would have thought she'd be on Diana's side, not mine. But if it weren't for her, I probably never would have figured it out. I wouldn't have thought that Diana had it in her to be unfaithful. I guess that under the right conditions, anyone can be a conniving whore.

I was angry, sure. But I needed all the facts before deciding on a course of action.

I hired a private investigator and found out about her love nest with Gavin. I also found out about the bank account that was bequeathed by her father. She hasn't moved any money out of it in all these years but I've still got my eye on her.

It turns out, I like monitoring her. I enjoy the steady reminders, the confirmation that I've been right to never let my guard down in this marriage. It proves what I've always known: you can't trust anyone but yourself.

It's high time Lizzie learned that lesson. I tried to tell her when we met up for lunch but she didn't want to hear it. Now the time for talking is over.

At least Diana's suffering. You can see how much she hates having Gavin around.

It's the only pleasure I've gotten out of this visit. I know those two parted on bad terms, that she ended it and he kept on stalking her. I decided to let it go on a while, just to punish her, before I stepped in.

She picked a real winner in Gavin Axelrod. I had the investigator look into him, too. Discovered his MO.

Gavin finds men who have money and then strategically goes after their wives and daughters.

Which means this is personal. It's a direct attack against me. Years ago, I let him off with a warning and that was my mistake. He tricked me, with all his shaking and cowering. I thought he knew better than to ever come back. But he'd been pandering to my ego, biding his time.

Based on what the investigator told me, Gavin might have preferred to steal Mari's husband's money, to make Genevieve his wife down the line, but it didn't work out. He had to settle for Lizzie. And my daughter is no one's sloppy seconds.

The fact that Gavin would dare to set foot in my house, the level of fucking disrespect involved in that—well, I'm going to love demonstrating who's king of this particular jungle.

THEN

SIXTY

DIANA

I need to see you. The text came from an anonymous number but the sender was obvious.

I'd expected this. You couldn't block a man like Gavin, not for long.

I was going to have to stab him through the heart. Metaphorically, I meant. Having killed once, I never wanted to do it again.

After our confrontation in his car, Gavin had left me alone for a few days, though I never really believed he'd gone away. He hadn't been leaving notes or parking in front of the house but the fact that I couldn't see him brought no relief. If anything, I'd been more on edge because he was still out there, a gathering storm.

My worst fear was immediately realized by his next text: *Lizzie's with me right now. I'll tell her everything unless you come see me.*

It was Saturday, and Lizzie had said she was with Maya. I prayed that she'd been telling the truth. I was debating how to respond when he sent a picture of her in his car. She looked giddy.

She wanted to take a selfie with my phone.

I was terrified, and furious. But I couldn't be mad at Lizzie. Sure, she'd lied but I'd lied plenty to my parents, too. Lizzie was just being a teenager, and a sheltered one at that. She was a defenseless pawn in Gavin's game.

I should have come clean to her about what was going on. It would have made me look terrible but at least she would have known not to go for a joy ride with Mr. Axelrod.

Could I text her that she was in danger? Would she believe me?

Sadly, I didn't think so. Gavin could have been telling her anything behind my back, elevating himself and denigrating me. My relationship with Lizzie was in tatters, which was just how he wanted it. He was the one in control.

Where are you taking her? I texted.

Somewhere special. She's really excited about it.

I felt like my heart was about to stop. Lizzie was a hostage victim and she had no idea. *Bring her home right now. Then I'll see you.*

I'll bring her home but you won't be there. You'll be at my apartment. We're going to talk—and do some other things—in private.

I was filled with rage and hate of a previously unimaginable intensity. I didn't know what I was going to do once we were face-to-face.

But maybe I'd surprise myself.

SIXTY-ONE

LIZZIE

I'm trying to seem older but I'm feeling so much younger. Overexcited, like when my mom used to promise me a special surprise.

She was so good at that, building up my anticipation and then introducing me to new experiences like trapeze or new foods like dim sum, even though that meant driving inside the loop. (Nothing unique, exotic, or thrilling was happening in our neck of the woods.) But she didn't do it often, so there was a lot of ho-hum in between. My life was like a movie where the good parts were spaced too far apart. It was a road trip where you kept asking, "Are we there yet?" in an increasingly irritated tone.

But when I asked Mr. Axelrod, "Are we there yet?" it was because I really couldn't wait to be alone with him someplace where no one knew us.

We'd already been driving an hour in the opposite direction of the city. I couldn't guess where we were headed and he'd made it clear that he wasn't going to tell me.

"Stop asking questions," he said flatly.

I'd hoped he'd be playful or flirtatious, that the car ride

would feel fun, but his mind was clearly elsewhere. He seemed quiet, tense, and remote.

He was playing a Van Morrison CD and he kept returning to the song "Tupelo Honey," which I liked, but come on, four times in a row? When I tried to talk during it, he shushed me.

"Was that your song with someone?" I asked. "Did you two just break up? You can tell me about her, if you want."

He laughed but not in an especially pleasant way. "I don't think that's such a good idea."

So I was right. There was someone. "I'd like to hear about her," I said. "Like, what happened? How long were you together?"

Instead of answering, he pulled his phone from his pocket. I wasn't wild about him texting and driving but I didn't want to act all anxious like my mother.

I watched his face as his thumbs moved. A minute later, he said, "Sorry, I'm going to have to cut this short."

He cranked the wheel and we went across two lanes and then careened onto the exit ramp. With a few left turns, he was headed back on the highway in the opposite direction.

There was no point in protesting, so I concentrated all my energy on not crying.

He noticed—Mr. Axelrod is nothing if not perceptive—and his expression softened. He cared about me, I knew he did. If it hadn't been for that other woman...

"We might do this another time, okay?" he said. "Depending on the outcome of my errand. You're very important to me. Don't ever doubt that."

NOW

SIXTY-TWO

DIANA

When I get home from seeing my mother, it's late and I'm beyond exhausted. I don't want to go upstairs and risk waking Ron. But I'm not as afraid of him as I once was, now that I have my inheritance.

Money is power, right? But it has to be properly deployed.

I settle on the couch downstairs with my laptop. I can't even think about what my mother revealed. Well, what she may have revealed. Even she doesn't know for sure what really went on between my father and me because she never went to find out. Instead, she left me to fend for myself.

All these years, I've been struggling with the fact that I killed my father. But had he actually deserved to die a whole lot sooner than he did?

What I know for sure: my mother didn't even try to protect me, so I'm going to be the mother she never was. I'll protect Lise, no matter what it takes.

I need to think about my next move. About whether it's possible to stop Gavin without actually killing him or if he'll always manage to skate away and find another victim.

Let's say I manage to save Lise. Is that really enough?

What about Genevieve and Mari and all the others? The people who fought and failed to bring him to justice while I was enabling and thinking only of myself and my own child?

Will other women wind up dying, women like Eve's daughter Hannah?

I've only just made Eve's acquaintance tonight. She's from Dallas and her daughter Hannah was Gavin's first wife. Or prior wife. I don't yet know for sure how many there have been.

It's almost midnight, and she and I have been going back and forth for the past hour. It started with a private message on Facebook. Eve said that she had some information about Gavin that might interest me. She'd been referred by a mutual friend, Mari.

I was touched that Mari would describe me that way and I didn't disabuse Eve of the notion, not at first. I learned that Mari and Eve had met through an unofficial Facebook support group for Gavin's victims, and those who love them.

Eve's daughter Hannah had met Mr. Axelrod when Hannah was a senior in an honors English class and he was the student teacher. It seemed important to Eve that I knew that her daughter was a bright girl. Had been a bright girl.

Eve had been suspicious of late nights at the school, of the new literary magazine where Hannah was the editor. There were lots of meetings between Hannah and the faculty adviser, Mr. Axelrod, yet the collaboration never produced a single issue.

Eve's spidey sense wouldn't stop tingling, especially when she was in his presence. Eve knew a predator when she was staring right into his dead, charming eyes.

But she felt helpless. She talked to Hannah about her concerns and got nowhere. She visited the school and got nowhere. Both Hannah and Mr. Axelrod seemed convincing when they said it was all above board, that nothing inappropriate was occurring. It still haunts Eve to remember how

Hannah had laughed and said, "Mom, quit being so overprotective! I know what I'm doing."

Eve didn't believe Hannah, and Hannah could tell that, and it became a wedge between the two of them that began in high school and never truly healed. Eve and Hannah weren't fully estranged, but they were distant.

So it wasn't just Lizzie and me. Gavin intentionally creates wedges and isolates his victims.

It feels oddly validating because I've spent so much time these past years beating myself up for what I had allowed to happen. What I hadn't been strong enough to prevent.

Now I can see that I never stood a chance. He was too practiced. He'd honed his craft, starting young, when he was just a student teacher right out of college. And who knew what he'd been up to before that?

In her sophomore year of college, during winter break, Hannah came home and introduced her fiancé, Gavin. She acted like it was totally normal, as if her parents should have no objections: "I'm over eighteen, Mom. I'm an adult." Once again, she added, "I know what I'm doing."

Gavin appeared to be a perfect gentleman, but Eve didn't buy his act. Only she had no influence, no positive relationship or pull, with which to convince Hannah that he was dangerous.

Hannah's dad was a very wealthy man, and he loved spoiling Hannah, especially if it would piss off his ex-wife, Eve. Eve surmises that Gavin Axelrod had discovered those dynamics when Eve was still in high school. Sure, Hannah was cute, but she wasn't the type to turn every head. She was naïve and insecure. She'd never really gotten over her parents' acrimonious divorce.

Despite Eve's objections, Hannah and Gavin married quickly, eloping to Vegas. Hannah's father took to Gavin right away, buying the newlyweds a house and two new cars.

Hannah stopped taking Eve's calls, so Eve doesn't really

know what was going on in the marriage. But just before their first anniversary, Hannah committed suicide.

Gavin appeared inconsolably bereaved. He sold the cops a story about Hannah's increasing depression and how she refused all his attempts to get her help. He also had an airtight alibi, so technically, he didn't murder her. But Eve suspects that he'd embarked on some sort of program of psychological torture where he systematically broke her down. Hannah had been down sometimes in her life but never clinically depressed. She'd certainly never been suicidal, not on Eve's watch.

I believe he's capable of that, I message her.

Hannah had a will. As in, a last will and testament. At twenty years old. There's no way she decided to do that on her own.

I'm sure he convinced her it was her own idea. My blood boils just imagining the conversation.

She left him everything. The house, the cars, every dollar in her bank account.

I wonder what happened to all that money because when I met Gavin years back, he wasn't living high on the hog.

Is he squirreling it away for the future, investing it, maybe? Hiding it offshore so he can make his getaway? Financing a secret life with another woman? Or has he used it as payment to silence his victims? In the case of Mari and Genevieve, he didn't need to buy anyone off; he had me.

I'm so sorry, Eve, I write, tears rolling down my cheeks. *I won't forget this, and I won't let you down.*

I'm not alone. I'm part of a community of survivors.

I once told Gavin, *This is over*, but he wouldn't let it be. Now he's going to wish he'd walked away when he had the chance.

SIXTY-THREE

LISE

I'm trying to sleep in the bathtub, which is about as comfortable as you'd expect. There is another room with a convertible bed, but if I go in there, then my parents will know that Gavin and I are on the outs.

I don't know why I care what they think anyway. It's not like I can ever have a relationship with them again.

My mother had an affair with Gavin and then lied about it. He lied about it, too, but then he told the truth. I suspect Mom would have taken this to her grave.

What if I have to get rid of all of them? I'd be entirely alone in the world.

Maybe that wouldn't be the worst thing ever, starting over from scratch. A newborn babe at twenty-two.

At least Gavin isn't talking to me through the door anymore.

What's he doing, though?

He still wants to marry me. He made that more than clear. So maybe that's what I should do. It would be the biggest fuck-you of all to my parents. And if it's the biggest mistake ever, if it thoroughly ruins my life, then that'll serve them right.

I used to like imagining them crying at my funeral. Isn't that completely fucked up?

No, this situation is. My life is.

I glance over at the medicine cabinet, and I think about Gavin's first wife. Hannah, that's her name.

Did she once feel like this? So confused, heartbroken, and humiliated that it seemed like there was only one way out?

THEN

SIXTY-FOUR

DIANA

It all changed when Gavin kidnapped my daughter. I changed, instantly.

There would be no more hoping, pleading, or begging. For Gavin Axelrod, those were all aphrodisiacs anyway.

Throughout the stalking, some small part of me had continued to feel sorry for him. After all, I'd never loved or been loved with such abject devotion. I couldn't understand that form of madness. Maybe, at times, I even felt flattered.

I didn't feel that way anymore. Gavin had lit a match and burned through all my compassion. Once I was heartless, the solution was obvious.

I was waiting outside his door, as instructed. "You dropped Lizzie at home?" I said.

"Of course. She's safe and sound." He gave me a smile of such pure and dazzling happiness—as if he had no memory or qualm about how he'd forced me here—that I felt capable of violence.

He didn't care what I felt, only what he felt. And what he felt, clearly, was horny.

Once inside the apartment, he started pawing at me immediately, trying to take off my clothes.

"No," I said, stepping back. "I don't want you."

"But you're here."

I stared at him wide-eyed and incredulous. "I'm here because you threatened my daughter. I had no choice."

"I never threatened her. Lizzie was having a great time. You could tell from her selfie."

"You're insane," I said. "This ends today."

"Oh, Di." He looked at me fondly. "That's just not going to happen."

I was angry, yes, but it was overlaid with calm. I trusted my plan. Trusted myself. "This will be our last interaction. If you see me walking down the hall, you'll turn and head the other way. Don't speak to me, ever. You won't be having any private conversations with Lizzie, either."

"Who's going to stop me?" He said it like we were flirting. Was he existing on an entirely separate astral plane? How had I ever thought this man could be my savior, or Lizzie's?

"If you don't leave us alone, then I'll be going to the administration," I said. "With Mari. She'll refile her complaint and I'll serve as a supporting witness. I'll say that you told me to intimidate her into withdrawing it the first time. I'll say that you've been grooming Lizzie, too. I have that picture you sent me, the one you took of Lizzie in your car."

"Come on, Diana." He forced a laugh, trying to seem unconcerned. But he was failing. "You wouldn't do any of that. Because if you did, it would expose the affair. You'd blow up your marriage and your relationship with Lizzie."

"Try me, Gavin."

"You're bluffing." I held his gaze.

He must have been able to feel my resolve because his face fell. Meanwhile, my heart rose. Because it was a win-win: He'd go away and leave me in peace, or he'd push me into telling the truth. Either way, I'd be living on my own terms again instead of in fear, at his beck and call. And maybe I relished the idea of destroying Gavin and my marriage in one fell swoop. I'd get to see what this new me would do once she came out the other side.

"Would you really tell lies like that?" he said. "I wasn't with Genevieve and I'm not grooming Lizzie. I'm not into children. I'm very much into adult women. As you well know."

"Strong women, right? That's what you said. But you've been the one lying all along."

"How could you do this to me? I love you more than anything. I've taken care of you and Lizzie. I'll continue to do that, if you'll just give me a chance. We can fix this."

I was immune to his pleas. "When you love someone, you elevate them. You don't use and degrade them."

"You've got me all wrong," he said sorrowfully.

"If that's true, then I'm willing to live with my mistake." I headed for the door and then said over my shoulder, "Don't contact me again or you'll pay the price."

In the coming days and weeks, I was terrified. I thought that he was hiding in the bushes, lying in wait, planning his next move. My threat rested on him being a rational actor but what if he really was not just evil but truly sick?

I wondered what he might be doing with Lizzie behind my back, if he'd told her anything about me. Given that she was so closed off, there was no point in asking. I had no way to police his actions.

Gradually, though, life returned to normal. A lonely normal, seeing as I'd lost Mari. Our group of friends sided with her, as expected.

Ron never even asked what happened, why there wouldn't be any more holiday parties. He just chalked it up to "women's drama." He introduced me to the wives of his work colleagues and they all liked me. Well, they liked what little I showed them. Our dance card was once again full.

As the months passed, Lizzie was willing to engage in small talk again, which was an improvement. But her walls never really came down.

Gavin did as he was told. He steered clear.

I dodged a bullet, I thought. *I'll never see Gavin Axelrod again.*

SIXTY-FIVE

LIZZIE

My relationship with Mr. Axelrod ended not with a bang, but a whimper.

After the aborted road trip, he became more professional. Distant. Detached, really. It hurt, though I told myself it shouldn't.

I was forced to realize these past months with him had all been a trick of the light. I'd been seeing what I wanted to see. He was my teacher, that was all. He thought I was smart and he liked my writing; he wanted me to reach my potential. Nothing more.

Since there was no literary magazine, I didn't have to keep trying to write short stories. I went back to my journal and my poems.

I also went back over every moment with him, feeling stupider by the second. He must have known the whole time that I was a kid with a crush and he'd been humoring me. So humiliating. But at least it gave me some new emotions to write about.

As time passed, Mr. Axelrod became his old, animated self

again. I assumed he'd gotten back together with his old girl-friend or found someone new.

I didn't allow myself to fantasize about him anymore. I was still getting A's. He wrote plenty of encouraging comments on my papers but he didn't seek me out and I followed his lead.

I did learn a lot that year.

One of the main things? That there was truly nothing for me in Houston. Mom was Mom, and Dad was Dad. Enough said. Maya and I were barely hanging out. Denver was cool but he got a girlfriend and started spending all his time with her. I was a little jealous because without the distraction of Mr. Axelrod, I could see what a gem Denver was. I'd missed my chance.

But that was okay. I had to just survive my senior year and then I could get to UT Austin, where they keep things weird. Where I'd be my fullest self. Where my real life would begin.

Yes, that was when I'd experience true happiness. And maybe love, too.

If I got lucky, I'd find a man just like Mr. Axelrod.

NOW

SIXTY-SIX

DIANA

I'm almost out of time. It's after midnight, which means Gavin's deadline has arrived. It's D-Day.

But I've got new hope, in the form of Hannah's mother, Eve. She directed me to contact her through the Signal app since it's the most secure. I'm sitting by the pool and we've been texting for the past hour. No more sharing sob stories. No, we've got to get to work.

Eve's been just where I am now. She's walked miles in my shoes.

In the months before Hannah's death, Eve had been at loose ends. Her motherly intuition was telling her that the situation was dire, that Hannah might not survive this man. Her friends thought she was paranoid, that she was overreacting, but she knew.

She'd contemplated having Gavin killed. She'd even gotten in touch with a guy—a professional—who could make it look like an accident. But at the last minute, she'd balked.

It's one of the great regrets of my life that I never said the word.
I didn't give the order.

Eve's guy is in Dallas. If I say the word—if I provide the funds—he can get on a plane and be here within hours. The job will be done by dinnertime.

Send Gavin out on some errand. He'll never come back.

I don't know why I'm hesitating. Gavin doesn't deserve to live. But do I deserve to make that call? Only God's supposed to decide.

I already did it once, with my father. He may have been a pedophile, too. *You're completely sure this can't be traced to me? Or to you?*

Of course I'm not sure. But isn't it a risk worth taking? So Lizzie doesn't wind up like Hannah?

Tell him to get on the plane.

I can still change my mind later. But I need to set this in motion. If I have to go to prison so that Lise remains free, so be it.

But first, I have one more Hail Mary. I can tell Lise about Hannah. I can show her what Eve wrote.

Sure, Lise dismissed me earlier when I told her about Mr. Axelrod's teen victims. But Lise knows, deep down, that Genevieve is one of those victims. She said it, not me. I have to hope that Lise is ready to listen to herself.

Once she sees Gavin for who and what he really is, she'll boot him from her life and join the team with Mari, Eve, and me to bring him to justice. Then I can avoid doing what I really don't want to do, ever again, not even to Gavin.

But if Lise's denial is too thick—well, that's why Eve's guy is getting on a plane. And if all else fails, I know the combination to Ron's gun safe.

Ron. I'm still going to have to deal with him, aren't I?

I sigh and lean back against the pool lounger, closing my eyes. I just need a minute to gather my strength.

When I awaken, Lise is standing over me. The sun is just coming up behind her and she's backlit like an angel. My beautiful girl, so in need of a rescue that she'll likely resist tooth and nail. She'll scratch and claw and continue to believe in her fiancé.

Because she loves him so much, or because she can't allow herself to be wrong?

Gavin preys on not just our naïveté but our fear of admitting we've been fooled. No one likes to be played for a sucker. Isn't there a saying about how pride comes before the fall?

Bad news for Gavin: I'm all out of pride.

But first, the sunrise. It doesn't look real. It's like a background set of a high school play, except that even now, the orange is incrementally becoming peach.

Gavin will be up and at 'em—at us—soon. He'll want to refute my facts with fiction, so at this point, my best move is to tell the whole truth and nothing but the truth.

So help me God.

"Could you sit down, Lise, please?" I say.

Is she glaring at me, or squinting to adjust to the light? Whichever it is, she obliges, perching on the lounger next to me. I'll call that auspicious.

"Our talk last night didn't go as well as I'd hoped," I begin, "and maybe that's because I wasn't being entirely honest. I mean, everything I said was true but there were things I left out. Essential things. The relevant history."

She's eyeballing me, and the silence is intimidating. But I've come too far to back out now.

"You deserve to know why I've been acting so strangely around Gavin," I say, "why I've wanted to steer you away from having a life with him. When you were in high school, in Mr. Axelrod's class, he and I really did have an affair."

"I know. Gavin confessed last night. So go ahead, tell me your version."

"I don't have a version. I have the truth." But I can see that she doesn't believe me, or at least, not in an automatic fashion. She's going to compare notes.

I'm too late. He got to her first and he's an expert at making his version seem real. Truthiness, rather than truth. It plays better, since it's less messy.

Gavin would make an excellent witness. There would be no slipups; he'd never admit to a failure of memory. He'd proceed seamlessly from start to finish, every word a perfect corroboration of whatever central narrative would be most compelling.

That's why I can't trust the system to handle someone like Gavin.

"When I first met Gavin, I hated myself," I say. "That's why his attention felt so good. I thought I finally had someone who really loved and understood me. Your father had little use for me, and you didn't—"

"Are you seriously blaming me?" Her eyes bug out.

"No, I don't blame you for anything. I blame Gavin."

The way she's looking at me with such contempt—this is his legacy. He worked hard to split Lizzie and me apart, same as he split Eve and Hannah apart. But I can't tell her that, not yet. I have to structure this correctly. I need to build this house brick by brick, only I'm a terrible architect.

Gavin, though, is a master builder.

I shake my head, feeling frustrated and helpless. I want to give up but I know that I have to keep going, for Lise's sake. Ironically, she's the only thing keeping him alive right now.

"It's not going to work," she says. She must be sensing my hopelessness. The sun is rising literally, but figuratively it's setting over my relationship with my daughter. "You can't cry your way out of this."

"I'm not trying to. I hate when you see me cry. Do you really think that I've spent my life wearing my emotions on my sleeve, hoping you'd take pity on me?"

It's such an obviously honest response that I can see it gets under Lise's skin. It runs counter to her narrative.

No, not hers. Gavin's. That's what I have to get her to see. She doesn't want to admit she's been his puppet, but she has. She didn't know how to guard against someone like him, same as I didn't. Same as Genevieve didn't, and Hannah didn't.

I know we have other things in common, too. We have a whole shared history that doesn't have anything to do with Gavin Axelrod.

"I love you, Lise," I say, "and I know you love me."

"Well, that's not even the question." She seems annoyed and yet it's the most reassuring indicator so far.

"What are your questions? What do you want to know? I'll tell you anything." I bet Gavin didn't make that promise. Or maybe he did, knowing how easily he'd break it. How comfortable he was replacing truth with lies, the way you might substitute skim for whole milk in a recipe.

No, that's the wrong analogy. It makes his actions sound harmless. All those little substitutions and you wind up with an entirely different dish, one guaranteed to make you very, very sick.

"He's poison," I say. "I believe that with every fiber of my being. I believe it so much that I was prepared to tell you the whole story this morning no matter how bad it made me look. Even if you never wanted to see me again," I blink back tears, "it would be worth it if you never saw him again. I have to get you away from him, Lise."

"Because you want him for yourself. Because you love him."

"No! I loathe him. I have for years now."

"You don't want anyone else to have him. You don't want him to be happy." She's throwing out possibilities indiscriminately. Desperately. And that's good for me, I think. At some point, she'll run out of excuses for him. Then his time will be up.

I glance toward the house. What if those glass doors open and Gavin comes walking out, spewing more lies? I suspect that he has a lot more power over her than I do.

I have to work fast.

"Okay," I say. "I'll tell you everything—the good, bad, and ugly about me. I bet in his version, the good, bad, and ugly are never about him, are they?"

"Just start talking." She looks past me, toward the sunrise, which is no longer. Now it's just a bright cloudless sky. We're in for a hot one.

So I start talking. When I get to the Christmas party, I see a light turn on in her eyes. She's remembering something.

"I guess technically, he didn't force me to have sex that night," I say, "but I didn't feel like I had a choice. I had to keep him happy."

"Why?" But I have a sneaking suspicion she knows why.

"I was terrified to lose him. I felt like everything would spin out of control if he left me when really, he was the reason it was so out of control. He kept me off balance. He wanted me to worry about you because then he kept the upper hand."

I can see her internal battle to maintain reasonable doubt. She doesn't want to lose Gavin because in her way, she's just as dependent on him as I once was.

"He figures out what you need most and then he becomes your main supplier," I say. "Like a drug dealer and an addict."

She scoffs. "That's how it was for you, but I'm different."

"Do you remember how bad things got between us when you were in his class? He said he was trying to empower me as a parent. I was supposed to come down on you, hard, so that you'd know you couldn't walk all over me anymore. You were supposed to see that I was a strong woman and then you'd respect me."

"It's not the worst theory."

"It was a disaster. You pulled away and shut down even more. Did you hate me?" *Do you hate me now?*

"I thought you were ridiculous, trying to act like some sort of badass. It so clearly wasn't you."

"Exactly. I didn't know who I was, and that worked well for him. He could make me into who he wanted me to be."

She looks away. Is this starting to sink in? Does she recognize her own story in mine?

"I did bad things, Lise, because he told me to," I say. "I alienated people. I hurt them." Tears spring to my eyes.

"Which people? What kinds of things?"

"I wish I could give you details but it's not my secret to tell. Just know that Gavin's the reason Mari and I stopped being friends. I did something awful because he said I had to protect him."

"You did something awful because he said to?" Her voice is mocking.

"I'm to blame for what I did. I had agency. Isn't that your word? But if you stay with him, he'll make you the worst version of yourself."

"He won't make me anything. I'm my own person."

"You met him when you were sixteen. You were impressionable."

"I was my own person then, too!" Her eyes are blazing.

"You were still a child. I know you didn't see yourself that way, that you probably thought—"

"You have no idea what I thought! You didn't talk to me. Not in any real way."

"I know. I'm sorry for that." I truly am, but we're running out of time. "I'm talking to you like an adult now."

"No. You're just trying to twist everything."

"That's what he does. Don't you see that? He pits women against each other and then he gets to walk away scot-free. That's how the trash gets passed."

"If you call him trash one more time, I'm the one who's walking away. I'm leaving and I'm never coming back." I sense that her threat is borne not of anger but of sadness. She's starting to see—she can't avoid seeing—and it's devastating.

I want to reach out to her, to tell her I understand, I've been there. I want to give her a hug; I want to let her cry on my shoulder. Hell, we can cry together. I'm barely holding it together myself.

"I was like you," I say. "Despite everything he'd done to me, I believed there were lines Gavin wouldn't cross. Until very recently—as in, a few days ago—I still thought he would never hurt children. All I wanted was for him to get out of my life and I didn't even try to hold him accountable. Now he's here, threatening you."

She's trying to scoff again, but there's less conviction this time around. I'm making headway. But will it be enough?

"I don't want to think what you might have to do if you become Gavin Axelrod's wife. What kind of loyalty tests you'll face."

"I'm not worried about that."

Because she still trusts him completely, or because she doesn't intend to marry him?

I tell her about how it ended. About the stalking. About how he alternated words of extreme love with extreme threats. About the day he kidnapped her.

"That's never happened," she says.

"I thought you were with Maya but he was driving you somewhere. He texted to say that you were with him and that I'd better meet him or else."

"Or else what?"

"I was too scared to find out. So I agreed to meet and he turned the car around. Do you remember that?"

Reluctantly, she nods.

"He used you to get to me. He knew that you were my Achilles' heel, and you always had been. I loved you so much more than I could ever love him, than I could ever love anyone."

There's a long silence, and I think maybe I've broken through. That I can avoid killing again.

SIXTY-SEVEN

LISE

"Tell me what you did," I say. "If you want me to believe you over Gavin, I need specifics."

Reading between the lines, it sounds like Gavin abused Genevieve, and Mom helped him cover it up. But that could just be what Mom wants me to intuit. She could be framing Gavin without saying it outright.

So they had an affair gone wrong. He'd told me as much himself.

"Did you really think I'd just take your word for it, that you've done some bad things and they've all been Gavin's fault? You're the one who chose to sleep with my teacher. You're not just some victim."

"I am responsible for my own actions," she says carefully, "but you need to know that Gavin is no ordinary person. He's basically a cult leader."

I laugh. "Do you even hear yourself?" I mean, that's ludicrous. "I don't even recognize the man you're talking about."

That's not entirely true. Some of her quotes do sound a lot like Gavin, like how he says he'll never let me go. Some of her details bump uncomfortably against my recollections, like how Gavin was taking me on a little road trip, texted someone, and then suddenly turned the car around. Like that Christmas party at Mari's. How I couldn't find my mom. How upset she seemed during the car ride home. How Genevieve had seemed so un-Genevieve-like.

Then there's how Genevieve was at the mall. I took some psychology classes, and she's like a textbook trauma survivor.

But how do I know that Gavin was really the source of the trauma? I won't, until I ask him. I'm sure he'll have his own version for that, too.

"Gavin tells me everything," I say. Sure, he didn't tell me about his first wife initially but now I know everything.

"Oh, Lise." Mom sounds compassionate. "Believe me, I know all about Stockholm syndrome."

"You and I are not the same!" I snap.

"No, we're not, but Gavin's the same."

Gavin told me that he never loved her. She was just a place-holder for me. Was he lying? Or is Mom lying now, trying to make their relationship sound a lot more serious than it was? I mean, I can believe it was more serious for her. She's basically admitted that she felt like a big fat nothing when they met.

Mom's making it sound like if he's some diabolical genius psycho.

That's not my fiancé. That's her bogeyman, and bogeymen originate in the mind.

Does it bother me, the idea of Mom and Gavin being together? Of course it does. It might take me a long time to let go of that.

Maybe I'm crazy, but I'm not ready to let go of Gavin. I've never met someone like him, never felt anything remotely like this kind of love. I'm afraid I never will again.

"You need him to be evil to absolve yourself of whatever it is you did," I say.

She goes quiet. "You're right," she says finally. "I did wrong even before Gavin came into my life. And when you showed up in that steakhouse with him, I thought that God was finally punishing me for everything."

"What's everything?"

She hesitates. "I'll answer that someday. But I don't want us to get distracted. You need to know that Gavin isn't here because he loves you. He's here for money and vengeance.

"Stop, I've heard enough." My breathing is shallow. "Why did it have to get to this point? Why didn't you ever just fucking talk to me, like, for real?"

"I didn't know how to be real with you, or anyone else. I felt like I had nothing to offer. Limited life experience, no wisdom. All I could tell you was what not to do. Don't get pregnant at sixteen, or if you do, don't marry an asshole." She looks at me, eyes bright with tears. "You wanted me to be a woman of agency but I wasn't. By the time you were a teenager, I knew I was nothing but a disappointment to you. Anything I said would have just confirmed it."

"That's not what I felt." Or maybe it was, but I don't want to say it now. Oh, wait, she's done it again. "See, this is how it always goes! I end up feeling sorry for you."

"Do you think I want it to be that way? I want to be someone you can respect. That's why I'm here, risking everything."

Risking everything to destroy my relationship. "You're ruining my life."

"I'm trying to save your life!" My mannered Stepford wife of a mother is suddenly screaming in the early morning hours so loudly that despite the large lot size, I'm sure our neighbors can hear.

"Well, you can't! I'm going to do whatever the fuck I want to do!" I scream back. Let them all hear.

She gets to her feet, and I do, too. We're about to have a

shouting match, and it's exhilarating. It's been a long time coming.

I'm finally getting to know my mother.

"You spoiled brat," she seethes. "I am out here laying myself bare and you still won't believe me. You turned thirteen and suddenly nothing I did or gave was good enough. I wasn't good enough. You couldn't have made it plainer. Are you proud of how you exerted your independence by shitting all over me?"

"I just wanted some personal space. You were breathing down my neck with your insistent, insipid questions. 'How was school?' 'How are your friends?' It was mind-numbing."

We're squaring off, and I have the sense that in her own way, she's enjoying this as much as I am. She circles me slowly, like she's stalking her prey, and I'm doing the same.

"I didn't know what to ask!" she says. "How could I, when you didn't tell me anything?"

She's nearly spitting the words at me. "You knew how much I loved you. You knew how desperately I wanted to be let into your life. And yet you gave me nothing. You're cruel, Lizzie."

"It's Lise." But it comes out low. Ashamed.

"That's just a façade. Underneath, you're still Lizzie. You came into this house determined to make me see things your way. You didn't talk to me; you talked at me. Or you just walked away when it suited you. Stormed away. You're still behaving like a child. Denying reality, believing in fairy tales. Look at me. Do you really think I'd make all this up about Gavin? I'm not the writer, you are! And I'm not the storyteller, he is!"

There it is. Mom's landed a solid punch and knocked the wind out of me. We're both standing still now, a couple of exhausted prize fighters.

"I know I wasn't a good mother to a teen girl, that my anxiety got the best of me, but I was a great mother before then. Admit it. Won't you just admit it? Please?"

"Yes," I say finally. "You definitely had your moments."

"I was a bad mother once I was overrun by fear, doubt, and insecurity. I couldn't think straight, so Gavin filled my head with whatever he wanted. What's he been filling your head with?"

I don't know. Right now, it feels empty.

I want to keep arguing that I'm my own person and always have been, that no one controls me, but I just don't feel sure of anything anymore. Mom would probably say that's how Gavin likes it.

Could she be right?

"Let me tell you the moment when I knew I needed to get away from him," she says. I can see that she's fighting back tears. Sure, I accused her of showing emotion in order to manipulate me but I didn't really believe that then and I don't believe it now. If anything, my mother is too restrained.

I don't want to hear about the moment she had to leave and yet, I'm transfixed. Mom is letting me into her interior life in a way that I never anticipated. But it's a scary place for me since my fiancé plays such an integral role.

He's her trauma, I realize.

"I did something on my own," she says. "Something terrible that Gavin never suggested. When I had you, I made a promise to myself that I would never behave like my mother did. I would show you a respect that I never received and for a long time, I upheld that. But then," her voice starts to crack, "one day, I just lost it."

"What do you mean?"

"I didn't trust Gavin anymore. When he told me you were fine, I thought he was lying or that he just didn't care enough to find out the truth. He wanted to shut me up. He was tired of listening to me go on about you."

"So what did you do, Mom?"

She lets out a shaky sigh. "I searched your room. I wasn't looking for drugs or alcohol or anything. If I had been, that might have been a reasonable excuse. But I was looking for your diary. I wanted to get in your head. I wanted to know what you thought."

"You read my diary?" I stare at her in horror because I know what's in there. All the awful things I said about her, all my fantasies about Gavin and my conversations with him.

"No. I didn't find it. Either you'd hid it well or you'd taken it with you. But afterward, I was relieved. I mean, I was ashamed mostly, but also relieved. It meant I hadn't crossed that particular line. I vowed, again, that I never would."

"Did you keep that vow?"

She nods solemnly. "That day was a reckoning. I realized how far I'd gone, and that if I didn't turn around, I might lose myself completely. I might never be able to come back."

"That's when you broke up with Gavin?"

"I tried to. Just to be clear, I hadn't been under his influence when I went through your room. That was me. I did that. But I knew, that to be a decent person, I could never be with him again. I needed to—" She stops talking, and I see fear spreading across her face.

I turn to follow her gaze and see that Gavin has slid the glass door open and is coming this way.

"This is your moment of reckoning," she says. She's speaking rapidly. "You're going to have to make a decision about what kind of person you want to yoke yourself to, and what kind of person you'll be. I can't choose for you, as much as I wish I could. I can only hope you'll do the right thing. Not for me, Lise, but for you."

Gavin's almost here, his face a mask of fury. But he's not looking at Mom; he's talking to me.

"I just want to make sure she really tells you everything," he says, "including what happened before she and I ever met. Has she gotten to the part where she murdered her own father in cold blood?"

SIXTY-EIGHT

DIANA

Lise looks horrified and stricken, which is entirely appropriate. Gavin has just outed me as a murderer. And it's not just any victim, but my father, Lise's grandfather.

"So she didn't tell you the whole truth," Gavin says, "only what she thinks is advantageous to her."

Gavin moves to Lise's side, feigning concern, but underneath there's a glimmer of satisfaction. He thinks that Lise will be so shattered and so disgusted by me that she'll have to turn to him for comfort.

Instead, she's backing away from both of us. "I thought Grandpa died of cancer," she says. "Is this true? Did you kill him?"

"Of course it's true!" Gavin interjects. "I wouldn't have said it otherwise. I'm sorry you had to find out this way, Lise, but I've given her plenty of time to come clean. She's a liar, through and through. Worse than a liar. She's a killer."

He's not wrong. And the way this is going, I'll be killing again soon.

Right now, though, I need to keep my focus on Lise. This is

between the two of us. Funny how if he keeps talking, if he persuades Lise to believe him, he'll actually be next to die.

"Your grandfather was in bad shape," I say. "He probably had only a few days left. He was out of his mind, calling me terrible names, making wild accusations."

"You wanted his money and you killed him for it," Gavin says.

"No, I didn't. Lise, listen to me." I turn to her urgently. "You have to believe me. Your grandfather said upsetting things. I was hurt and I stepped out of the room. I could hear that he was struggling to breathe and I—"

"You didn't help him," Gavin finishes. "You didn't do CPR or call the paramedics until you knew it was too late. That meant you could walk away with the money. Lise, she chose $50K over her own father's life."

Lise's horror deepens.

"I told Gavin that story years ago," I say. "And you know what his reaction was? Pride. He told me what a strong woman I was. And you know what? It turns out he was right." He looks at me in surprise. "Because I killed the man who'd abused me as a kid."

"You never told me that part!" Gavin's looking at Lise again. "Do you see how depraved your mother is? She's willing to say anything just to avoid taking responsibility for what she's done."

Lise is obviously torn. She doesn't know who to believe.

"When I told Gavin what I'd done, I was racked with guilt about it. I didn't know about my dad. I only found out yesterday. I went to your grandmother to ask her for a million dollars. To pay off Gavin. That's how much he said it would take for him to break your heart."

"No." Lise shakes her head. "This is all madness."

"It is, baby," Gavin says. "It's madness, and your mother is psycho. Sitting here accusing her dead father—who she killed—of being a child molester."

"My mother told me," I say rapidly. "She said that my father used to go into my room late at night and she never said or did anything about it but she understood why I did what I did. She knew that I killed her husband and she was okay with it. She absolved me. Not only that, she gave me the money."

"A million dollars?" Lise asks. "To make Gavin go away?"

"Yes! I can prove it. I'll show you my bank account."

"You can't possibly be buying this." Gavin and I are both pleading our cases to Lise. "I don't know what that money is for, but it's not for me. I'd never leave you. Didn't I ask you to elope with me last night?"

"You did." Lise looks like she's about to pass out.

"Your mother is obsessed with me," Gavin says. "She's jealous and she's vicious. She'll say absolutely anything."

"I'm telling the truth," I say. "In your heart, you know that."

"No," Gavin says. "I'm telling the truth. That's what you know in your heart." He steps close to Lise, boxing me out. "You never knew until now what your mother's capable of. I hate that I had to be the one to show you. But you need to trust me on this: If we walk out that door and never see her again, it's no loss. She's a terrible mother and a terrible person."

Lise is staring down at her bare feet as if she's never seen them before.

"Marry me, Lise," he says. "You're the only one I've ever truly wanted."

"He's right," I say. Lise and Gavin both swivel toward me. "I am a terrible person. Gavin is also a terrible person. You should walk out of here and never see either of us again. Then you'll be free. You'll be safe."

This is the only way out, I've suddenly realized. If Lise leaves both Gavin and me for good, then he has no more ammunition. There won't have to be any more killing.

"I did kill my father," I say, tears rolling down my cheeks, "and maybe he was abusing me, maybe he wasn't. Maybe it never happened or maybe I've suppressed the memories. But what I know for sure is that when he couldn't breathe, I didn't lift a finger to help him. I left him there to die alone. I was never punished for it. So maybe I deserve a life sentence. That's what it'll be to lose you, Lise."

Gavin shakes his head. "Unbelievable. Just listen to her over there, trying to manipulate you, Lise."

Lise keeps her eyes on my face. I can tell she needs to hear this.

So I continue. "The other thing I know? When I was a kid, my mother had her suspicions and she didn't even try to protect me. I've devoted my life to protecting you, Lise, and that's what I'm doing right now. I pray to God that Gavin loses you, too. You deserve better than the both of us."

I stare at Gavin. I've just proven that I'm willing to make the ultimate sacrifice because of how much I love Lise. What's he got?

"Your mother is the one who asked what it would take for me to get out of your life," he says. "I told her a million, knowing that I had no intention of going anywhere. I wouldn't leave you, not for any amount of money. But that money exposes her for the manipulator that she is."

"So it's true? You were blackmailing my mother?" She's staring at him like she's never seen him before. Like she never wants to see him again?

Fingers crossed.

"I wanted that money for us." He's taken her hand, imploring, and she lets him. "It's for our future. I thought that once we had the million, we could leave and never come back. There's nothing for you here, Lise. This shouldn't be your family anymore. Let's start our own."

He moves in even closer, whispering, and I can't make out the words but I know exactly what I'm seeing. I recognize it all, in sequence: love bombing, guilt-tripping, implied threats. This is where all his earlier efforts—all the grooming—could bear fruit. When she was sixteen, he put in all that time and effort to figure out what made her tick.

But I can tell that it's not working, not completely. Lise hasn't said one word, hasn't even made reassuring noises. Her eyes keep flicking over to me.

Right now, she needs her mother. I'm going to stay here, no matter what.

Gavin's agitation is mounting. Finally, he whirls on me. "Get the fuck away from us, Diana!"

'No," I say. Quietly. Firmly.

I'm daring him to try to make me go away in my own house. To put his hands on me. If he does, he'll have shown his true colors. There's no way Lise would leave with him after that.

Would she?

I'm not afraid. This final showdown has been a long time coming, and I feel ready. Calm. Maybe that's because I've got an ace in the hole: Eve's guy on the plane. If Gavin has an accident, it'll be because of his own recklessness.

Gavin's starting to come unglued. Lise can see it, too. She's looking shaky. But she's still silent. She's been silent so long.

"Your mother is a desperate woman," Gavin says. "She was desperate back then and she's desperate now. It's pathetic, actually. When you were in high school, she couldn't talk to you at all so she tried to get me to do her bidding. She used sex to control me. But what you and I have, Lise, goes so far beyond that."

"Does it go beyond what you had with Hannah?" I pipe up.

"You shouldn't talk about that, Mom," Lise says. "That's a low blow."

Speaking of low blows... Lise finally speaks and *that's* what she says? She's criticizing my lack of decorum?

He's trained her well.

"You're right," I say. "We shouldn't speak ill of the dead. Hannah was a beautiful girl. Her mother's told me all about her."

"Shut the fuck up, Diana!" Gavin screams so loud that I can see his tonsils quivering.

Lise takes a step back. But she doesn't flinch, which makes me wonder whether she's already seen this side of him. If she's accepted it.

"Isn't it suspicious that Hannah killed herself before their first anniversary?" I say. "She was twenty years old and had a will where she left everything to Gavin. Everything that her rich father had bought them, including a house, two cars, and—"

"She doesn't know what she's talking about, Lise," he says. Once again, he closes the gap between them, taking her by the arms. "I'm sorry that I wasn't honest sooner about my past with your mother. I'm sorry that she is who she is. You shouldn't have to deal with any of this."

All I want is for her to meet my eyes. Then she'll know the truth. But she won't.

"We leave here and we don't look back," he says. "Let's fly to Vegas and get married today."

She finally glances over at me, and he grips her arms tighter.

"I can't be a part of this family," he says. "I can't have anything to do with your crazy parents ever again."

Music to my ears.

"Marry me today, Lise, or I'm gone. I love you passionately, painfully, and I need to know that you love me the same way. I have to know that you're not going to believe some woman spurned. A woman who killed her own father and then lied about him being a molester. Prove that you love me like I love you. That you would go to the ends of this earth for me like I would for you. Say yes, Lise."

No, Lise, tell him to go to hell where he belongs.

"Marry me today, Lise," he repeats, "or lose me forever."

I'm so focused on the spectacle in front of me and the choice in front of her that I hadn't even noticed Ron making his appearance. "Move away from my daughter," he says.

He's holding a gun.

"You've got it all wrong, sir," Gavin says to Dad, putting his hands up in surrender. "I'm just trying to talk to my fiancée. We're thinking of eloping today, and your wife—who you hate, for good reason—is trying to come between us."

My head is spinning, and it's a challenge to remain upright. Is it possible that both Mom and Gavin love me a lot? They're both so convincing. But they can't both be telling the truth. So who's lying?

"Move away from my daughter." This time, Dad gestures with the gun, and Gavin does as he's told.

"You don't have the full picture, Ron," Gavin says. "If you only knew all the secrets that Di has been keeping from you—"

"Shut up, Gavin." Dad is staring at Gavin venomously. "You think you know my wife better than I do? What kind of chump do you take me for?"

I feel like I should be saying something but I'm bleary and slow. Is this what it's like to be in shock?

"I can only imagine how it looked when you were watching from across the lawn," Gavin says. "But now that you're here, you can see that there's no danger. I was actually trying to convince Lise to elope with me today."

"Sounds pretty dangerous to me," Dad says. The gun is still fixed on Gavin.

"I made a terrible mistake all those years ago, being with Diana," Gavin says. "I'm very sorry, sir. But cut to half a decade later and I love your daughter more than anyone in the world. I want to marry her. I'm not here for money, only for lo—"

"Enough of the bullshit." With that, Dad shoots Gavin right in the chest. In the heart.

Gavin falls down, face forward, and it doesn't take a genius or a doctor to know that he's dead, instantly. Dad's done plenty of hunting, and he was shooting to kill.

I let out a strangled cry and now I'm on my knees next to Gavin. I don't touch him, though. Maybe it's because I've never touched a dead person or because I don't know what to feel after what Mom's said.

When he came out on the lawn, it's like he was hypnotizing me, just like he once hypnotized her.

My gut had said Mom was telling the truth, but my heart kept calling Gavin's name.

Would I have married him, despite everything? Or would I have lost him forever? I don't know because my father took the choice out of my hands.

"Get in the house, both of you." Dad gestures with the gun. He sounds entirely calm, just like he did the entire time he was talking to Gavin. I've just witnessed an execution.

I look to Mom. She wanted Gavin to disappear from our lives and now she's gotten her wish. Why doesn't she look happier?

She murdered her father. My father murdered my fiancé.

What the hell kind of family is this?

"Move," Dad says, a little louder, like Mom and I might be

hard of hearing. Mom starts walking and I follow. Dad is behind us, the gun lowered to his side now.

Once we're all in the kitchen, he locks the glass doors, and I start to laugh. I mean, the home invasion already occurred. Dad took care of the intruder.

Mom and Dad are both staring at me and I realize that I've been laughing for a long time. That I sound hysterical. That I'm also crying.

Am I still in shock, or emerging from it?

Mom comes over to hug me and I neither respond nor resist.

"We need to get down to business," Dad says. "The neighbors must have heard you all arguing with Gavin, which is good. Then when I came out, he was holding on to Lise, violently. I told him to get away from her and he wouldn't. You were in danger, and I had to act."

Dad's getting our stories straight.

"We're not going to bring in any of the history. There was never an affair with Diana, and the visit had been going well. No one had any beef with Gavin. This is a tragedy, period."

With the manner of a quarterback diagramming the final play of the game, Dad goes over what we supposedly saw two more times, wanting Mom and me to commit his version to memory.

I've had enough of men and their versions.

"I'll explain that I was half asleep," Dad says, "but I knew that I needed to protect my family, so I got my gun. I needed to protect my women. I did what I had to do. I have the right to defend my property."

As in, Mom and I are his property.

"Lise, you should be the one to call the police," he says. "Sound upset about your dead fiancé, okay? That shouldn't be tough. You look upset." He sounds pleased with that, as I've been well-cast in the role.

I'm not the grieving fiancée, though. Mom was willing to lose me to save me; she was telling the truth.

This is not a loss; it's a net gain. Now Gavin can't stalk me the way he once stalked Mom. He can't do to me what he did to Hannah. And probably to Genevieve, too. How many others have there been?

I'm done taking orders.

"Before I call the police," I say, "I need to know something. What are you planning to do next, Dad? Let's assume you get away with shooting Gavin. You're on the verge of becoming the CEO. Are you planning to divorce Mom and leave her with nothing?"

He glares at me like I'm betraying him, as if I have no right to reveal what he told me in private at the lunch to which he summoned me. As if he has any right to expect loyalty after the way he's treated me my whole life. And he's treated Mom a whole lot worse. She deserves to be compensated.

Then there's how she was likely treated by her own father, and her mother, too. Mom's made a ton of mistakes but she's tried hard to protect me. Now it's my turn.

"Don't worry about what I'm going to do," Dad says. "Just make your call."

He still thinks he's running the show, just like Gavin did. They worked over Mom, and they've tried to work me over, too.

But there's a new sheriff in town.

"That's not what happened," I say. "With Gavin. We were all just talking. It was heated, yes, but he wasn't attacking anyone physically and you knew that. When you told him to step away from me, he did. And you could have shot him in the leg or shoulder, but you went for the heart."

He looks to Mom. "She doesn't know what she's saying. She doesn't know what she saw. Maybe you need to be the one to make the call instead of her."

"She sounds pretty clear to me, Ron," Mom says.

Dad's eyes are bulging. He never expected a mutiny. "I saved you both!"

"Yeah, you're a real hero, Ron." Mom and I share a look that's not quite an eye roll, but it's adjacent.

"You shot him dead on purpose," I tell Dad. "You're a murderer." Then to Mom, "We both know what we saw."

"We do," she says solemnly.

For once, we're on the same wavelength, Mom and me. We're about to free ourselves from two terrible men in one go.

SEVENTY

DIANA

After Gavin's body was cold in the morgue and Ron had been arrested, I texted Mari and Eve with the good news.

To Mari, I added, *I know this won't make up for my past actions but I hope it helps you and Genevieve find some measure of peace.* Mari texted back three emojis: fireworks exploding, fingers crossed, and a heart.

To Eve, I wrote via Signal: *Glad I didn't need your guy after all. For the first time ever, Ron was handy around the house.* She sent me a laughing/crying emoji back. I'm planning to go visit her soon in Dallas.

It's not that I find Gavin's death and Ron's ruin to be funny, exactly. It's more like poetic justice.

I don't know; I'm just trying to unpack it all in therapy. Lise convinced me to go.

She also convinced me to rent a house in the inner loop in Houston. Then she moved in. My grown daughter has become my roommate. It's not the ending I ever pictured but there's a certain twisted logic to it.

Ron's out on bail, confined to his dream house, and Lise didn't want to go back to the apartment she'd shared with

Gavin. We both have so much healing to do. We're in family therapy together, and she has her own individual therapist, too.

The unsaid is being said. It can come out like a firehose or a trickle. I'm not going to lie; it's overwhelming to feel so much. Sometimes I really miss being repressed. But I'm grateful that Lise and I are finally getting to know each other.

Sometimes she's compassionate toward me, sometimes angry. At moments, she's filled with guilt and shame. It runs the gamut but at least she's still here. So there's hope.

I've realized that I never got over what Gavin did to me five years ago. It took a lot of energy to push down memories of Gavin and all the related emotions, to keep trucking along like nothing had changed. Like I hadn't been changed.

I still don't know what Father did to me, or how it altered the course of my development. Who would I have been if not for...?

I have no idea. And it turns out there's not some simple way to recover memories. While I don't remember my father being inappropriate, I don't know that he was appropriate, either. My suspicion is that he was underinvolved in some ways and over-involved in others. I used to think that my mother was the destructive parent with her coldness and impossibly superficial standards but now I believe my childhood was defined by destructive influences.

My mother gave me an inheritance but that doesn't mean I owe her a relationship. She didn't buy forgiveness. I consider that money to be reparations.

Lise and I haven't been in touch with Ron, and I haven't been in touch with my mother. We don't owe our abusers and enablers anything, not until we're stronger, and even then, forgiveness isn't for them; it would be for us.

Now that I'm seeing clearly, I'm ready to do my part to stop the remaining Gavin Axelrods of the world. That feels like the right form of penance.

Lise and I are both in the market for our life's purpose and I'm thinking that I might have found mine. There's far too little awareness of the issue of teacher abuse, and almost no legislation or meaningful action by schools to prevent and address it. Every day, the trash gets passed, and students like Genevieve are the ones to suffer. I'm going to work to change the system.

Lise sometimes laughs and says, "Mom, you're up on your soapbox again," but I think she's proud of me.

I know I'm proud of her. Here we are, just two women of agency, finding our way out of the dark.

SEVENTY-ONE

LISE

So yeah, I'm back in Houston, living with my mom, though we're in a way cooler neighborhood, one I never even thought she'd consider.

I could say that I stayed because she needs me to help her prepare for the divorce. It's not untrue. She really is terrible at dealing with the lawyers, skewing soft and nonconfrontational. She's tempted to just make a deal and end it all quickly even though it's obvious that Dad's been hiding money their whole marriage. I would never let someone—

Well, I guess I should never say never.

She does need me, though. I'm cheering her on from the sidelines as she becomes an activist, if you can believe that.

I'm pretty impressed, and I'll tell her that one of these days. It's just that the words keep getting stuck, maybe because I still have a lot of anger toward her. She did fuck up in innumerable ways. It's not at all okay that she had an affair with my teacher, though I understand it a little. He was diabolical and she's kind of a babe in the woods. Kind of a babe, all around, and at some point, lots of guys are going to be sniffing around. I'll need to vet them.

Not that I'm entirely sure how to spot a sociopath myself. Maybe I can take a class in it. Going back to school does hold some appeal.

Which brings me to the fact that I don't know what I'm going to do next. I'm still pretty damn lost.

I've always been down on Houston but life inside the loop isn't so bad. Denver's moved back in with his parents but he prefers to come down to my new neck of the woods. We meet up a few times a week, like a support group. Losers Anonymous, we call it. But we laugh when we say it. He's not a loser, which means I'm not one, either. We're just young adults. This is how it goes. We're launching.

I've suspended my job search because I'm still kind of a mess emotionally. But once I'm healthy enough, I'll probably apply for positions where I'll get to travel the world.

When that happens, I might actually miss my mom. We've been finding ourselves, together. We're obviously not the same age chronologically but we're in the same developmental phase.

What I'm most embarrassed to admit? I still miss Gavin. We shared a lot of great moments when I was sixteen and over this past year. I know my mother puts them all under the heading of "grooming," but I think it was a real relationship, that he did love me, in his way.

Mom thinks he was a monster, plain and simple; I think he did monstrous things. She calls him a pedophile but I think he was only attracted to teen girls who looked like women, not children.

Maybe these are just semantics, and I'm still trying to make excuses for the man who, unfortunately, I did really love. A man who did hold enormous sway over me.

My therapist is helping me to excavate and exorcise, parsing and separating my thoughts, tastes, and opinions from his (the ones he inculcated back in high school as well as his more recent influence). Sometimes I'll find myself humming a song and I'll think, "Do I really like that? Or do I just think I'm supposed to because he did?" In other words, how well do I really know myself?

Denver says that to some extent, that's the process every young adult goes through, including him. We're inundated with influences all the time, steeped in them like tea. Then we have to spend our lives distinguishing the signal from the noise, deciding what we want to keep and what we want to throw out. He's pruning, he says, just like me.

I have to believe that I'm not some file that's been permanently corrupted. I'm still young, right? I intend to seek out all sorts of new influences. The key might be diffusion. Never take anything exclusively from one source. Always cross-check. Trust but verify.

It sounds exhausting but exciting, too. Maybe that's what life is.

Dad's out on bail, at home with an ankle monitor. He's been texting, asking me to visit.

Since Mom and I are the prosecution's star witnesses, a judge warned Dad to back off or be charged with witness tampering. During the hearing, Dad broke down in tears, saying, "I just want to be with my daughter again. There's so much I didn't know to appreciate until..." Then he was too overcome with emotion to speak.

I'd never seen anything like it. Even Mom thought it might be genuine. But she still doesn't want either of us to communicate with Dad at all until after the trial. "Once we've told our stories—once we've told the truth—then you can visit him in prison as much as you want," she says.

I do think Dad should go to prison. He assassinated Gavin. I don't believe that it was done to protect me, at least not primarily; it was to protect Dad's ego, which is the property he cares most about defending. But maybe this experience has humbled him and transformed his perspective.

Mom says if that's the case, why isn't he taking a plea deal? Why is he taking it to court, knowing what a strain it will be on Mom and me to testify against him?

She's probably right and he's the same old dick. But he is still my father. I'm just trying not to look too far ahead.

At some point, I might want to give him another chance, if he earns it. I mean, Mom's changed so much, and I have, too.

I'm not going to let Gavin turn me into a furious coward who's so afraid of getting hurt—of getting victimized—that I'm barely living. I won't go through the next eighty years with a tortoise shell.

Who knows what'll become of us? I get a little thrill when I write that. I mean, a year from now, we could be anything.

Watch this space.

SEVENTY-TWO

MARI

This has turned out so much better than I ever could have hoped. When I first found out that Lizzie—excuse me, *Lise*—was back in town, parading around her new fiancé who also happened to be her old teacher, I was livid. I mean, this is my turf. How fucking dare Gavin Axelrod set foot here ever again after what he did to my daughter?

But now he's dead, which serves him so completely right, and Diana's family has basically been decimated. Ron was about to be a CEO and now he's going to prison instead, with his own wife and daughter testifying for the prosecution. Delicious.

Diana took Gavin's side over mine years back—as in, took the side of an abuser over her best friend, allowing him to walk free—and I've been furious with her ever since. Furious enough to embark on an ill-fated affair with her husband.

It's not like I ever loved Ron, or any of the others; my heart truly belongs to Nelson. He knows that, which is why he can wait them all out. He's secure enough to realize that I'll always come back to him.

I decide when a relationship begins and ends, not the men.

Did Ron really think he could just use me to work out his anger at Diana and then throw me away? And Gavin really believed that he could abuse my daughter and then fuck my best friend right in front of my house during my Christmas party?

It's not like I've been sitting by idly since then. I worked on my revenge for years, learning about teacher misconduct and connecting with the parents of Gavin's victims. I put all that knowledge to use in mentoring another parent. She was the one who got the school to pass the trash that is Gavin Axelrod. I made sure he knew good and well that I had a hand in his destruction.

Alas, Mr. Axelrod always lands on his feet, and he decided to go to Austin and hook up with Lizzie/Lise. Which turned out to be a fatal mistake.

It was just so sweet, getting another chance at retribution through Diana's house call. And then Ron murdering Gavin—I couldn't have even dared to dream of anything so wonderful. Talk about killing two (jail)birds with one stone.

I've always planned on letting Ron get right to the CEO's door before starting a smear campaign in the neighborhood. I'd gathered a whole arsenal of accusations that were ready to be unleashed at the most advantageous—i.e., most damaging—time. I wanted him to be able to taste that promotion before it was ripped away from him.

More than that, though, I've always wanted to fully and completely destroy Gavin Axelrod.

Now my daughter can finally heal. I know that I will. I mean, I'm feeling better than ever.

I love when it all comes full circle. The universe works in such beautiful and mysterious ways, don't you think?

A LETTER FROM ELLIE

Dear reader,

I want to say a huge thank you for choosing to read *The Son-in-Law*. If you did enjoy it and want to keep up to date with all my latest releases, just sign up at the following link. Your email address will never be shared and you can unsubscribe at any time.

www.bookouture.com/ellie-monago

If you think others should read this book, please consider leaving a review. It makes such a difference helping new readers to discover one of my books for the first time. And I'd love to hear what you think.

You can get in touch on my Goodreads.

Thanks,

Ellie Monago

goodreads.com/elliemonago

ACKNOWLEDGMENTS

This novel was inspired in large part by the four-episode documentary *Keep This Between Us*. Until I watched, I had no idea how pervasive and unchecked the problem of inappropriate teacher-student relationships is in U.S. schools. Grooming and passing the trash are far too common. More awareness and legislation are desperately needed in order to protect young people. While thrillers aren't generally known for their consciousness raising, I hope that my book can create some valuable conversations.

I owe a huge debt of gratitude to the filmmakers (Amy Berg, Jenna Rosher, and Kristi Jacobson) and am in awe of the brave survivors who allowed their stories to be told (Cheryl, Heaven, and Alisson).

As always, a big thank you to the phenomenal Bookouture team (Harriet Wade, Richard King, Kim Nash, Jess Readett, Alba Proko, Hannah Snetsinger, and Peta Nightingale) and to my loving and beloved family and friends.

PUBLISHING TEAM

Turning a manuscript into a book requires the efforts of many people. The publishing team at Bookouture would like to acknowledge everyone who contributed to this publication.

Audio
Alba Proko
Sinead O'Connor
Melissa Tran

Commercial
Lauren Morrissette
Hannah Richmond
Imogen Allport

Cover design
Jo Thomson

Data and analysis
Mark Alder
Mohamed Bussuri

Editorial
Harriet Wade
Sinead O'Connor

Copyeditor
Ian Hodder

Proofreader
John Romans

Marketing
Alex Crow
Melanie Price
Occy Carr
Cíara Rosney
Martyna Młynarska

Operations and distribution
Marina Valles
Stephanie Straub
Joe Morris

Production
Hannah Snetsinger
Mandy Kullar
Ria Clare
Nadia Michael

Publicity
Kim Nash
Noelle Holten
Jess Readett
Sarah Hardy

Rights and contracts
Peta Nightingale
Richard King
Saidah Graham

Dear Reader,

We'd love your attention for one more page to tell you about the crisis in children's reading, and what we can all do.

Studies have shown that reading for fun is the **single biggest predictor of a child's future life chances** – more than family circumstance, parents' educational background or income. It improves academic results, mental health, wealth, communication skills, ambition and happiness.

The number of children reading for fun is in rapid decline. Young people have a lot of competition for their time, and a worryingly high number do not have a single book at home.

Hachette works extensively with schools, libraries and literacy charities, but here are some ways we can all raise more readers:

- Reading to children for just 10 minutes a day makes a difference
- Don't give up if children aren't regular readers – there will be books for them!

- Visit bookshops and libraries to get recommendations
- Encourage them to listen to audiobooks
- Support school libraries
- Give books as gifts

There's a lot more information about how to encourage children to read on our websites: **www.RaisingReaders.co.uk** and **www.JoinRaisingReaders.com**.

Thank you for reading.